THE MOVER

JC Garton

RIVERSONG
BOOKS

An Imprint of Sulis International Press
Los Angeles | London

Library of Congress Control Number: 2019906297
ISBN (paperback): 978-1-946849-44-1
ISBN (eBook): 978-1-946849-45-8

Riversong Books
An Imprint of Sulis International
Los Angeles | London

www.sulisinternational.com

Contents

To past, present, and future lgbtq+ youth, *it gets better*, I promise.

CHAPTER 1

"Are we there yet?"

Eddie wasn't quite sure how she ended up in the passenger seat of her step-mom's beat up Toyota that morning. Just how did Natalie do it, win every single argument without raising her voice? Her step-mom had even convinced her to pack and load the car by herself.

Witchcraft, I bet. Eddie groaned to herself.

With a book on her lap and earbuds half-hanging out of her ears, Eddie sat in silent hell. They had been in the car for well over an hour and a half and getting comfortable wasn't an option for Eddie. Duffle bags full of clothes and reusable bags full of dry fruit, granola bars, and bottles of water were stuffed neatly around her short legs. In the backseat, next to her sister's car seat, sat three sleeping bags, a big garbage bag full of colorful, cellophane-wrapped Easter baskets, and several pairs of dress slacks.

"Why did we have to bring all of this crap anyway," Eddie asked, chewing her gum extra loud. "It's like a 1950s bunker in here."

"Are you the one driving?" Her step-mom asked.

"No, you won't let me drive. You don't trust me, remember?" Eddie said, emphasizing the words 'trust me' with fingered air quotes.

"Because you don't understand the necessity of things, child," her step-mom replied. "For starters, you don't see the point in wearing a seat-belt. You also fail to see the point of listening to music at a reasonable volume. And we brought 'this crap' because I don't want to stop every five seconds, and because it's cheaper. Do ya know how much a bag of Lays costs at a gas station?"

"No," Eddie said. "But I'm sure you're going to tell me."

"Six bucks. Six bucks for a bag of chips." Her step-mom was becoming hysterical. "It's highway robbery."

"Nat, no one is asking you for chips. Oh my god, it's not that deep. Calm down."

"Chips," Sam screeched from the backseat. "Doritos! Cool Ranch! Fritos!"

"See, now look what you did," her step-mom shouted, over the loud rock music playing in the background. "She was asleep back there. Damn it."

"Nuh uh, was not," her baby sister dissented. "And I'm hungry."

"Good job, Edwina. Now you get to entertain her 'til we get there."

"For Christ's sake," Eddie scoffed. "Are you kidding me? I didn't do anything."

"Don't use the Lord's name in vain."

"Oh my god." Eddie's patience had worn thin. "You go to church like twice a year. Besides, it's just a friggin' word."

"Are you going to give me a lecture on religion now?"

"No." Eddie refused to take her step-mom's bait. She was looking for a reason to fight, and Eddie wasn't going to give her one. "I'd much rather hang out with a classroom full of preschoolers than suffer through that crap again. I'll just sit here like a good little girl instead."

"Good," Natalie replied. "And stop swearing. Now do something with her until she falls back asleep. Do you hear me back there? It's going to be awhile before we get to your father's, so you best stop squirming around."

"It's a rehab facility." Sugarcoating the reason for the weekend trip didn't make it more manageable. Eddie wasn't a child anymore, and she saw it for what it really was. "Stop acting like it's his home."

"It has been his home for the past several months," Natalie corrected her step-daughter. "Why do you always have to be like this?"

"Whatever, man. It's his life." Slipping her hand between the seat and the car door, Eddie tickled her sister's feet. "You know I don't care one way or the other. Eddie's coming to get those piggies! Watch out!"

Eddie's family hadn't seen their father in nine months, and to her knowledge, he was still at the rehab center getting treatment for being a drunk who had inadvertently messed up everything. He was a dick. Everyone knew this, but his oldest daughter was the only one brave enough to say it.

Eddie rolled her eyes at her step-mom, then looked out the window. She loved her dad, but she wasn't ready to just forgive and forget like Natalie had suggested earlier that morning. For the past several months, he had put his family through the wringer, and she wasn't sure she wanted to see him. No, Eddie knew she didn't want to see him. He was an asshole, and she was entitled to feeling pissed off.

As the Toyota went up and down each mountain like an Appalachian roller coaster, all Eddie could think about was the melting snow. Spring was rapidly approaching, and this time of year was always the most difficult for her. Winter was the worst. Her bio-mom was gone, and now her dad was gone too, but at least he was still alive. Why was her family life utter crap? Did everyone have these problems, or was *her* family an anomaly?

She cranked up the volume on her iPod and blew an enormous pink bubble.

Bereavement would be a lifetime process, the grief counselor would always say during their sessions.

But Eddie knew. She would never get over this crap. How could she? Every day was a miserable reminder that her bio-mom was dead. Eddie bent her head forward in contemplation and rested it on the cool glass.

Her father had looked sickly the last time she'd waved goodbye to him. *When was that? September? October?* Eddie shook her head at the memory. At some point in his life, he had gone from being a healthy, athletic man, to a being shriveled up, worthless POS. His pictures from college featured a man she had never known. No, that man was gone, and what had been left was more like the nasty stuff cicadas leave behind in trees during springtime.

Until last year, Eddie's father had been a computer repairman, but after dicking around one too many times, lost his job, forcing Natalie to bear the brunt of the bills. Natalie barely made enough to pay for groceries at Walmart, let alone the mortgage on their double-wide and a car payment. Their new car had been replaced with the clunker her step-mom now drove.

Eddie couldn't imagine how much Natalie had to sacrifice to be both parents. She was a strong person.

Eddie looked at Natalie's reflection in the glass and smiled to herself.

Her step-mom was short, pear-shaped, had long blonde hair, and dressed in pink almost exclusively.

They got along. For the most part, any sway. Their feuding never lasted long.

Just this morning they had gotten into an argument over the seat-belt, and it subsequently set the tone for the drive. Nat was okay when she wanted to be, though Eddie would admit this to no one. Her step-mom was a caseworker at a local shelter, and luckily for her, Eddie had no interest in after-school activities, which made her available to watch Sam while Natalie worked funky graveyard shifts.

It wasn't easy, but they made it work without their dad.

Natalie had her faults, sure, like killing every plant in the house and correcting people if they said the word "ain't" (that really bothered Eddie), but she truly saw the best in people and wanted to help them. Natalie was pretty cool.

"Are you in the mood for some hot chocolate?" Her step-mom poked Eddie in the shoulder. "I'm suddenly in the mood for something hot and something chocolaty."

"But what about the cost of chips?" Eddie asked, turning down the car radio. "Can you really afford such a luxury item?"

"To hell with the chips. Smart ass. Do you want something to drink or not?"

Natalie took the next exit and drove for two miles until she found a gas station. They were still a few hundred miles away from the rehab center, but it did feel good to get up and stretch their legs. Eddie also needed to use the restroom.

"Here, let me get her."

Eddie helped unbuckle her little sister, and gently lifted her from the straps of the car seat, then Natalie graciously extended her arms and motioned for her to go on ahead. Once inside the gas station, Eddie located the restroom.

A key. She would need a damned key according to the sign on the door. She hated gas stations that required patrons to ask the cashier for keys, especially when you had to be *a paying customer* (whatever the hell that meant).

Lots of things irritated her.

Eddie reluctantly walked over to the cashier but was pleasantly surprised when a pretty young woman turned around and smiled at her.

"Hey, what's up? Can I help you with something?"

Cropped and dyed black, her hair was the first thing Eddie noticed. The thick, black-framed glasses that were too big for her heart-shaped face were a nice addition too. A fist-sized rainbow button attached to her gas station smock was the last thing Eddie noticed. *Jesus Christ*, Eddie thought. *She is really cute.*

Eddie returned her smile.

"Yeah, hey. Can I possibly get the key to the bathroom? The door is locked, and there's a note hanging on it." Eddie took her hand out of her hoodie pocket and motioned toward the back of the store. The young woman nodded, then handed her the key. *Damn*, Eddie thought again. *Why can't they make them like that back home?*

On her way to the restroom, Eddie thought about her girlfriend, Alice, whom she hadn't seen in over a week. They had not been on good terms the last time they had spoken. *Had they ever been on good terms?* They had been dating for nearly a year, but then two weeks ago, Alice suddenly got overly protective and possessive of Eddie.

Things got really weird.

At first, Eddie had been cool with the extra attention and the texts and phone calls, but then when Alice made a scene in front of their friends, Eddie decided it wasn't cool anymore, and suggested they spend some time apart.

The incident at the movie theater was what set her over the edge.

No one should ever spit on you.

After that, Natalie had started asking pointed questions about Alice's clingy behavior, but Eddie wrote her off as being nosey, always dodging questions and ending any conversation before Natalie could psychoanalyze their damn relationship. Alice was the most important person in Eddie's life at the moment, and her first real love, so she kept telling herself that she just needed to set better boundaries with Alice, that she could change. Eddie just needed to figure out how to help Alice, maybe offer to help her study, share some of her burden.

Because if there was one thing Edwina Burke was good at, it was problem-solving, especially people-problems.

After Eddie paid for a large cup of coffee, she walked outside and lit up a cigarette. She knew that Natalie would have a hissy fit if she saw her smoking, so she attempted to duck behind a large ice freezer on the other side of the gas station. Things were going well until her step-mom discovered her, flying around the corner like a bat out of hell, immediately scolding her for smoking in front of her little sister.

Natalie was super cool about nearly everything. Except for Eddie's cigarettes.

At first, Eddie thought it was an act, a way to weasel into her heart, something out of a crappy Hallmark Channel movie or something, but after moving in with them, Eddie decided Natalie was the real deal. Hell, she even let Alice spend the night three weeks ago for the first time, fully knowing that they were messing around.

Smoking was the one thing that Natalie would not abide, however.

"Uncool, Edwina. Super uncool." Her step-mom was not pleased. "Now get your bony ass in the car."

With a shrug, Eddie glanced at Natalie's car and saw Samantha drinking a sippy cup and pointing her stubby finger at her from behind the window. Of course, Eddie knew it was bad to smoke, *wrong*, *evil*, *whatever*, but she hadn't been able to quit since she started three years ago. To her credit, she had made several attempts in the past—even stopping for a full twenty-six days—but recently, she found herself becoming anxious over every little thing, and smoking calmed her nerves.

Eddie took one last deep draw, then smooshed the cigarette out on the freezer.

"Yeah, yeah. I know, I know. I'm sorry, Nat. It's a cancer stick, and I'm an idiot for smoking when my mom died from cancer. Spare me the damn lecture." Eddie placed the cigarette back in her pants pocket and prepared herself for the worst.

"Move. In the car. Now." Thankfully, her step-mom's bite was less severe than her bark.

After a minute-long staring contest (that Eddie lost), the two women got back into the Toyota and pulled onto the two-lane road.

"You smell like crap, by the way. Roll down the window."

Eddie turned her head, puzzled, and then looked at Natalie as if she were suggesting murder. "Are you kidding me? Nat, it's freaking freezing out there, like with snow and stuff."

"Oh well," her step-mom croaked. "You sure seemed warm enough when you were standing outside, or would you prefer that I pull over and have you stand outside for twenty minutes to air out your stinky clothing?"

"Oh my god, fine," Eddie bristled. "No need to be melodramatic. Jesus Christ."

"Hey, what did I just tell you? Watch your mouth in front of the kid."

"Whatever, man." Eddie slid her earbuds back into her ears and tried to drown out the terrible 90s music now blaring from the car stereo. "Just drive and leave me alone." After just a couple hours of being alone with her family, Eddie was starting to get cabin fever, and she needed a break.

It took them five hours and twenty-two minutes to reach their final destination. The rusted jalopy pulled up to the rehabilitation facility at a quarter past five. The drive had been long, but scenic, and Eddie had been able to finish her book. It had been a good one. Wizards. Kings. Elves. An interesting, quick read. Unlike the boring crap she was being forced to read in senior English—John the Savage was the last person she wanted to think about over Easter weekend.

After Natalie secured a parking space, she opened up the car door and took in the sights. It was colder up north, and a significant amount of snow had fallen and covered the ground, leafless trees, and bushes. Eddie closed her book, then bent down and began gathering the bags that had kept her company for over five hours.

While Eddie was climbing out of the car and juggling what felt like a hundred bags, a tall man wearing blue scrubs came to greet them. To Eddie's surprise, her father had buzzed his red hair and wispy, red beard, and had noticeably gained several pounds. Before Natalie and Eddie could move out of one another's way, her father threw his arms around both of them, squeezing them tight like biscuits in a foil can. Eddie had never seen her father look so healthy in all her life. Maybe before her mom died, but certainly not since then. He looked like an entirely different person.

Natalie turned to greet him with a kiss, and he released them from his vice grip. Eddie and her father considered each other for a moment like two cowboys sizing each other up before high-noon, and then he offered to carry the bags for her. Trying hard to keep it together, Eddie nodded and accepted, then followed him into the large, stucco building.

"Come this way," he said, leading them up the front stairs. "I have a room set aside for you and your sister. You have no idea how glad—I am so glad to see you, Edwina. I didn't think you'd come."

Then he knew her well.

This new hopeful look in her dad's eyes made Eddie want to cry—or take a knife to a couch cushion. All the hatred and anger she had felt towards him had contorted into something different, something complicated, something she didn't quite understand. Eddie knew that he had made her family suffer, but he looked so clean, so good, *so sober*. This added to her confusion.

The interior of the enormous building resembled a motel. While clean and preserved, it had the normal wear and tear of an older building. The lobby was enormous, and several visitors sat on couches, trying to talk to one another about the basketball game that was showing on one of the large, flat screen TVs. Scattered all over long tables were health and fashion magazines, and small children played with blocks and cars on the floor. A few teenage girls sat by themselves and looked around, no doubt talking crap on their relatives and the other teenagers who occupied various seats in the room.

Looking at the girls from out of the corner of her eye, Eddie suddenly felt very self-conscious. She hadn't thought to dress nicely for this occasion—instead wearing whatever she had hastily pulled out of the dryer that morning: a pair of black skinny jeans, a black hoodie with a band logo on the front, and a pair of striped black and gray socks. And as if to make matters worse, her hair was no better—haphazardly shoved up under a beanie, with fiery, orange vines poking out from underneath it.

Eddie was a hot mess, and she knew it.

"Hey shortstop." Her father's gentle voice sliced through the bittersweet pie of self-deprecation that Eddie was currently serving herself. Squeezing her shoulder, he then asked her to have a seat with the rest of the visitors. "I'm glad you're here. I've missed you."

After another long, hard look around the room, Eddie could tell that it was going to be a long four days.

Fortunately for Eddie, her stay in the lobby lasted all of ten minutes. A nurse dressed in blue and white scrubs came to greet the families and directed them toward their rooms. Eddie and Samantha were allowed to share a room while Natalie took her belongings to her father's room. They had a nice dinner in a large dining hall, during which the rehab clients were encouraged to share their personal stories of recovery.

When it came time for her father to share his journey, Eddie felt a strange twinge of sympathy for him. He informed everyone how his first wife had died, how he had been unequipped to handle the responsibility of rearing a teenager by himself, and how he eventually turned to drinking as a way to cope with the long hours at the office and the dirty, empty house he had then shared with his daughter. Her father also spoke about being fired from his job, and being unemployed for several months for the first time in his adult life, sharing with everyone just how embarrassing and shameful it had all been. He turned to Natalie and begged for her forgiveness, and told her how much he missed her, how pleased he was to see his family again. Her father then met Eddie's eyes and smiled, ending on that note.

After dinner was over, the families made sundaes with one another, then returned to their separate rooms to settle in for the evening. Eddie was thankful for the parting. She knew her sister would fall asleep as soon as she put her to bed. Eddie was also thankful for the windows that had screen coverings and opened from the inside.

Lighting up a cigarette, she sat very close to the screen and silently prayed that the smoke detector would not go off. It had been a *very* long day.

In the morning Eddie awoke, only to find her sister curled up beside her. She watched Sam's tiny chest rise and fall, rise and fall, with great interest. Eddie loved her little sister best of all. Even though Eddie had been slowly warming up to Natalie, she had loved her sister from the very beginning. Eddie had always wanted a younger sibling, but her bio-mom had been very firm with a one-child-only policy, often sharing horror stories of her own crowded childhood with Eddie.

Samantha. Sammy. Samwise. Sam.

Sam would be four next month.

With fair skin, honey blonde curls, and azure eyes, Sam looked more like her mom and their dad. Sam and Eddie shared cute button noses, but that was the only likeness. Eddie, with her chestnut-colored skin and slender build, had never much looked like either of her parents. Not really. The ginger hair she got from her father, and the curls from her mother, but that was about it. Her mother was much darker and prettier than Eddie could ever hope to be.

Back when Eddie was in middle school, she would find herself at odds with her appearance, often wishing that she had been born darker or lighter so that she maybe could fit in more easily at school and church.

As Eddie got older, however, she realized that both sides of her family loved and accepted her as she was. From time-to-time, her freckles and orange hair still got on her nerves, and fitting in always seemed impossible, especially at school. Sam would grow up to be a lovely woman, whereas Eddie would remain an ugly, flat-chested dwarf, like some mucked up version of Snow White.

Sam wriggled beneath Eddie's arm, suddenly pulling her back into orbit. She was awake now and ready to play, dammit.

"Oh Sammy," Eddie said, softly running her fingers through her sister's fair hair.

In response, Sam only giggled, then turned around and put her feet in the air.

"I love you so much." Sam was so perfect, so pure. Nothing she did could upset her big sister. "If anyone ever tries to hurt you, I swear to god I will friggin' kill them."

Samantha nodded, got down from the bed and walked over to the front door, then performed an interpretive dance. "Uhhh."

"What is it?" Eddie asked. "You gotta pee? Alright, kiddo. Come here."

By the time they reached the lobby, it was a quarter till ten, which meant they were late. Really late. Everything would be Eddie's fault, too. She could just hear the bitching now.

"Hell—we gotta bolt, kid."

The first thing Eddie saw when she got to the cafeteria was her parents sitting together, laughing and sharing a bagel with one another. This was not the reaction she had come to expect from always-on-time-never-late-don't-take-shortcuts-Natalie Burke. But once Eddie realized they were in the clear, her jaw muscles relaxed, and the tension slid from her shoulders onto the floor like an empty backpack.

"Hey, we're over here!" Beckoning the two girls toward the table with a wave, her parents did not seem to mind their tardiness, her father instead planting a kiss on Eddie's cheek, and scooping his other daughter up into his arms. Sam welcomed his embrace and responded appropriately like the helping of cheerful, golden laughter that she was. Her little sister giggled with great mirth, then threw her arms around her father's neck, and shrieked as loudly as a cockatoo. "Daddy!"

The room soon fell silent, and everyone turned to stare at the pig-tailed cherub in purple overalls. Her father didn't seem to mind. "It doesn't take much to please them at this age. Come here, you!"

Eddie rolled her eyes, picked up a plate, and sat down next to Natalie. *Still* not ready to forgive. *It's going to take more than blowing a damned raspberry on my cheek.*

Natalie placed a knowing hand on Eddie's back and rubbed it. "Morning, sunshine."

With extraordinary effort, Eddie struggled to accept the current situation, loading her plate with scrambled eggs, a handful of berries, and some white toast. Her father, now trying to play nice, handed her a packet of grape jelly.

"I made sure to tell them that you're a vegetarian, Ed. So there's plenty of food for you." Eddie nodded in response and bit into a strawberry.

"Cool," she replied, with a mouthful of fruit. "That was nice of you." Eddie wasn't good at feigning indifference, but he wasn't going to just weasel his ass back into her life so easily.

He's trying so hard, she thought to herself, shutting her eyes. The thought was comforting, especially if her disinterest was causing him pain. It was petty to think like that, but she couldn't help it. He had abandoned them, and she felt that he had not suffered enough. *Trying isn't enough. He has to prove himself.*

"So tell me, what's been up?" Her father was annoyingly cheerful, and Eddie would need coffee and a cigarette if it kept up.

"I don't know. Just school. Same stuff, different day. You know." Natalie was glaring at her, but Eddie continued, "Graduate in a couple of months, haven't really narrowed down any of my choices. Probably just go to Huntington Junior College. Take some art classes. Get out of there as fast as I can."

Her father leaned toward her, his chin resting on a balled fist, and said, "If you don't want to go to HJC, we can make it work. Don't sell yourself short. You're a gifted artist."

"I'm not the one who's settling. I haven't settled for anything." The words had more bite in them than intended, but her father didn't seem to mind. "I'm being realistic. I don't even really want to go to college, you already know this."

"I do know, honey. But think about your-." With a black look, Eddie cut him off.

Don't you dare say 'mom.' You leave her out of this, you son of a bitch.

It was a crappy manipulative tactic, and Eddie wasn't having any of it.

"Alright, well, time to change the subject," Natalie intervened. "We are thinking of getting a dog, Andy."

"A dog?" Shock replaced the sadness in her father's voice.

"Yes, his adoption will be finalized next Thursday. His name is Jasper."

"Thursday?" Her father asked. "Next Thursday? I thought we were supposed to discuss everything as a family, and aren't you allergic to dogs?"

"Huh, that's funny. Like we did with you leaving the family to come here and live for a year?" Again, her father didn't take the bait, but this time Eddie could see the pain in his eyes immediately after she said it. Maybe she had gone too far, maybe she hadn't. It was too late now, though, and besides, she was tired of pretending that everything was normal, nice, copacetic.

Everything was a damned mess, and everyone in the room knew it. There was no magic pill that could make this experience any more bearable—for any of them. The human mind is a delicate thing, shaped by one's reality, and the reality here was more like a nightmare.

After brunch was over, a short, stocky man in a gray three-piece suit stood before the room and cleared his throat. Much like Eddie's school cafeteria, the chatter died down in patches, and all turned to face him as if he *were* a principal getting ready to address a rowdy assembly.

"My name is Walter Crabtree," he said. "I am the house manager of Recovery Works. As you can see, we are blessed here at this facility. We are able to offer 24-hour care to our patients. We are able to do this through grants and generous donations from various charities. Well, yesterday, a spokeswoman from the university came to visit a relative and left ten tickets with us. These tickets are for the fine arts center downtown. A traveling exhibit opened last week and being the director of the center, she was able to present us with these tickets. We thought it would be a nice opportunity for the children to get to know one another. If your children are interested in attending an, ahem, unofficial field trip of sorts, please meet with one of the chaperons after brunch. I believe it would allow the parents time to become reacquainted as well and give the children a much-needed chance to socialize."

A chance to get away. To break free. This was like a dream come true to Eddie.

After the short man finished running through planned activities for the day, Eddie turned to her father and nodded vigorously.

"Uh yeah, absolutely. I'd love to get the hell out of this place." Even though the idea of hanging out with noisy mall-rats wasn't her idea of bliss, she absolutely loved art and couldn't wait to get out of this bizarre facility. She was glad it was working for her father, but it reminded her too much of a hospital, and hospitals were bad. They're where parents go to die.

Eddie needed to breathe.

And smoke.

Chapter 2

As usual, Eddie got turned around in the arts center and found herself lost amongst various works of art. Keeping up with the small group of kids had proved useless because no one actually gave a crap about the art. All they wanted to do was take selfies and share memes with one another. But not Eddie. For her, art was an escape, one that forced you to leave your parachute behind.

The upstairs portion of the arts center was her favorite, featuring unique sculptures of gray naked men and women made by local art majors, and awesome, expensive paintings of nobles, kings and queens, complete with golden and bronze frames—or at least that's what she assumed from the frames and attire they were wearing in the portraits. At the ripe old age of seventeen, Eddie was no art historian.

The art was absolutely breathtaking.

Eddie appreciated art in a way that was indescribable.

At first, art had been a tool for coping with the death of her mother, but after the first two years, it had blossomed into something more—a full-time passion. Through the art courses offered at her middle and high school, she developed a deep, personal love of making stuff with her hands. She loved the way the clay felt in her hands, wet and cool to the touch.

After a few minutes of being deeply absorbed into her surroundings, Eddie realized how just how eerily silent this corridor of the arts center had become.

No more laughing. No more noisy kids. No more selfies.

It was slightly unnerving, but she did enjoy the stillness immensely. She knew that Natalie would not approve of her accidental detour and that she, more than likely, would be punished for ditching the group at the water fountains and exploring the halls by herself. But she had to do it—some unseen force had compelled her to ditch the dodos and research this unknown part of the island.

Ornate masks lined the walls, and tarnished suits of armor could be found in nearly every room. This seemed overdone to Eddie, and she did not quite understand the organizational skills, but then again, she was no curator, so she continued to gaze at the art with great interest.

After exploring a room full of remarkable colonialware and weaponry, Eddie stumbled upon a tiny room housing only two pieces of art. The room seemed sterile. It reminded her of the rehab facility. She didn't like it.

The first piece of art was a chair, placed in the middle of the room. A fairly simple chair, upholstered in a rich, goldenrod colored fabric, it had sturdy wooden legs with intricate carvings.

"Whoa, cool," Eddie said to herself, crouching down on her hands and knees to get a better look at the patterns. Fiery swirls going this way and that way consumed the dark mahogany legs. She had never seen anything quite so whimsical before, especially not on something that looked like it belonged in a fancy museum.

Eddie stood up and shifted her backpack on her shoulders, then rubbed her eyes and looked at her watch. *Weird.* It was after seven, yet no sounds made their way through the halls—and she was getting hungry.

When Eddie walked back over to the doorway and peered into the vacant hallway, she suddenly realized that she had somehow gotten completely disconnected from *everyone* in the arts center. At what point had she strayed from the group of fellow rehab brats? She couldn't remember, growing nervous and agitated.

Eddie vigorously rubbed her hands on her pants as if to wipe away an unseen substance. A panic attack would not do. *Not now.* She walked back to the chair.

The second piece of art was a framed painting; unlike the others, in that, it had a modest wooden frame and was slightly tilted and propped up against the chair. Eddie took the painting into her hands. On the canvas was a scene depicting a lanky, elderly man conjuring up a spell of some sort, over an old, rusty cauldron, complete with gray plumes of smoke welling up from the big pot. The tall thin man, with long white hair and a dark brown robe that engulfed his wiry frame, towered over several people, who were lying on the floor with looks of exasperation on their faces.

It had to be the tackiest piece of art in the building—it seemed so out of place, like one of those velvet paintings of dogs playing poker that you'd find at the flea market. She turned the painting over.

No name anywhere. What the hell.

Now clutching the painting in her hands, Eddie stared into the piercing green eyes of the tall man. They were unsettling. A moment later Eddie found herself overcome with fatigue and exhaustion, a sudden dizzy spell forcing her to drop the painting on the floor, and find solace in the chair. She hoped someone from her cohort would find her soon.

Eddie waited as patiently as she could, opening and closing her eyes slowly, but eventually found it too difficult to shake the inexplicable feelings of fatigue.

It was bizarre, like being trapped in one of those funky dreams where you know you're asleep, but you can't control the things you see or feel.

I'm just tired. Eddie hadn't gotten enough sleep last night, and she was pooped. *Yeah, that's it. But why now? And why so strong?*

Eddie tried to stay awake, but the desire to close her eyes for good was winning. Each eyelid felt as heavy as a bag of sugar.

Aw, crap. It's no use. Maybe just for a couple of minutes.

She pulled her knees up under her chin, leaned her head and shoulder against the soft velvety fabric, and closed her eyes. Eddie didn't know what was happening. She knew that if staff caught her, she would be in trouble because she was breaking some serious rules and maybe even the law—but at that moment, Eddie didn't really care. Finally, she let a wave of warmth overcome her and drifted off into a deep sleep.

•••

It's got to work. It just has to.

Aldous had been up for thirty-nine hours trying to perfect the spell. Graduation was less than two months away, and if he couldn't get this stupid simple spell right, there was no hope for him. And there never would be. Everything his father believed about his incompetence and futility would ring true.

He removed the thick, brown-framed glasses from his head and rubbed the bridge of his nose. Boy, was he exhausted. He put his glasses down on the desk, closed the book sitting next to them, and reached for a plate.

Tilting his head to one side, he eyed the slice of cake.

How long has this been sitting here? How old is it?

Had Vada left it there yesterday, or the day before yesterday, or the day before that?

Aldous murmured something inaudible to himself, shrugged a half-hearted shrug, and then took a bite.

Over the past two days, Aldous had been so busy that he had forgotten to eat. A piece of stale walnut cake would just have to do. He took two more bites and placed his fork down on the table. He needed something.

Milk.

Aldous stood up, walked over to his large wooden armoire, retrieved an enormous black cloak from within, then walked over to the mirror and examined his face and hair.

He was a lanky boy—a young man, really—freakishly tall, gaunt and wiry, with long white hair that fell way past his shoulders and appeared silver in the moonlight (or so some of the children taunted). Dreadfully pale and possessing a slightly crooked smile, the tall boy had an unfortunate sliver of a gap between his two front teeth.

Spectre. Aldous hated the way he looked.

Hmpf. Nothing had changed since the last time he had braved a glance.

Sylph. He rolled his eyes. *Freak.*

Aldous wasn't a particularly unsightly fellow, but you couldn't tell him that.

No, once Aldous Molhata set his mind to something, it was all or nothing.

He walked over to his closet, picked up a pair of black leather boots, then walked over to his bed, and sat down, gently pushing aside the moving lump to his right.

The fox. *His fox.* The enormous animal on his bed looked at him, then looked at the boots in his hands. Aldous followed his eyes. The boots were covered in mud, but he couldn't remember the last time he had been outside in the rain.

Hell, I can't remember the last time I even went outside. For anything.

In fact, Aldous seemed to be losing his grip on most things these days.

No, his focus was set on nothing other than mastering these last few spells.

Was he losing his mind in the process, though? Either way, he didn't care—Aldous might not be the best suuga in the world, but by the stars, he would be mediocre. He owed his waja that much.

After a minute that seemed to defy the actual composition of time, Aldous pulled the cloak over his head, walked over to his desk, and picked up a large candelabra, then ducked under the door frame on which he normally hit his head. Remnants of the bump on his forehead from last week, when he had rushed out of the room because of a forgotten spell book in Waja Sanjay's room, suggested that he proceed with caution.

With a wry grin, he gently closed the door, and then rubbed the knot.

The hallways were quiet and dark, and only a few pendant lanterns offered their luminous assistance to Aldous. He wasn't supposed to be wandering through the halls past midnight, but since he was an upperclassman and lived in the haunted halls, he would not likely encounter another. He rubbed his arm with his free hand. It was drafty. And silent. Aldous wasn't afraid of the dark, nor did he truly believe these halls or rooms were haunted. After his mother died, he had sauntered through these halls for days, crying and calling her name. But no one came. Not even an apparition of another.

When Aldous finally came upon the descending staircase, he could see shadows swiftly dancing across the ceiling like tiny black imps celebrating the witching hour, and flames from the lanterns smashing into the glass panes angrily, indignantly fighting against the unfriendly draft. Somehow it seemed much darker tonight, a shade of darkness beyond the blackest of black, extending itself well down into the winding stairwell.

Aldous clutched at his cloak and hurried down the stairs, for he knew with certainty that if the headmistress caught him, he would be in for it. The last time he had been caught, she forced him to clean the chalkboards and erasers for three weeks. He had coughed up dust for much longer than that, and his fingernails had been left horribly brittle.

When Aldous was halfway down the stairwell, he decided to climb onto the handrail, wrap his legs around the top pole, and ride the rest of the way down. He felt incredibly silly and foolish, but the darkness seemed to be chasing him at a speed that he couldn't possibly out-walk.

Suddenly the idea of creeping alone at night didn't seem so bright.

The brass end-cap of the handrail came abruptly, however, and forced Aldous to slide off the banister rather slowly.

For a moment he sat in pain beyond words, and then suddenly remembered the fallen candelabra.

Aldous, you are quite the idiot at times, aren't you?

After slowly pushing himself away from the floor, he picked up the silver candlestick and walked rather sheepishly until the pain subsided. Aldous rejoiced the fact that he was the only one awake to witness such foolishness.

When Aldous finally came upon the over-sized kitchen, he decided to make a small basket of food to store in his room until he figured out the intricate workings of those darn spells. He set down the candlestick and proceeded to inspect the room.

Five sinks, six iceboxes, four stoves, two ovens, an enormous cauldron, and a dark pantry that seemed to stretch well into the next kingdom. He walked over to one of the iceboxes and discovered several bottles of sheep's milk within. With a click of his tongue, he retrieved two chilly bottles from the top shelf and set them on the large wooden island in the middle of the room.

After loading his arms up with several glass jars, he walked over to the island and placed them beside the milk. What he needed was food that he could store in his room for longer than a day.

Bread. Loaves of good, crusty, hard bread.

It was an odd feeling, this. Aldous had never before been in the kitchen at night, despite having the unspoken permission to go mostly wherever he pleased. Being the headmaster's son did have some perks, and this was certainly one of them.

Aldous lifted the candelabra high above his head to see more of the room. A blackness covered everything not touched by the candlelight. It was alarming. If he could find a few loaves of bread, he wouldn't bother with cheese or anything else; for it was becoming increasingly apparent that his presence was not wanted in this part of the school.

As Aldous approached a large bread box, he heard something.

A loud clatter to his left.

The unmistakable sound of pots and pans spilling onto the floor.

Aldous jumped and swiftly turned around, but couldn't see very well in the dark because he had left his glasses in the bedroom. With his heart now racing as fast as a falcon, he waited for more movement.

Noise.

Anything.

Aldous stood as still as a dead man for several minutes, but nothing else happened. All he could hear was the sound of blood rushing through his ears. Maybe he was wrong. Maybe this part of the school was truly haunted.

Aldous didn't want to find out, however, so he rushed over to the bread box, took out two loaves of bread, placed them on the island, and then searched for towels or rags to wrap them in. *I've got to be swift. I have to get out of here.*

While wrapping the bread in a sack, he felt something move behind him, turning him into a panic-stricken gargoyle within seconds. Now frightened beyond words, he surveyed the dark kitchen as best he could, before setting his eyes on a knife block at the end of the sink. Any sudden movement and he would endanger himself. So he closed his eyes, counted to ten, then lifted the candles to eye level, and turned around.

"Who's there?" He whispered. But no reply came.

Then after a deep breath, he said to no one in particular, "Look, I know that I'm not supposed to be down here, alright, but if you'll allow me to gather my belongings, I will be out very shortly." Still, no reply came. "OK, you win. I'll just be on my way then."

Feeling as though he might faint, Aldous placed his hands on the wooden island and braced himself, for he was not a very brave young man. But then he saw a shadow dart beside him, and he shakily raised the candlestick to get a better look.

It was his fox, standing there, with a wheel of cheese in his mouth.

"Are you kidding me? It was you this whole time? You nearly scared me into an early grave. What are you doing down here, snooping about? You could have given me a heart attack, you know. Have you been down here this whole time?"

The fox wagged his long, wispy tail in response. He had probably seen Aldous hit the brass butt of the rail and fall off, as though he had been hit with a baseball bat in the groin, too.

"You're wrong, you know that? You're a demon's hound. Now get over here." Aldous shook his head and wagged his finger at the large animal. "Stay close to me and don't go wandering off. You probably woke the headmistress, and she will not be pleased to find a wild animal scavenging through her pantry. And don't give me that look—you *are* wild. You are a fox. And where did you find that cheese?"

The fox pointed his nose in the opposite direction. Aldous in return placed his hand on the tall animal's ruff and followed him into the pantry. There, he found several blocks of cheese, stacked neatly in a large wooden case, behind jars of candied yams. He picked up two blocks and patted the fox on his head.

"Thank you. I know that you were trying to be helpful, in your own diabolical way, but next time, try not to be so clever. Don't be a, you know, fox about it." The fox shook his head at the terrible joke and snapped his long fangs at his tall companion.

Feeling far less frightened now, Aldous strolled over to the wooden island and placed the various items in a basket that he found hidden within the island's shelves. He lifted up the basket and looked at it more thoroughly. Obviously used for storage, the basket was worn, and some of the colorful weaving had come undone. He shook the dirt from the basket beside the island. The fox sneezed.

Hey, I am down here you know.

Aldous considered the fox.

I may be wild, but I don't want soiled fur. You never brush me anymore, and it is becoming increasingly difficult for me to reach my back. Bad bones, you know.

Aldous placed the basket back on the island and put his bony hands on his hips.

"It's not my fault you like playing in that horrid forest. I have tried washing you repeatedly, but you seem to run off every time I locate a bar of lye. Convenient, huh?" The fox sniffed in response and gently sat down on his haunches, defiantly licking his left paw. "You're an absolutely nasty creature, you know that? Nasty and cunning, and I'd like for you to stay out of my head. Do you hear me?"

Aldous harrumphed, turned back around, and began filling the rickety basket with the bottles, loaves of bread, and blocks of cheese. He wasn't sure he would be able to fit all the foodstuffs in the basket, but he would try. Balancing the basket in one hand and the candlestick in his other might prove tricky, especially since the bottom of the basket was looking more and more unreliable every time he placed a bottle in it. The fox was as helpful as a sack of potatoes, and there was no way he would allow Aldous to place anything on his back. The fox stopped cleaning his paw to sneer at Aldous.

"Bother you, then. You can feed yourself!" Aldous looked down at the fox, stuck out his tongue, and furtively arranged the broken basket and candles in his arms, then nudged the animal with his boot, nodding toward the darkened hallway. "Up you go." The fox stood up and stretched his long torso, then walked around in a circle.

"You're like a big prissy house cat, you know that?"

The fox, ignoring the jab, sniffed the air and turned his head toward the area where the pots and pans had fallen a moment earlier.

"This is rather uncomfortable," Aldous bristled. "Can we be on our way, or are you ready for another nap?"

Without waiting for an answer, Aldous ambled towards the hallway, leaving the fox behind.

"Bloody dog. You're quite worthless, really."

Hey, I heard that. I am a fox. Not a slobbering idiot, waiting for my next bone. Thank you very much. And I thought you might like to know that I wasn't the one who made that iron fall out of the closet.

Aldous turned around to face the animal.

This fox was a sly one, oh yes, but a liar he was not. It was then that Aldous decided to make a dash for the stairwell. If something or someone was lurking in the shadows, he didn't care to find out. Things were considerably bad at the moment, what with the end of school in sight and his ever-shrinking support system, but he wasn't ready to dance with eternal darkness quite yet.

As Aldous scurried up the marble stairs, scalding wax spilled down onto his wrists and fingers, the jars in his arms clanking together so loudly that they could wake the dead (assuming they weren't already awake, that is).

By the time he reached the top of the stairs, Aldous was drenched in sweat, and shivering, more exhausted now than he was before he left his room. If Aldous were to hazard a guess about the time it took to race up the stairs carrying a ramshackle basket full of junk to get to his room, he would say approximately thirty-seven years. He pulled the slipping basket back onto his shoulder, re-positioned the candelabra in his sweaty hands, and glanced up at a large iron clock on the wall.

Nearly two o'clock.
The all-nighters are finally catching up to me.
Something has to give.
Things have to change.
I need a miracle.

After he reached his door, Aldous sang a low chant, and then a blue light traced the corners of the door, slowly moving in all directions, like newborn snakes emerging from their nest for the first time.

This is good. It's working. Finally.

The seal on his door was still intact, and while he knew that an ogre or troll could very well bash it in with one swift movement of their fist or club, he found solace in this simple majik.

Aldous walked cautiously into the darkened room, eventually setting the basket of goods on a large wooden chest next to his nightstand.

Aldous.

"What is it? Is something wrong?" Aldous whispered to his fox, raising the candlestick outward.

I think it's alive.

"What? What's alive? What are you talking about? Where?"

There, by the bed. Look.

The fox was right. He usually was, though Aldous would not tell him as much, especially not tonight.

On the floor lay a small thing, compact and curled up in a ball, and dressed in all black. After tiptoeing over to the tiny black mass, Aldous bent down on one knee to get a better look, holding the candles up above his head.

"It's a girl, or maybe a boy. I'm not sure," he said, and then slumped against his dresser. "Good grief, you are one for histrionics, aren't you?"

Aldous bit his bottom lip and thought about everything that had happened that night. Why did everything have to go wrong? It had been there when he left. He was sure of it. No one could have broken that seal. One week of rationing his desserts, two weeks of non-stop bartering, and three sleepless nights trying to deactivate the loud siren that went off every time you exited the room—that's what he had sacrificed for the spell.

And for what? An underclassman?

The protective seal was useless after all if a first- or second-year suuga could find their way into his room so easily. He wanted to bang his head against the wall but didn't. It would cause too much noise.

Well, what are you going to do? Sit there and pout all night?

"No, you hateful thing. I am going to get it a blanket and a pillow, and then send it on its way in the morning. What is wrong with you?"

Aldous liked doing things for other people. It made him feel good, needed. He was good at taking care of things. He liked being of help to others and watching them grow. Forget-me-nots, wounded bloodhounds, saplings, whatever—he was a nurturer, whose gifts were wasted simply because of his gender. The First Kingdom was no place for a male sujii.

"I wonder how that little sprite got here," Aldous said to no one in particular, now leaning back on his elbows. "I don't think I've ever seen you."

His unexpected guest had a very pleasant face, and he wondered how someone's face could hold that many freckles. Quickly remembering that he was ignorant of their age, he felt strange and maybe even a little wicked. From the other side of the room, the fox snorted loudly in response, and Aldous chucked a pillow at him.

"Oh shut up you," he whispered, leaning over to extinguish the candles on his nightstand.

•••

When Eddie opened her eyes, the only thing she could see was darkness and small flecks of white light. The floor was cold to the touch, and someone had placed a blanket on her. It was quiet, which meant it was "lights out" at the rehab facility.

Just what time is it? What the hell?

Had someone found her in the arts center and brought her home? Had she been that out of it that she couldn't remember getting into a van and being driven home? What the hell happened to her? What was wrong with her?

She was afraid to lift the blanket now.

What if she ended up in the hospital instead because something terrible had happened? What if she was in juvie for messing with that crappy art? Thoughts flooded into Eddie like an angry current.

*It wouldn't be the first time I found myself in a hospital without my knowledge or consent.*But things had worked out then, and they would work out now. All she had to do at the moment was focus on her breathing and count in multiples of five.

Five. Eddie slid the blanket down her face, and then after a few deep breaths, opened her eyes.

Ten. She didn't want to move.

Fifteen. She didn't want to breathe.

Twenty. This feels wrong.

Twenty-five. Something is off.

Thirty. The breathing exercises were not working, and Eddie soon found herself paralyzed, as fear, doubt, and confusion slithered their way into her heart like a summer's weed.

Behind her, a door opened, and the shadow of a tall figure crept along the walls of the room. The sound of walking and claws scraping the floor added to the terror that now dictated Eddie's every breath and every movement.

Had she been kidnapped and taken to some weird house in the sticks, probably one of those dilapidated houses they'd passed on their way to the rehab facility?

The sun-faded Confederate flag painted on the van-on-cinder-blocks-combo was a dead giveaway. Eddie didn't know why she hadn't realized it sooner. Her body started to shake like the engine of an old pickup, and she was afraid her captors would hear it.

C-a-l-m d-o-w-n.

If they discovered Eddie was awake, the real horror would start—chains, hooks, reruns of Caillou. Who knows what these freaks had in mind? Now consumed by anxiety and fear, Eddie was startled by the sudden sensation of a heavy animal plopping down on her legs.

"Will you get off of them? You are not a cat." To Eddie, this person did not give off axe murderer vibes. They had an accent unlike hers, but she was from West Virginia, and that was easy to do if you were from any of the bordering states. The large dog now asleep at her feet did not seem murderous or territorial, either. She decided she would try opening her eyes again—a little at first anyway, just in case the soft-spoken man was, in fact, wearing a hockey mask.

After her eyes adjusted to the light, Eddie could see the tall figure opening what appeared to be a small glass cage. Standing a few feet away from her, the robed figure whispered into the empty container, and a tiny flame appeared in what she could now see was a lantern, not a cage. The person then flipped back their hood, revealing their face and hair, confirming her suspicions: a man, or perhaps a very, very tall boy.

"Hey there, little one. Did you sleep well? Do you need anything? A glass of water, perhaps?"

At first, Eddie said nothing, still afraid, not wanting to say the wrong thing. The boy had a friendly face and did not appear to want to hurt her, speaking slowly and moving carefully as if to reassure her of this. Eddie didn't think this boy could hurt someone's feelings, let alone their arm or leg.

"Come on, don't be shy. The sooner you tell me what you need, the sooner I can get you back to your dorm. It's just… that seal. I mean, I worked on that seal for days. And you just—you broke it. I don't see how you did it." He paused briefly and then continued. "At this point, I'm not even concerned with why you did it." Eddie chewed on her lip and locked eyes with the boy. Large, piercing, and a profound color of green, his eyes looked familiar—but how could that be? Eddie had never met this boy.

"I'm sorry," Eddie replied. "But I have no idea what you're talking about. I don't know how I got here. I don't even know where here is."

Aldous stared at her for a second, taking in her unfamiliar face and black clothes.

"What do you mean you have no idea?" He asked. "I'm not going to hurt you, but I don't appreciate being lied to."

The room grew darker when Aldous raised his voice, sending a chill down Eddie's spine.

"What the hell are you even talking about? I'm not lying to you. I don't know who you are, or where I am. I just woke up on this damned floor," Eddie said. "With that dog next to me. Like who do you think you are, talking to me like this." Not waiting for an answer, Eddie continued, angrily. "Look, if you don't want to believe me, fine, that's on you. Not on me. But I'm telling you, I have no idea where the hell I am. And I didn't break no seal, so you'd better stop saying that."

Aldous had been at Ashkak's since he was a boy, which meant that he had interacted with many different walks of life. Students from every kingdom attended this university, and every villager knew that it was the best school for learning and practicing the craft. Not just anyone could attend—you had to be hand-picked and placed in a cohort that you would best serve. There was little tolerance for rule-breaking, and Ashkak's required a strong mind and body, which meant no room for idleness or story-spinning. The child's claims only further annoyed Aldous.

"Right. So, you just appeared out of thin air, did you?" He asked, tersely.

Eddie didn't appreciate his tone and said as much.

"I don't know what the hell your deal is, but you need to chill out," she replied. "Something happened here, and neither of us believes one another. Clearly. Thing is, I don't give a good hot damn if you believe me. I know that I'm telling you the truth. Besides," Eddie said, now eyeing Aldous. "How do I know I haven't been kidnapped? That you're not some creep who snatches girls when they're asleep, like some messed up version of Prince Charming?"

Aldous crossed his arms and replied, "Kidnap? Who got caught in whose room? You're pretty hostile for a burglar."

Eddie leaned forward and adjusted her toboggan. "What exactly is it that you want from me?" When Eddie got angry, you could tell she was from the mountain state. It's what she referred to as her almost-not-quite-white-trash-half, the half that often got her into trouble.

But if Aldous minded, it didn't show.

Actually, her accent and manner of speaking intrigued him. Much like dough being rolled and stretched on a table, Eddie's words were drawn out and carefully formed in her mouth. She talked slow and fast at the same time, the cadence of her voice unlike his, or anyone else at the school, for that matter.

"Are you finished?"

"I guess so," Eddie grumbled.

"Good. Are you hungry? How about some breakfast? There's some bread and cheese over there if you'd like some. And some milk, too. Hang on. I'll get you a plate."

Eddie nodded, hungry enough to eat an entire bag of bread. She got to her feet and wearily followed Aldous over to the table.

"My name is Aldous Molhata, in case you don't already know," he said, the latter half of the sentence whispered unnecessarily.

The first few steps Eddie took were shaky like she had forgotten how to walk. Once she reached the desk, she lost her footing again and stumbled back into Aldous, like a foal learning how to stand on its newly born legs.

"Whoa. Hey, are you alright? Did you stand up too fast?"

"Maybe. I'm not sure," Eddie said. "I don't know."

The young man blinked, then carefully let go of her wrist. "Are you sure you can stand? Do you want to sit back down?"

"Yeah. I think so. I'm OK," she answered. "My name is Edwina, by the way, Edwina Burke, but most folks just call me Eddie. And thanks."

After she filled her plate with food, Eddie looked around the room.

To her right, hung dark velvet drapes high above the desk, and to her left, sat a tremendous bed, one fit for three men. She considered Aldous. He was tall, yes, but as thin as a wraith. Her eyes then darted to the dog now sitting on the bed licking its front paws. It balked, holding her gaze.

"That sure is a pretty dog you've got there. Big as hell, too."

"Yes well," Aldous said. "Don't let his demeanor fool you. He has a bad attitude. I mean, he won't bite you, but he makes messes and gets into everything. Here you go. Let me get you a napkin."

"This isn't poisoned, is it?"

Aldous shot her a dark look.

"I kid, I kid. Jeez. But seriously, dude," Eddie said, lowering to the floor. "This spread is freaking a-m-a-z-i-n-g. It looks like wedding food or something. Is it cool if I eat here?"

"Oh, you don't have to do that. Hang on, let me get you a chair."

Eddie was fine with sitting on the floor. Back home, when there weren't enough chairs at Thanksgiving or Christmas, they sat on the floor, in the kitchen, in the living room. It didn't matter to them. No one made a big deal about it. But before Eddie could voice dissent, a chair moved from one end of the room to the next. With her eyes now as wide as saucers, she exclaimed, "What the hell was that?"

"What do you mean? Surely you've seen a chair before?"

"Don't be a smart ass. That is not what I'm talking about. And that—why are you using lanterns? Is the electricity out, or something?"

"Would you like to sit in the dark instead?" Aldous asked. "Because I can make that happen if you want."

Ignoring his threat, Eddie chewed the food in her mouth slowly and thought about everything—the furniture, the candles, and lanterns, the way Aldous spoke, the fancy food in her mouth. At first, things hadn't seemed so strange—in the dim light—but now that she could see how high the ceilings were, and just how different Aldous looked, a weird, uneasy feeling began to grow in the pit of her stomach.

"Where am I? Where are we, I mean?"

"In my dormitory," Aldous said.

"Dormitory? Rich people word for bedroom in a school."

"Yes," Aldous chuckled. "I suppose you could say that. Are you really that out of it? Maybe you hit your head?"

"I definitely did something. I feel weird."

"Well, eat that food. Maybe it will help. I'm going to make it lighter in here for us—with some lanterns—so that we can actually see each other when we're talking." Eddie did not miss his emphasis on the words 'with some lanterns,' but she refused to give him the satisfaction of seeing her annoyed, so she ignored him and began asking questions instead.

"What's the name of this place?"

"Ashkak's," Aldous replied. "Really, Eddie?"

"Why are you dressed like that? Halloween isn't for another six months."

"Dressed like what? You snuck into my room, you're eating my food, and now you're criticizing my clothing? I had no idea criminals could be so demanding. Would you like a foot rub as well?"

"Ew, no," Eddie said. "I ain't into that kind of crap. But I could go for something to drink. What have you got?"

"Is milk OK?" Aldous wasn't trying to be combative, but Eddie was making things difficult.

"Yeah, that'll work."

With the room now illuminated by candlelight and lanterns, Eddie watched Aldous as he moved. His height, his hair, his face, everything about him was unique. When he spoke, it was like watching one of those shows on PBS, where the men wear makeup and have black moles, and the women wear big poofy dresses and fan themselves a lot. She had never heard of Ashkak's either. Granted, she was from a small town in West Virginia, and she had never seen, heard, or tried lots of things, but she felt like a foreigner in this room. If there was a fancy, rich kid boarding school type of place anywhere near her dad's rehab center, it was news to her. The only logical explanation that she could provide wasn't all that logical and didn't explain nearly enough.

"You never answered my question," Eddie said, holding a glass to her mouth.

"What question?"

"Why are you dressed like that? Like a…wizard or something."

"A wizard? I am not a wizard," Aldous objected, with his back turned to her.

"No, because that would actually be logical, in some weird way. I guess you just like dressing like that?"

"Wizard? I swear, Eddie, we've got to get your head looked at."

"What kind of school is this?"

Turning around with his hands in the air, he answered, "The best kind. The kind where you learn and practice the craft."

Despite already knowing the answer, Eddie asked anyway. "What kind of craft? Like crocheting?" *Please don't say witchcraft. Please don't say witchcraft. Please don't say witchcraft.*

"It's hard to put into words really, but I can show you." At that, Aldous clapped his hands together and whispered into them. Within seconds, a little yellow bird appeared inside. The bird chirped loudly and then vanished into thin air.

"I have lost my freaking mind," Eddie said, before collapsing onto the floor.

By the sound of her head hitting the hardwood floor, Eddie could wake up with a concussion, so Aldous got down on his knees, pulled her head up into his lap, and brushed the hair out of her face. Her brown skin was covered in freckles, and she had flaming orange curls that rested underneath a black knitted hat.

Aldous had been mistaken—she was not a boy or a girl, but a woman nearly grown. Staring down at her, he knew why he had never seen her in the halls. Because she was not a student.

"God, I'm still here," Eddie croaked. "I was hoping this was a dream."

"Oh thank the stars you're alright. You gave me a good scare."

Steadily raising up from his lap, everything came smashing into Eddie's brain like a wrecking ball—the chair, the bird, the school.

"Where am I? Who are you? What is this place? How did you do that with the bird? And why is that dog so friggin' big?"

The two friends exchanged glances with one another, then returned Eddie's puzzled look.

"Crap," Eddie shouted at the top of her lungs. "I mean, what is that? How are you able to pull birds out of thin air like that? Am I on one of those weird Japanese TV shows where the announcer is going to emerge from underneath the bed?"

"You're not a student here, are you?"

"No," Eddie said. "What gave it away?"

"Surely your village has a waja, though."

"A what? What the hell are you talking about? Village?"

"Actually, I guess some of us prefer to practice majik behind closed doors," Aldous replied. "Forget I said that."

"Magic? Like pull-a-rabbit-out-of-a-hat magic?"

"I suppose so, if the spell were powerful enough to create both the hat and the rabbit. Yes, I think you could do that."

Spell. Words that a wizard or witch recite in order to bring about some *magical* scenario.

Eddie shook her head. "This isn't real. This isn't happening. This is not friggin' happening."

Aldous and the fox exchanged glances again.

"Is it possible that you have no idea what I'm talking about? That you've never seen anyone work majik before?"

When Eddie did not return his smile, Aldous looked down at the fox, then back at Eddie, and back at the fox, then back at Eddie again, before finally saying, "You've never seen majik worked before." It was as if *Aldous* needed it repeated in order to believe it himself.

Eddie slowly nodded with wide eyes. "Yes."

For the next few minutes, Aldous sat across from Eddie in silence. No one moved. They hardly breathed. Neither the boy nor his fox knew how Eddie had gotten into Aldous's room. The fox walked over to Eddie and nuzzled her with his wet, black nose.

Now trying to break the awkward silence, Eddie placed her hand on his head and said, "Uh, your dog is very beautiful. And sweet."

The fox shot a look at Aldous.

"Yea, he's not a dog. He's a fox. And he's not a pet. He's—he's something different entirely, actually." Aldous looked down at his hands. "And he quite fancies the way you smell."

Scratching the fox's chin, Eddie asked, "How do ya know that he likes the way I smell? And what's 'something different entirely'? Who's a good boy?"

Aldous lifted his head and finally looked at her. "Well, because he just told me."

Eddie shook her head. *Of course the fox can talk. Why shouldn't he? Pigs probably fly around here, too.*

"And to answer your other question, he's more of like a guard. But not like a guard dog." The differentiation was clearly important to Aldous. "If that makes any sense. He's an animal that is bound to me by majik, not friendship. My lyärgo."

Magic. Eddie thought about that word and then thought about Ashkak's. Aldous didn't have to say it, because she knew in her heart of hearts that she was no longer in West Virginia. Her new companion did not seem nonplussed by her sudden arrival, however. She wished she shared his sentiments.

Opening her mouth, and then closing it, Eddie fought back question after question while Aldous messed with something on his desk. *Odd,* she thought to herself, admiring his profile and white hair, *he's actually kind of cute. In a weird wizardly sort of way. Cute?* Aldous was right—she must have hit her head harder than they thought. This place had gotten her all twisted up inside, and she didn't know her up from down. *Cute.* Eddie dismissed the notion immediately.

"You should really try to sleep some. Your eyes look OK so it's unlikely that you'd go to sleep forever, but if you're worried about it, I won't be able to go to sleep so I can check on you. It's no big deal."

"Are you sure you're not going to murder me while I sleep?" Eddie wasn't entirely opposed to the idea, but could she really trust this boy she had just met?

"I promise. Now take that pillow and rest your eyes."

Resting her eyes was all Eddie could do because sleep never actually came. She lay there with her eyes closed, praying to God that he/she/they/whatever wake her up from this wretched dream. Aldous moved around the room, tip-toeing back and forth, trying his best not to wake her. He seemed like a nice enough guy, a little combative at times, but nothing Eddie couldn't handle. After rolling around on the floor, Eddie finally sat up and removed her hat.

Aldous was standing at his desk, with a book in his hand, working on something Eddie guessed was homework. Did Ashkak's even have homework? Just what kind of school was this? Were wizards required to take trig and AP Lit? Eddie shook her head and then stood up.

"Hey," Aldous said. "Can't sleep?"

"Are you kidding me? You sound like a horse when you walk. Who could sleep with that kind of noise," Eddie replied, folding the blanket Aldous had lent her.

"Good. I'm glad you're up because I've been thinking. We need to figure out some things, but first I have to finish this paper, and then we can put our heads together. OK?"

"OK. Sounds good to me. Hey, did you happen to find a backpack anywhere? It's this little black bag, and you put stuff in it. It's got zippers and compartments."

"I know what a backpack is, but thank you for that riveting description, Miss Burke. And yes, I did. It's over there by the bed."

Eddie placed the folded blanket on the bed and walked over to the backpack.

Slivers of sunshine had found their way onto the bed and floor. It was morning Eddie discovered as she pulled the drapes to one side. From where she stood, several of the buildings appeared to be made of white marble, with dome-shaped rooftops that were covered in black and silver shingles. The only comparison Eddie had was the Taj Mahal from her world history textbook, but she was fairly certain that she was not in Southeast Asia.

After she'd had her fill of mountain peaks and rooftops, she took a step back and inhaled a deep breath. "Too high. We are way too high. How many stories is this school?"

"Hmm," Aldous replied. "Oh, nine."

"Nine? Holy crap, man. I don't know how you're able to do it."

"The school is the oldest in the First Kingdom, and it's the largest. I don't know why, but they just kept building upward, instead of expanding outward. It's kind of weird, I guess, and I'd never thought of it until now."

"Are you finished with your paper yet?" Eddie found it hard to control her eagerness. "Because you just said 'kingdom' and I need some information like stat."

Aldous threw up five fingers in response, indicating either five seconds or five minutes. Eddie didn't mind; although she was curious about her surroundings, and when he was ready, she was going to unleash an avalanche of questions upon him.

Instead, she turned her gaze from the window to Aldous and watched him work. His skin was sickly looking and white like an eggshell, but not as bone white as his hair. His other features were fairly unremarkable, but the way his smile touched his emerald green eyes made Eddie uneasy because he had a great smile.

It was a phenomenal smile.

She couldn't remember looking at a man, or boy, like that in a long time. At school, church functions, or football games, it had never gone beyond a bored glance. Eddie then thought about the boys back home in West-by-god-Virginia—strapping, young bucks, obsessed with cheap beer, four-wheelers, and deer hunting. Oh, and they clung to their homophobic slurs like a used dryer sheet. Not all of them, of course, but a lot of them. The ones she knew wore faded blue jeans and boots covered in mud and often topped off their attire with Mack trucker hats. Oh yes, Eddie knew their kind real well and knew to stay away from them, never accepting a ride home from school, even when it resembled hurricane weather outside. Aldous, on the other hand, was as tall and thin as a telephone pole, and the boots on his feet were sleek, black, and covered in mud, definitely not fit for hunting.

"Are you a human?" Eddie finally asked, eyeing Aldous's eyebrows.

"What's a human?"

Eddie had her answer, but clarified further anyway. "Ya know, like a man, or whatever?"

"I'm not a man yet, but I will be soon."

"How do you give birth?"

"What? I'm not capable of giving birth." The incredulity in Aldous's voice did not faze Eddie, however.

She pursed her lips together and asked, "How then? Do y'all lay eggs?"

"What are you getting at? We are not birds or snakes."

"So, you give birth by…?"

"Pushing a baby through the birth canal. Jeez, what is your problem? Why do you need to know this stuff right now?"

Aldous was uncomfortable, which Eddie found oddly reassuring in a way. "I am just making sure that you're not an alien."

"An alien? Like someone who does not belong?"

"Yeah, like those little green guys with laser guns and big flying saucers. They land in your backyard and try to take you back to their home planet. Sometimes they do weird things to cows."

The fox and boy looked at each other, then Aldous said, "I believe you are the alien in this scenario, Miss Burke."

Eddie did not have a response to that.

For a good stretch of the morning, Eddie and Aldous took turns asking each other questions over cups of tea and a rather dubious-looking piece of cake that Eddie politely declined.

"His name is Mister Fluffy, in case you'd like to know, but you're more than welcome to keep calling him a dog," Aldous said, placing his plate on the floor in front of the big animal. "He doesn't mind."

The fox's ears twitched in disapproval.

"What? Wait a minute. This majestic animal's name is Mister Fluffy? This animal that can communicate with you using some Stephen-King-Firestarter-brain-thing. How the hell did you come up with such a goofy name?" Eddie reached out and caressed his long black ears. "Dass a good boy."

"Why," Aldous responded, clutching his chest. "Is he not fluffy? And I do think 'majestic' is a stretch."

"Don't be an idiot." Eddie had seen better acting in Sunday school.

"I'm not sure what his preferred name is. He won't tell me. Stubborn animal."

"That doesn't take away from how dumb it sounds."

"Yes, well—I have some questions for you, too—when you're ready—but if you've got more questions for me, let's hear 'em."

After looking out the window earlier, questions had swum through the ocean of Eddie's mind with so much force that she thought she was going to be seasick. But now she saw an opportunity for relief and decided to take it.

Aldous met her gaze with a warm smile and raised a cup in the air. "Anything. I'll answer anything."

Eddie began, "In that case, I suppose I'd like to know *everything*." Aldous blinked. "Ya know, who you are. Where we are. What life is like here. How magic impacts your daily life. Are there limits to magic? Are there side-effects?"

Aldous bit his lip, nodded, and replied, "How about this? For every question I answer, you have to answer one of mine."

Eddie took a sip of her tea. "Fine by me. The ball's in your court, jolly white giant."

"OK," Aldous said, straightening up. "Hit me with your best shot."

"How old are you?

"Easy. Nineteen. How old are you?"

"Almost eighteen," Eddie replied. The answer brought a smile to Aldous's face. "Why are you smiling like that?"

"No reason. Next question."

"How long have you been here at Ashkak's?"

"Hmm," Aldous said. "Since I was a child. We moved here because my father accepted a teaching position here."

"Do you like it here?"

"It's alright, I suppose. Things are a lot better now than they were back then, I guess."

"How come?" Eddie could feel her curiosity about the boy growing. "Boring?"

Aldous shrugged. "I don't know. My mom got sick after we moved."

"My mom's dead, too."

Aldous smiled. "I'm sorry to hear that. I know how bad it can get."

"Thanks. What's your next question?"

"Your village. Where's it located?"

"Alright," Eddie said. "Let's get one thing straight, Gandalf the Gray, I don't live in a village. I live in a small town—Milton, West Virginia—but I'm sure you have no idea what the hell I'm talking about." A town. The word conjured images of storefronts and busy cobblestone streets, but somehow Aldous knew Eddie didn't live in that kind of town. "What's your sister's name?"

"Astrid," Aldous replied.

"Sam," Eddie then offered, immediately. "Samantha, actually. My sister's name is Samantha. You keep saying that you're not a wizard, but it sure sounds like it."

"Suuga."

"What?"

"I'm suuga," Aldous corrected Eddie. "We're called suuga."

"Soo-gah."

Aldous nodded. "And sujii."

"Soogey?"

"No, not quite," Aldous laughed. "Soo-ji-ee. We're spell-casters."

"Oh, so like a witch?" Eddie spoke slowly for dramatic effect, but Aldous seemed unaffected.

"Sort of, but like I keep telling you, witches exist in fairy-tales. Sujii are very real and very powerful. Suuga are the other half of the coin. For example, I am suuga, and my sister is sujii."

"That sounds an awful lot like witches and wizards to me, but whatever. Earlier you said something about a village witch. What were you talking about?"

"Ah yes, the waja."

Eddie took another drink. "The what? Walljaha?"

"Close." Aldous laughed again. "Wah-jah. My partner. I am her wah-jah as well. That was two questions, by the way."

"Yea, because this," Eddie said, motioning with her hands. "Is obviously more interesting than me." She pointed an index finger at her chest.

"I think you're interesting. I mean, just look at you. We're different—that's all."

"What the hell is that supposed to mean?" Eddie knew the answer even though she had asked. All it took was a quick glance to know that the two of them were as similar as cinnamon and sugar. Aldous looked like something straight out of Masterpiece Theatre, and she likes something out of a Hot Topic catalog. "Are you and your partner going to leave this place and find a village of your own?"

"While that is the plan, I am not so sure. Caoilainn and I aren't on the best of terms. We haven't discussed the topic in a good long while. She hates me, actually, which is just as well because I can't stand her."

"Hmm," Eddie replied. "That doesn't sound like the best ever."

"No, it's not. Anything else of importance? How about you? What do you do in your spare time?"

"I like to read, I guess, and I make stuff with my hands."

"What kind of stuff?" It was Aldous's turn to show interest in his new guest.

"Ya know, like jewelry. But not corny stuff. No beads and yarn. I don't mess with that. I like to work with metal."

"Metal? So you're an artist then." Aldous's green eyes sparkled like the emeralds they were, and Eddie found it hard not to stare into them.

"I suppose so."

"That's really cool," Aldous said, with awe. "I'd love to be able to create things with my hands."

"What? You mean like that damn bird you pulled out of nowhere?"

"That's not the same thing, and you know it."

"Why not? It seems to me that we are both *crafty* in our own ways. See what I did there? Get it? Sometimes I crack myself up."

The fox and Aldous exchanged looks.

Chapter 3

After lunch, Eddie opened her backpack to find two small containers of aspirin and Xanax, some Chapstick, a toothbrush, a hair pick, a red marker, a tiny bottle of body wash, her iPod and ear-buds, two pairs of leggings, and two shirts, she was overcome with gratitude. Natalie was right. Overpacking could be a good thing. Eddie got dressed, then swiveled around and waited for Aldous to do the same.

After he changed into a pair of khaki slacks and a gray turtleneck, looking more like a regular boy and less like someone from Lord of the Rings, Aldous excused himself from the room. Eddie changed her socks and threw a flannel over the black t-shirt she had slept in. The toboggan then came off as she searched for a mirror, and without much effort, found one sitting on Aldous's nightstand. She ran the pick through her bouncy curls.

Last month when her girlfriend had shaved her head, she nearly talked Eddie into shaving her own. Eddie was still unsure if it had been the right decision. A soft knock at the door interrupted Eddie's thoughts before could think any more about her life—her other life.

She called out, "You can come in. I'm decent."

Aldous looked much taller now and his facial features even more severe—greener, thinner, harder.

He looks like a porcelain doll. But not like one of those expensive ones, more like one of those dolls that you find at a thrift store that's been on the shelf for years because it's too creepy to add to your collection.

"I'm not going to lie—this." Aldous made a circular motion at Eddie. "Isn't going to be easy to explain. I will have to come up with some elaborate story that I'm sure no one will believe, anyway." He walked over to the window, his fingers now hooked on the belt loops of his trousers.

Eddie noticed that he had taken the band out of his hair, letting his thick locks flow down his back like a frothy waterfall.

His hair is so white, like the first undisturbed snowfall of winter.

An urge to run her hands through it overcame Eddie momentarily. *What? No.*

Then as if hearing her thoughts, Aldous turned around and smiled.

Did he hear my thoughts? She looked down at her feet in case he had. *Oh hell.*

"Are you alright? Have I said something weird?"

"Hmm." Eddie sat down in a chair and kicked her backpack out of the way, then said, "You can't read my mind or hear my thoughts, can you?"

Aldous belted out a hearty laugh and showed his slightly crooked teeth in response. A joke had been made, and Eddie had missed it.

"No, Edwina, I'm afraid I cannot hear what you are thinking. Nor am I able to read minds or move through dreams or see the future. My powers are relatively limited, especially for someone my age."

It's weird.

This is weird.

He's weird.

Aldous was weird, undeniably different. Even in this world of magic, Eddie could tell that he was different from the rest, despite having never met the rest. She had always assumed magicians had long white beards and old, wizened owls or clever black cats for companions, but that was something she read in books or saw on television. In reality, Aldous was a smart-ass and fought with his animal two-four-seven. At times, the two fought like brothers, or so it seemed to Eddie from the one-sided arguments her new acquaintance often had with the animal.

"Ya know, if we're being completely honest here," Eddie said out of nowhere. "The only exposure to magic I've ever had was that time Alex Moore had a magician at his ninth birthday party and he did some card tricks. Dude's name was Ralph Lombardo—he was the size of a school bus, and he smelled like farts. He actually kind of sucked now that I'm thinking about it."

Aldous raised his arms and put them behind his head. "You talk a lot, you know?"

"Jesus. Sorry." Eddie felt as though she'd been punched in the gut. "I'll just stay quiet from now on."

"Hey, that's not what I meant. It's not a bad thing. I'm just not used to it."

"What?" Eddie asked. "You mean talking?"

"Yeah, unless it's with that jerk over there." Aldous pointed to the fox. "Telepathy isn't all it's cracked up to be. Other than track meets, I don't really go out of my way to hang out with other students. I mostly just keep to myself."

"Well, if you talk to your fellow peers the way you talk to me," Eddie said. "I'm not surprised."

"You don't let up, do you? Well, believe what you want, but I'm glad that you ended up on my floor."

•••

Ashkak University was, as Eddie would come to find out, similar to her high school back home. Many of the same types of kids graced the halls of this fine institution—freaks, assholes, art kids, dorks. There were cliques, and students played sports, and some played musical instruments (some for magical purposes, some not). Kids got bullied, and there were wallflowers.

Eddie didn't ask, but she secretly wondered which kind of kid Aldous was. So far he had been unpretentious and relatively friendly, answering her questions without belittling her or making her feel unwelcome. Occasionally, he would refer to a small group of friends, but other than that, he didn't seem to care about making or keeping therm. Not that Eddie blamed him, of course, friendships in high school could be as fickle as a Kentucky winter.

"Simone is a genius. One of two female suuga at Ashkak's," Aldous explained. "Her ability to transmute surpasses even the most adept instructor. I think everyone is secretly afraid of her, but no one wants to say anything, probably because her parents are powerful diplomats."

"What about you?" Eddie asked, trying to process everything they had discussed in such a short period of time.

"Me? Oh, I'll be lucky to graduate at all. I'm afraid I'm not the greatest student in the world."

Big, spectacular things were expected from his friends, but poor Aldous was a wiz at chemistry and horticulture, and those sorts of abilities were not praised at this kind of school. Kids were graded on their ability to steady themselves on a flying carpet and transform into different animals. There was little room for Marie Curie-types at Ashkak's.

"Isn't your dad like a big deal around here, though?"

Aldous laughed. "Yeah, like I said before, he is the headmaster."

"And?" Eddie asked.

"And what? I'm definitely not a star pupil, if that's what you're asking, and my da knows it. If he weren't the headmaster of this school, I wouldn't be here. He would love that."

Eddie turned to look at him. "Damn, aren't you being kind of hard on yourself?"

"Not at all. I'm just being realistic," Aldous said, with a shrug. "No matter how hard I study, or practice, I cannot master spells. It is that simple. I've been doing the same stuff for years, and still I am forced to wear the brown robe."

Much like the belts Eddie received in karate, the color of one's robe at Ashkak's symbolized how far a student had come in their studies and mastery. Aldous still wore the brown robe, which apparently was the same color of robe that many first and second-year students wore. He was in his sixth and final year. Eddie felt sorry for him.

"My sister is a first year, and she wore the brown robe for like a month. It was humiliating, despite her reassurance that it wasn't. I'm not mad about it, though. Not at all," Aldous said. "I know she is meant for greater things than being some village waja. I don't know how, but she has been able to practice majik since was a toddler. It made for a very interesting childhood, I'll tell you that much. She drove our first governess absolutely mad."

"I don't think you're being fair. I've been here for less than a day and I can tell that you're not an idiot."

"Thank you," Aldous said. "That's very reassuring. I'll be sure to add that to my short list of accomplishments."

"Hey." Eddie punched his arm softly. "I'm being serious here. I don't know nothin' about seals or turning into animals or pulling birds out of thin air, but I know that you're a lot smarter than you realize," Eddie said. "I don't know what kind of crap you were fed growing up, but I don't think there's anything wrong with you."

Aldous gave her an unreadable look and said, "Just give it time. I'm sure you'll change your mind."

Eddie sighed.

Some people measured their worth by applying other people's standards. It never made sense to Eddie. If something wasn't working for her, she just quit or abandoned it, and she certainly didn't give a flying frick about other people's opinions when it came to how she viewed herself. Aldous was funny and sarcastic, easy going, and incredibly knowledgeable about a range of topics. Since getting over her ax murderer fears, the two had hit it off.

Eddie shook her head. "You're wrong."

For the rest of the afternoon, Aldous and Eddie shared food with one another, and discussed books, spells, herbs, and charms at length. They looked over maps, and Aldous pointed out where in the Four Kingdoms they were. Eddie did her best to hide her excitement.

"There are four kingdoms. We're in the First Kingdom, right here. That's what it's called, by the way—though I'm not sure that's what others call us," Aldous admitted. "They may have different names depending upon where in the world you are. The First Kingdom is completely land-locked as you can see, with the Second Kingdom being partially covered in water, and that right there is the Third Kingdom—well, it's basically an enormous island, really. Lots of exotic creatures. Sea serpents. Lots of fishing villages. That sort of stuff. I've never been to the lower kingdoms, but I do have relatives who live in the Second Kingdom on my mom's side. My da doesn't really speak to my mom's family much anymore, though. But I do visit with my gran every spring. She lives a few hours away."

Aldous talked about magic with such passion and interest that Eddie found herself wishing she had been born in one of the Four Kingdoms, and not boring-ole-broke-ass-West-Virginia. She also caught herself looking at Aldous and paying more attention to his features than she normally would, smiling and looking away, or pointing to something else on the map every time he caught her. It was a bizarre, foreign sensation.

After dinner, they shared a pot of lavender tea and iced lemon scones for dessert from the dining hall. Aldous had been gone for what seemed like a decade when he returned with an armful of confections and a big jar of loose tea leaves. That evening, they spoke for a bit about her life in West Virginia and what things were like back home.

"Yeah. Natalie is alright, I guess. She's got a lot going on right now, but she's a decent person. I don't know what my dad would do without her. I mean, her patience is never-ending. I don't really know how she does it. And she always knows what to do. Like, if you're having problems, she's the best person to go to. My dad is not good in a crisis situation. I like her alright. She's a good mom to Sam."

"How old is your sister?"

"Four, or almost, whatever," Eddie responded. "She's great."

"Aren't all little sisters?"

Eddie shook her head in disagreement. "I don't know about all little sisters. My cousin Deidre is a terror, and I know her brother, Eric, hates her. She once found some pictures on his phone and sent them to everyone in his address book. Nobody wanted to press charges, but they both got grounded for the rest of the school year. And honestly, serves him right. There's no telling who he was sending those pictures to."

"What's a phone? And what kind of pictures?" Aldous seemed more interested in the latter than the former.

"A phone is like a little box that you carry around with you, and you are able to talk to another person using it, like you can be in a different room or a different state and call someone from the phone. Does that make sense? I'm not sure if I'm explaining it correctly."

"A box? You speak into the box and a voice appears?" Aldous said, glancing over to a stack of woven boxes in the corner.

"Not that kind of box. It's made of plastic and metal and crap. Some phones even fit in the palm of your hand. OK, so do you have to be in the same room with the dog in order to communicate with him?"

Aldous smiled at the animal beside him, who was now glaring at the both of them, and then said, "No, there can be some distance between us."

"Can other people hear your thoughts?"

"No, just him, and vice versa."

"Alright then," Eddie said. "Imagine having the ability to talk to another person like that, but instead of your mind, you have a little contraption that helps you do this. No magic, just a battery." She could see the wheels turning in Aldous's head.

"So what kind of pictures are we talking about here?"

•••

Later that evening, Aldous excused himself from the bedroom and let Eddie change into an old pair of bedclothes. Mister Fluffy stayed behind and picked through their leftovers on the floor. Eddie undressed and donned a pair of Aldous's long underwear. The shirt was entirely too large, so she decided against wearing the pants (because the waist would fit, but the legs were far too long), and instead wore the shirt as a nightgown. The shirt fell well below her knees, and even though she had to roll up the sleeves, she made it work. She then slipped her feet into a pair of large wool socks and pulled them up to her knees. Looking down at the clothes, Eddie couldn't help but feel as though she had been transported to the top of a beanstalk and not the bedroom of a teenage boy.

Aldous knocked on the door and Eddie invited him back into the room. After a few minutes of fooling around with books on a bookshelf, he walked over to where Eddie was sitting and placed a large, dusty book on her thighs and bare knees.

"Go on, open it."

"Alright," Eddie said, carefully opening the book. "It's not going to suck me inside like The Pagemaster, is it?"

"What? Pagemaster? I have no idea what that is. But no, it won't suck you in, silly. It's just a book."

"OK." Eddie scrunched her nose. "I highly doubt that anything here is *just* anything."

Aldous adjusted the brown frames on his face. "Alright. So you're probably right, but go ahead anyway."

Inside the book rested hundreds of over-worn caramel colored pages, marked with grease and black fingerprints—and upon further inspection, it was not *just a book* as Aldous had suggested: it was his mother's spell book. Technically, Aldous explained, he wasn't supposed to have it and could get into serious trouble if it was found in his room, but he had gone to great lengths to get it any way, and wanted to share it with someone.

Eddie fingered through the pages with a shared interest.

"Within this book, you'll discover the best kind of yarn for flying carpets, love spells, fortune telling, how to ward off djinn, the best kind of glass for crystal balls, how to make charms and amulets, the best wood for broomsticks and wands—all of it. My mother was a studious sujii, and recorded nearly everything. That's why every page is covered front to back with information regarding this stuff."

Eddie brushed her fingers lightly across the ink and smiled. It was a lovely keepsake.

"It's wonderful, Aldous," Eddie said, stifling a yawn. "Thank you for showing it to me."

"We're not through yet. Keep turning the page until I tell you to stop."

"OK." All of the reading in low light was starting to get to Eddie. "But I'm not sure I can go on much longer."

"There," Aldous exclaimed, placing a finger on a page that read in big, bold letters: TELEPORTATION.

Aldous said the word aloud. It didn't seem real. How could something like teleportation be real? Is that how Eddie came to be sitting on this tall boy's sofa? She didn't want to consider the possibility, not really. But if the rules of logic were still intact, it meant that magic had brought her here, and that if magic existed here, it existed back home, too.

"Teleportation. Are you familiar with the concept?"

"What? Like traveling through time and space, or whatever?"

"Perfect summation," Aldous replied. "Yes. Is it a thing where you live?"

"Aldous." Eddie didn't take her eyes off the book. "None of this stuff is real where I live."

"Except that you're here." Aldous's voice had taken on a sing-songy quality that Eddie didn't like.

"Except that I'm here." Eddie half-expected a smart-ass quip about magic being real, blah blah blah, but Aldous said nothing in return, instead choosing to run his finger along the words on the page.

Hope suddenly coursed through her body.

Could this book contain the way home? Would she be able to leave tomorrow? Perhaps the next day?

Aldous adjusted his glasses and began to read. "Pay attention now, burglar sprite, because this concerns you." Eddie stuck her tongue out at him. "There are three ways to teleport, which are outlined below." He held up three fingers.

Eddie rolled her eyes. "Will you just read the damn thing?"

"'It is important to remember that not all three spells will work the same way, however, and whatever works for me may not work for you, and vice versa. So far only one of these spells has worked for me, and it just so happens to be the most complicated.' Of course it is," Aldous bristled. "'In order to complete the first spell, you will need seven twigs from an Althean tree that has not yet died, but is in the last throes; five ripe sunberries, three small locks of hair (presumably the hair of the traveler), and an object through which you can pass.' Hmm. I'm not entirely sure what that last bit means about 'an object through which you can pass.' Perhaps this is an older movement spell. Something archaic. I've never heard of someone passing through an object. Let's look at the other spells."

Eddie looked at the unreadable words with a frown. "Wait, so is she saying that the spells work differently? What does that mean? Does she mean they won't produce similar effects?" She had never heard of an Althean tree, nor did she know where to find sunberries. Were they related to sunflowers? Did they taste sweet or sour? Were you supposed to eat them? The impossibility of everything now rested squarely on her chest like a cement block and it was becoming harder to breathe. Aldous lifted the book from her lap and began pacing the floor with it in his hands. They did not go over the other spells as he had suggested.

Now feeling somewhat ill and deflated, Eddie walked over to Aldous's bed, positioned herself next to the fox, and began stroking his coarse fur.

Mister Fluffy would make a kick-ass emotional support animal.

Eddie was afraid now. If her new friend couldn't figure out what had brought her here and why, then she may never see her family again. It wasn't the world's greatest family by any stretch of the phrase, but it was her family, and she belonged with them.

The next morning Eddie found herself lying awake in Aldous's bed. The last thing she remembered from last night was getting in the bed with Mister Fluffy. Aldous must have let her sleep. She stared up at the ceiling.

Things were a damned mess. The spell book had not offered Eddie much hope after all. Things were still unclear, and despite Aldous's reassurance that he would help her get home, she didn't feel very confident.

Just as Eddie was getting up from the bed, a door opened. Wearing nothing but a towel around his waist, Aldous returned with wet hair and a smile—and for the first time in her life, Eddie looked at a boy's bare chest with interest. She turned away in haste, hoping that he had not seen it.

What the hell? Just what the hell is happening to me? Have you lost your mind?

"So, um, I'm sorry for stealing your bed last night. I wish you would have told me to move. It's cold in here and it's your bed."

Aldous grabbed a pair of socks from his dresser, then went to look for a robe in his closet.

"Nah. Don't worry about it. I couldn't really sleep last night anyway. I'm glad someone's getting use out of the darn thing. Besides Fluff likes it when pretty girls shower him with attention. Don't you, you old narcissist?"

Aldous had intentionally (or unintentionally, it was hard to tell because of his tone and manner of speaking) called her pretty. Eddie wasn't used to compliments, especially from straight boys. It shouldn't matter to her that he thought she was pretty, but somewhere deep inside her chest, her heart stirred.

You don't know this person. Are you insane?

With his back to her (and still wearing a towel), Eddie braved one more glance at the boy's bare back.

Aldous's shoulders weren't very broad, and he was as pasty as Elmer's Glue, but Eddie couldn't deny how attractive she found him. When she turned around again, she caught Mister Fluffy eyeing her as if he could read her thoughts.

I'm just looking. Nothing more.

After gathering an armful of clothing, Aldous informed Eddie that he would be back, and that she could get dressed in the meantime. *Getting dressed would be so much nicer if I could take a shower*, she thought, while rummaging through her backpack. A shower. Thinking back on a conversation she had had with Aldous, the thought of staying in one of the girl's dorms had initially made her nervous, but also excited because that meant showering. *Finally.*

Eddie changed her clothes and waited for Aldous to return.

When Aldous stepped through the doorway looking like something from a Disney movie, Eddie had to bite the inside of her cheek to keep from smiling. Now wearing a floor-length brown robe with a silver cord tied around his narrow waist, Aldous's thick white hair hung past his shoulders and covered most of his face. His black boots had been replaced with a pair of brown leather ankle boots, and he carried a brown leather satchel at his side. Something was missing though, and when Aldous emerged from the closet wearing a long, conical, brown hat, Eddie nearly lost it. He was a wizard—or suuga, whatever—and now he looked like one. She felt like biting herself again.

"Whoa, would you look at that," Eddie said. "This shit is surreal."

After a quick gander at his reflection in the mirror, Aldous removed his hat and angrily shoved it into his satchel.

"Oh I know, it's an absolutely horrid thing. The hat. It's mostly ceremonial, but one of my instructors requires that you wear it in his class. It looks stupid and funny."

"I honestly don't know what to say to you right now." Eddie stared at Aldous in disbelief. "My mind is blown. This whole thing is almost too much for me to comprehend. I mean, you look *incredible*. Straight up like Merlin or some junk."

After that, Eddie watched Aldous's every move with great anticipation. Would the others wear similar hats and robes? Did he carry a wand? Did the others? With her black clothes and country drawl, fitting in would be impossible. She swallowed.

"Hey, look at me." Aldous picked up Eddie's backpack and handed it to her. "You're nervous. Try not to be. It won't be that bad. My friends aren't vicious, a little overbearing maybe, but they're good people. If I didn't think the headmistress would somehow find you, I'd let you stay in my room until we figured things out. She has some sort of sixth sense about this stuff, though. Are you ready?"

Eddie took the backpack from his hands and eased it onto her shoulders. It felt heavier somehow, because the weight she now carried on her shoulders couldn't be measured in pounds or ounces.

Jesus H. Christ. What have I gotten myself into?

"Alright, I am," Eddie replied. "I mean, as ready as I could be in a school full of witches and wizards, ya know, but I'm not making any promises. I'm just letting you know right now. Will there be coffee by any chance?"

Aldous whistled to his fox and opened the door. "Come on, then. I'm not sure, but I'll try to find you some. Yeah?"

You know it's not necessary to whistle at me. I'm not a dog. You just want to show off for her.

Mister Fluffy jumped down from the bed and stretched his front paws, then walked over to Eddie and rubbed against her legs. She silently wished that she could stay in Aldous's room all day and play with the damn thing instead and skip out on meeting his friends. Eddie had no idea what she was walking into. What if these people had two noses, or tails, or walked on their hands instead of feet? Aldous looked normal enough, but was he? Was he really that normal? Just what was normal in this place, anyway? It wasn't that Eddie shied away from friendships—they just didn't come easy to her. She never knew what to say or what to do, and when she did say something, it was usually too late, or inappropriate. If Eddie possessed a magical gift, she was sure it had something to do with scaring away other people.

Eddie followed Aldous out of the room.

With his hand still on the doorknob, he said a few words to himself before taking a step back and bumping into Eddie.

"Is that the seal I broke? It looks like miniature fireworks being set off. Will the light hurt you?"

Aldous replied, "It could hurt you, depending upon its efficacy. But remember, I'm not sure it actually works. I did everything in my power to make it work, but don't forget who you're talking to." He patted the leather satchel which now held the brown hat. "Come on, it's this way."

"One more question and then I'll shut the hell up."

"Hmm?" They walked side by side down the poorly lit hallway.

"What am I going to tell people? How will I answer their questions? What do I do? When they ask me where I'm from, I can't exactly say the rolling hills of Appalachia, now can I?"

At first Aldous said nothing, instead focusing on his feet, that were carefully descending the staircase, but then, as if changing his mind in mid-step, he turned around and collided with Eddie abruptly. "Oh stars, pardon me!"

"Aw hell, dude." Eddie snarled, heading face-first into his torso, and nearly losing her footing. "Careful. Jesus Christ. I know I'm shorter than you, but come on. I'm not that short."

"Oh yeah, I'm sorry. Are you OK? Here let me help you. Well, I suppose we could tell everyone that you're my cousin."

"Cousin?" Eddie raised an eyebrow at this suggestion.

Aldous's skin was as alabaster as her bedroom walls, and his eyes were brilliantly green. He was also significantly taller than her, and didn't have a mole, zit, or freckle anywhere that Eddie could see. Back home her dad's side was full of freckled Gingers so she fit in well enough, but Aldous looked and carried himself like a walking blizzard. No, it would be a stretch. A long stretch.

"Uh, dude? I am not sure that will work. That would be like saying the sun and the moon are related."

Now looking down at her orange hair and freckles, Aldous nodded his head in agreement. "Darn. Maybe you're right. Besides, it would be difficult to explain why I have never mentioned you before," he said. "I could tell them that you're from another kingdom, I suppose. That your parents are off on some perilous quest. That you're a friend of the family, perhaps? It has happened before in emergency situations. Students have stayed here for a few weeks while their parents were indisposed."

"A quest? What kind of quest?"

"Don't worry about that. Just let me do all the talking."

But Eddie didn't want to let Aldous do all the talking.

"I have a bad feeling about this," she said.

As they got closer to the end of the stairwell, Eddie could hear faint sounds of laughter and chatter. She gripped the banister with white knuckles in response.

"Oh hell, man. I don't know about this. I am started to freak out over here."

"Look," Aldous said. "You just traveled through time and space by yourself. You're still alive. You've got all of your limbs and your wits. You've managed to get this far with just a backpack. I'm not sure how it happened, but I do know it happened for a reason. Currently clueless as to what that reason is, but we will find out, I'm sure. I promise you that I will get you back home, and if we're lucky, all in one piece."

"Gee, thanks. I highly doubt that being an accidental intergalactic hitch-hiker means anything in the grand scheme of things, but I'll add it to *my* short list of accomplishments—Edwina Burke, Time Lord."

"I don't know what that is, but we're almost there. The dining hall is just beyond that area. Don't worry. Just take a deep breath and remember that I'm right here. If you need to, take my hand and I'll get us through the day as pain-lessly as possible. Everything will be alright, Eddie."

"If you say so."

"Are you ready?" Eddie nodded once.

"Alright, off we go."

CHAPTER 4

As Eddie and Aldous made their way through the busy halls and rooms, Eddie tried to absorb their surroundings. Everything was beautiful—every piece of carefully carved furniture, every high vaulted ceiling, every snot-faced kid crying—everything. It was as if she had taken a step out of Aldous's messy bedroom and taken a step into a magnificent cathedral. With Aldous's hand now in hers, things didn't seem so impossible. They would get through the day, and hopefully the night.

In the banquet hall, there were hundreds of youths, ranging in ages from pre-tween to nearly grown. At the long tables sat girls and boys alongside young men and young women dressed in colorful robes and long, conical hats. The tables were covered in fine porcelain dishes and silverware, and huge decanters full of amber-colored liquid were being passed around. The younger students sat closely next to one another and spoke loudly, while the older teenagers attempted to act more mature and subdued, but Eddie knew that act all too well. Everyone is a big dork until they're like 35, and even then they've just found better ways to hide it.

These kids ain't foolin' no one.

As Eddie and Aldous approached a large dining table, he gently squeezed her hand and let it fall to her side. "Deep breaths now," he said, gently.

"Right." Eddie felt as though she might faint.

"Almost there."

"Aldous, over here!" A young lady with curly blonde hair and a blue hat that matched Aldous's, beckoned them toward her and her friends. She had a lovely round face and long locks of yellow hair that fell beyond her waist. The person sitting next to her was as equally enchanting—tall and slender, with dark brown skin, and black stubble that covered her head. Eddie found it hard to tear her eyes away from the full lips and haunting brown eyes.

God, she looks like one of those women from a Victoria Secret's Catalog.

When the tall girl smiled at Eddie, she felt her face flush. *So I do still like girls.* It was a comforting thought. A familiar thought in an unfamiliar environment. Seconds later an overwhelming sense of relief came crashing into Eddie. She had no idea what the hell was going on. Things weren't nearly so complicated back in West Virginia. She just wanted to go home, where things were black and white, gay or straight. Except...she wasn't black or white, and now she wasn't so sure she was gay.

Does finding Aldous attractive kick me out of the club? What is happening to me?

Sitting on the other side of the table was a pretty young lady with flawless, fair skin and fire engine red hair that was bound together by two leather straps, set in long braids on both sides of her face. She had long brown eyelashes, a pair of stormy blue eyes, and vermilion lips that covered a set of perfect white teeth. Eddie saw the way Aldous looked at the girl when she greeted him and was made painfully aware of her own grubbiness.

"Hey everyone. This is my childhood friend, Edwina Burke, but she goes by Eddie. And for Pete's sake, don't call her Miss Burke, unless you want a lecture on outdated, misogynistic honorifics." Aldous could feel Eddie's laser gaze on the side of his face, but this only made his smile bigger. "She is staying with my family for a few weeks until her parents come to get her." All eyes turned to Eddie and suddenly, her heart began to race so fast that she could feel her pulse in every limb.

Somehow she managed a weak wave and a side-smile. "Hey. Hey there. What's up?"

"Hello Edwina, my name is Vada." The yellow-haired girl was the first to speak. "This here is Simone, and across from us sits Caoilainn. Are you hungry? Here, take a saucer. I'm afraid all of the larger dishes have been taken," she said, now eyeing Aldous. "There's plenty of cantaloupe, sweet ham, and custard-filled pastries to go around, however." Then with a furrowed brow, Vada bit her lip, and paused. "And somewhere there's a pitcher of grape juice going 'round, though you might have to take it from the children by force." She scooted over and placed a hand on the bench beside her. "Come on. There's no need to be shy. We won't bite." Vada was polite and welcoming, and Edwina could see why she and Aldous were best friends.

The five companions quickly filled their plates and glasses after Eddie and Aldous took their places at the table. Aldous quietly picked at the ham and strawberries on his plate for the next several minutes. Eddie saw his demeanor change almost immediately once he sat down next to Caoilainn, becoming stiff and silent, and focusing most of his attention on chewing and keeping his face turned towards his food. He said nothing to Caoilainn, but greeted her with a nod and poured himself a glass of juice. Caoilainn took three bites of her pastry and politely excused herself from the table. Afterwards Aldous's jaw unclenched, and he turned to Eddie, releasing a great sigh.

Jeez. He must really hate her.

"Good god Aldous," Simone said. "Is it always going to be like this?"

"What do you mean? I'm not the one who acts like she's invisible. She's the one who didn't say anything and wasted an entire pastry. Look, she even left her plate."

"Do you really think things are going to work out if you two keep pretending that the inevitable isn't happening in a few months," Vada added, reaching for said pastry. "Ew, this is peach. No wonder she didn't want it."

"I really don't care. Not anymore, I don't. I'm over it."

"But she's your waja," Simone said. "One day you will be business partners. Are you planning on giving her all of your customers and living under a rock while she reaps the benefits of a good education?"

"The benefits of a good education? God, you sound like my father. Besides, it doesn't matter. I'd much rather share a rock with worms and grubs than share a village with that girl."

"Oh bloody hell," Vada said. "You're being absurd."

Aldous shrugged and said, "Whatever. Are you going to eat that?"

•••

Of the morning classes she attended, only one instructor gave Eddie a difficult time—Waja Abjou, a powerful suuga who dealt in movement majik (and who leered at her with suspicion during Aldous's lengthy, spotty explanation for the visit).

"Interesting," Abjou said, folding his hands atop the messy table. "Her parents are slayers, you say? From where?" He turned from Aldous to her. "Hmm?"

Aldous nervously shifted in his chair and wrung his hands. "Uh—from the Second Kingdom, sir."

"And just what are they fighting?" Abjou asked, with an eyebrow raised.

"Water dra–dragons in the Northeast." Aldous felt himself butchering the explanation. "Sea serpents."

Waja Abjou's eyes narrowed as he put his hands on his hips and stared at Eddie with an unsettling interest. The class steered its collective interest toward the orange-haired girl, too.

"I see." After a long pause, Waja Abjou turned to Aldous. "Aldous, is Edwina mute?"

Startled, Aldous replied, "No, sir. Surely not."

"So you will not be speaking for her the entire time she is in my class?"

"No, sir." Aldous looked down at his hands. "Forgive me. I will not."

"I take it the Headmaster has approved of this little arrangement, Mr. Molhata?"

Aldous did not look up, instead chewing on the end of his pencil and nodding slowly in response. "Er—yeah."

"Very well, then. I hope so, for your sake, anyway. Miss Burke, if you are ready to learn about teleportation, find yourself a seat. There are a few students out today, so you may sit in one of their seats if you wish."

Since most students were already paired up with one other, it was awkward finding an empty seat. Eventually, a dark-haired boy wearing a blue robe flagged Eddie over, and she took the seat next to him.

Eddie positioned her backpack up on the table and pulled out a pen and notebook that Aldous had given her. She was nervous, and no matter how many times she tried to reassure herself, Eddie could not get rid of the anxiety looming overhead. She dropped the backpack on the floor and kicked it under her chair. The boy sitting next to Eddie flashed her a smile when she looked his way.

God, my nerves are freaking shot. What I wouldn't give for a cigarette right now.

Everything that Waja Abjou said in class went straight over Eddie's head. It was like being in French class all over again. Just what the hell was hyperspace? And wasn't telefrag a video game term? It was back home. Eddie would have to memorize an entire dictionary in order to learn even the basics of movement majik, which was unfortunate given that this class could unlock the key to sending her back home.

When Waja Abjou informed the students they would have to work together in pairs to solve a problem, Eddie felt dread settle in her stomach. She would have to talk to this person sitting next to her and it would be excruciating. Eddie wasn't a shy person normally, but she felt out of her element, like a lone apple in a bowl of oranges. Most of these students had grown up with one another. They had been children together and were now coming of age. Pairs would soon relocate to villages spread throughout the Four Kingdoms and they would likely grow old together, or at least know each other until they died. Building new friendships seemed like a daunting task, and somewhat useless given that Eddie could vanish at any moment.

"Hi there. Eddie, is it?" The dark-haired boy asked, reeling Eddie back into reality. His accent was familiar, but unlike any she had heard at the university thus far. It sounded European...Italian, maybe? Eddie shot him a curious glance, one that did not avert his gaze when it met his eyes.

"Yes, Eddie." The sentence sounded awkward coming from her mouth, as if he were the one named Eddie, and she was addressing him. She regretted speaking immediately. "I mean, I'm Eddie, not you." She sighed. Why did she have to be so verbally clumsy? Is this how she sounded to Aldous? She desperately wanted to shrink down in her seat and hide under the table.

"Of course you are. My name is Salvator."

Waja Abjou wrote a complicated word problem on the chalkboard, then exited the room, taking with him a crocheted, lavender scarf and an oversized black leather bag. Abjou was an odd character. He and Eddie shared a similar skin color, but he had long black hair, which he kept in a thick braid down his back, and wore noisy cowboy boots with silver spurs. The silver spurs were not nearly as intriguing as the enormous golden hoops he wore in each ear. Without a long hat and an oversized robe, he hardly fit in with the students.

All it took was two seconds of the instructor's absence to get the room going. The students talked over one another, and soon the room came alive with banter. The scene was familiar to Eddie in a way that made her feel homesick. It wasn't the school she missed, nor the few friends she kept close, but the way the students reacted as soon as the teacher left the room felt universal: their captor had left, and everyone was rejoicing. That's how it worked in her school, too.

Eddie noticed that Aldous was watching her out of the corner of her eye, so she turned to meet his gaze. He returned her smile. It was apparent from the way the two were ignoring each other, that he and Caoilainn had already solved the problem—that or they didn't care to. The paper Salvator had set on the table was still blank. Class would soon be over and everyone would return to the dining hall for lunch.

Eddie wanted nothing more than to go back to Aldous's room and bury her head under his blankets. Due to their shaky excuse Waja Abjou was now suspicious of Eddie and she could not fault him. A dingy biracial Ginger in wrinkled black clothes with a peculiar accent. It wasn't like she didn't completely stand out or anything, and the answer Aldous had provided in regard to her parents' whereabouts had been atrocious.

"Eddie? I think I figured it out." It wasn't until Salvator said her name that she realized she had been lost in thought again. The paper now contained diagrams, symbols, and formulas that meant nothing to Eddie. She wouldn't be able to understand it even if she tried.

"Oh, I'm sorry. I'm afraid I'm not very good at word problems. You should have seen my ACT scores. Pa-the-tic."

"Do you want to try it?" His brown eyes sparkled with mischief. "Or should I?"

"What? Oh, you mean, the two of us? Try this spell?" Actually casting the enchantment with Salvator had not crossed Eddie's mind, because she had already written it off as impossible. When she saw the excitement and anticipation glittering in his eyes, however, she eventually caved in with a half-smile and a shrug. "Sure. I suppose it wouldn't hurt, would it?" What would happen if she teleported back into the arts center? That would be a good thing, wouldn't it? That's what she wanted, wasn't it?

Salvator took the piece of paper out of her hand and stood up. "Alright then. I will try it first."

He then pushed his seat away from the table and held the document out in front of his chest. After clearing his voice loudly, Salvator recited the words written on the paper four times before vanishing into thin air.

"Mulah andril revole anha." The spell Salvator had cast seconds before then visited every pair of students in the classroom, producing similar results. Kids sat in their seats laughing and carrying on one minute, and then the next, they were gone.

Eddie stared at Salvator's empty seat in horror for several minutes until someone placed a hand on her shoulder, knocking her back into the seat. Is that how it looked when she had disappeared? Simple and efficient? Where was the fanfare, the disintegration, the flickering of lights? Anything? Was the act of teleportation really this mundane?

"Are you alright?" Salvator's deep voice startled her. "It worked. We did it. You should be proud of yourself. Transfer students from the *other* kingdoms often have trouble learning majik." His choice of words contained a hidden meaning that Eddie couldn't decipher. Just what had she done? Sat there while he did the math and cast the spell? That hardly seemed worthy of recognition.

"Oh yeah, cool. Thanks."

"Now you try."

The enchantment had worked for Salvator, but when Eddie tried it, nothing moved. Not even the pencil on her desk. She stared at the paper, trying to understand why it had worked for him but not her. It couldn't be the way she was pronouncing the words, because he coached her through enunciation and nodded vigorously when she got them down. Eddie wondered if it took more than words to make a spell work—maybe it took actually believing in the spell. If that was the case, Eddie would never leave Ashkak's.

"Don't worry about it. I'm sure you'll get it, eventually. Movement majik comes easily to those who do not seek it. Remember that. It'll happen for you. Just keep at it."

After the bell rang, Aldous got up from his table and walked over to her.

"Hey there, are you hungry?" He asked, intentionally ignoring Salvator.

Eddie didn't know if her nerves would let her eat, but she desperately needed to get out of the room. She felt as though she were suffocating, as if air was being sucked out of her lungs by a large vacuum.

Eyeing Aldous, Salvator excused himself from the table and walked over to where Caoilainn sat. From the wide smile that appeared on her face, it was easy to see that Caoilainn preferred Salvator's company. Eddie could read the discomfort written across Aldous's face and felt sorry for him. Salvator was friendly and encouraging, and not to mention tall, dark and handsome.

"You know, I really hate that guy."

Eddie picked up her backpack and touched Aldous's shoulder. "Yeah, I can tell. Come on," Eddie said." Let's go get some sandwiches."

"And some coffee."

"Yes," Eddie replied. "I'll take a whole pot, please."

CHAPTER 5

The dining hall was as loud and unruly at lunchtime as it had been at breakfast. Servants walked across the room with pans full of hot rolls and big pots full of creamy carrot soup. The food at Ashkak's was amazing. By the end of lunch, Eddie was so stuffed she thought her pants might burst open if she shifted the wrong way.

"What are you thinking about?" Eddie asked, watching Aldous, who was staring into a mug of steaming tea.

"Hmm? Oh, just thinking about what we learned in Abjou's class today. I think it will come in handy. Did you understand any of it?" Eddie shook her head at his question. "I didn't think so. I imagine it would be difficult to understand majik if you were not majikally inclined," Aldous said. "I'm sorry. I was thinking that maybe after school was over we could mess around with that spell for a bit? Who knows? We might get lucky. Either way, it should be exciting."

Eddie considered this, then laughed at his enthusiasm. "You are by far the most unusual person I've ever met, like seriously."

With a frown, he whispered into the cup, "Believe me, I know. It's not the first time I've heard that."

"Yo, I didn't mean that as an insult." Eddie's face was as serious as a broken bone. "I'm being serious."

"Right." Aldous took another sip of tea and placed his cup down on the saucer in front of him. "Would you like to step outside for a moment?"

Thinking of her cigarettes, Eddie replied, "Hell yeah. Lead the way, magic man."

To her amazement, students were allowed frequent breaks throughout the day, unlike Eddie's high school where everything was over-structured and sterile, a poor environment for learning. It was no wonder everyone hated high school. Sure, Eddie enjoyed learning, but the rules were punitive, not constructive, and the content they learned was as boring as a sack of flour. Eddie could remember being in her freshman English class reading a book about a man who could travel through mirrors, and how the teacher had scolded her because she was reading the *wrong* book. How can a book be wrong, she had argued with the teacher. At least she had been reading, right? Besides, star-crossed lovers weren't really Eddie's thing, and who falls in love with someone the very minute they lay eyes on them, anyway? Shakespeare had been a melodramatic hack.

It was chilly but beautiful outside. Aldous had taken Eddie to his mother's gardens with the intention of showing her various types of magical herbs and non-magical herbs used for healing. He wasn't sure, but he didn't think sunberries had ever grown in these gardens. Still, it was worth a second look.

"Sunberries," he explained with a kind of raw fascination, "are more of a wild plant, one that refuses to be domesticated. It is even rumored that sunberry vines can run away if they feel vulnerable or threatened." Aldous didn't go on to say whether he believed these claims, but Eddie was fairly certain she knew how he felt.

Red and orange leaves covered the dying grass, and crunched loudly beneath their shoes, as they weaved in and out of the foliage. Eddie was enchanted by the mesmerizing scenery.

Once they were far enough away from the building and immersed in the foliage, Eddie withdrew a cigarette from her pocket and began to fumble around with a broken lighter. The picture of a naked lady encasing the lighter had been peeling and cracking for some time, and it had been only a matter of time before the brass-base gave out.

"Freaking piece of trash. I swear to God."

After several attempts, Eddie still couldn't get the damned thing to light.

Admit defeat, she angrily thought, shoving the lighter back into her pocket. *All I want is a damned cigarette.* Then without notice, Aldous gently took Eddie's hand into his and waved his other hand over the cigarette.

"Here," he said. "Allow me."

Within a matter of seconds, the tip of the cigarette caught fire, and Eddie took a long drag off it, then exhaled loudly.

"Hell yes. Thank you. You're a real lifesaver, ya know that?" Eddie dismissed the irony of the statement.

With her hand now in his, Aldous led Eddie over to an old rusted metallic bench, one that had obviously been resplendent at some point, but was now worn from age and weather. Waging a silent war on her clothes, Eddie just knew that if she sat down on the bench, fleets of gold and silver paint would charge her black clothes like a determined cavalry. Reluctantly, she accepted the seat anyway and continued to smoke in silence.

Aldous looked at the plants, some dying, some thriving, and said, "You know, this is my absolute favorite place in the world. I can come here, and nothing else matters. After my mother died, I would pull weeds like a madman. It's all I could do to keep from shutting down. I'm afraid I was too ignorant of plants then to determine which ones were weeds and which ones were plants."

"Ya know," Eddie replied, after taking another drag. "Even weeds have their place in the world."

Aldous nodded. "I think you're right. When I was a child, I used to think that I was that weed, just trying to fit in with the flowers. Now I don't know what I am. Or who I am to become. Everything just feels so hopeless at times. Do you know what I mean?"

A gentle breeze tugged at Aldous's long, white hair and brown robe, forcing him to clutch at the dark cloth. In the direct sunlight, his hair was as white as lamb's wool, and his pale skin looked almost translucent like parchment paper, with blue veins barely visible beneath his skin. His eyebrows were bright silver—not white as Eddie had once thought—and mostly hidden underneath his large brown frames. Looking at Aldous this way was like staring directly into the sun: it felt good at the time, but there was no telling if there would be repercussions. Eddie held her breath. Aldous was as bewitching as the idea of majik itself, and somehow even more alluring with his hood pulled over his head. Eddie exhaled.

What the hell is happening to me? Do I actually have a crush on this guy?

The realization hadn't been sudden necessarily, but it did catch her off guard, and Eddie wasn't prepared for it. She knew that from her interactions with Aldous, they got along well and that their connection *had* been sudden, but Eddie wasn't one for reading into things. Besides, she had known Aldous for two-and-a-half days and planned on going home tonight, and had a sneaking suspicion that Aldous was jealous of Salvator because of Caoilainn, a woman who beat Eddie in nearly every way. His waja was leggy and busty, Eddie had noticed at lunch, after Caoilainn removed her robe and placed it on her lap. The woman turned heads as soon as she entered a room.

Eddie rolled her eyes. *Whatever.* She didn't want to like Aldous, and with any luck, she would leave soon, and these feelings would hopefully stay here.

"That thing stinks." Aldous let go of Eddie's hand and motioned to the cigarette, the declaration leading her to uncontrollable laughter. "It's horrid, really. I don't know how you stand it. Good grief."

Aldous was, if anything, completely honest with Eddie, and that was a relatively foreign concept to her. Alice never treated her this way. Her girlfriend was mean and jealous and made Eddie feel horrible about herself. Not that Eddie viewed Aldous as a potential boyfriend, of course. She hadn't known him that long. Aldous just happened to be extremely easy on her eyes and kind and generous. She groaned to herself.

This is stupid. Eddie felt helpless. "God, you sound like my step-mom."

"Look, all I'm saying is that it can't be good for you. Nothing that smells like that can be good for you," Aldous replied. "I mean, you're sitting there, inhaling smoke into your lungs. That's like standing next to a burning house and just asking for smoke poisoning."

"Alright, alright. I get the picture. Jeez," Eddie said, putting the cigarette out on the bench. "Now you really do sound like her. Y'all should start a damned club."

After a few deep breaths of the crisp, autumnal air, Eddie turned to Aldous, and they both stood as still as a fence post. Aldous was the first to speak. "Are you alright?"

Eddie nodded, then placed her hands in her pants pockets. "Yeah, it's nothing. I'm sure it will pass."

"You sure?"

Around them, the wind howled and moved through the trees like a pack of angry wolves.

Eddie rubbed her sleeves, then slapped her arms. "Well, I certainly hope so."

"Alright. Well, in that case, we have two classes left to go. We've got calisthenics next."

"Calisthenics? You mean like gym?" Gym was Eddie's least favorite subject.

"It takes places in a gymnasium, yes. Follow me."

Aldous led Eddie out of the gardens and back into the building, where they soon found themselves standing in a loud, busy hallway.

"And then?" Eddie had to raise her voice in order to be heard by Aldous.

"Za'tari," he replied with similar force. "Which is my favorite class, and our last stop for the day. You can sit with me if you'd like. We don't have assigned seats."

Eddie considered this for a moment, then asked, "So, do you learn about plants in Zay-teree?"

"Yep," Aldous said, enthusiastically. "And animals. Za'tari. Say it with me. Rolls right off the tongue."

"Whatever you say," Eddie said. "That's going to take me a few tries. I have another question."

"OK. But seeing as how I've answered forty-three of your questions, and you've answered, like eight of mine, I'd say we are not even."

Eddie put her hands on his back and heaved him forward through the crowd.

"What happens if a suuga messes around with sujii magic? Is it that big of a deal?"

Aldous shrugged in response and pulled the hood down over his head so that Eddie could no longer see his face. She let go of his shoulders and tried to match his pace.

Aldous began, "It is forbidden. If a suuga is caught tinkering around with plants or animal majik, anything having to do with sujii craft, they could be expelled from the school. Any school that teaches the craft, for that matter. If a suuga could practice sujii majik, it would give him an enormous advantage over another person, or opponent."

"What? Why?"

Aldous opened the door for Eddie. "Too much majik (or power) is looked down upon by the Elders. Are you ready for this, because it's heavy information?"

Eddie mouthed *yeah* and shifted her backpack uneasily.

"The Emperor of the First Kingdom is the one who handpicks the Council of Elders. There are fifteen of them, and they are the most powerful sujii and suuga in all of the Kingdoms. It's left up to them to decide who becomes a waja and who stays in the villages throughout the Four Kingdoms. Do you follow?"

"Yes," Eddie said. "They control everything and decide your fate."

"Pretty much. They have the capability to strip you of your majik and banish you from our kingdom. Then, you have to beg your way into either the Second or Third Kingdom. It's not a path most (if not all) suuga—or sujii—would want to take," Aldous said. "It means demotion. It means selling trinkets at the side of the road with bands of roaming thugs. It means having your identity taken from you. Everything you've ever known, gone."

"Jesus H. Christ," Eddie said, bewildered by this new information. "There are a lot of rules here."

•••

The locker room was one of Eddie's least favorite places in the world for a number of reasons.

She glanced around at the other girls. Eddie had always been uncomfortable with her body, but being around young women such as Vada and Caoilainn made her hyper-aware of her physical shortcomings. Both women were round and curvy in all the right places. Eddie would have been fine with having just a ¼ of their assets. If it weren't for her hair, she could easily be mistaken for a boy. In fact, she had been, several times.

Eddie was short, just barely 5 feet tall, angular, and as flat as a tabletop. No matter what she did or how much she ate, she remained at an even seven stones. Her prior attempts to hide her body included having poor posture, wearing baggy clothes, and stuffing her bra (which she did only twice in the seventh grade). Nothing seemed to help.

Eddie followed Vada and Caoilainn out of the locker room and looked around the simple gymnasium where she eventually spotted Aldous amongst a group of boys and waved. He was wearing a tight blue shirt and black running shorts. Aldous was lean, but his legs were unusually muscular.

Oh, right. He is a runner. Of course, he would look like that underneath his clothes. What is wrong with you? Stop thinking about what's underneath his clothes.

Eddie hated gym, hated it with the passion of a thousand burning suns.

It didn't help that smoking had greatly compromised Eddie's lung capacity, either. A short jog would have her on the floor in minutes. Eddie knew she needed to quit, that she just needed to be done with it already. Smoking could kill her.

I'm going to quit. Eventually, she told herself. *In time. But not today.*

Shortly after Eddie stopped fuming about exercising in front of some random ass kids, her eyes settled on Simone and Aldous who now stood side by side in a small group. They soon began jogging, and Eddie found herself entranced by the sight of Aldous jogging. She really liked looking at him, and it was becoming a problem.

"Hello Edwina," Vada said, seemingly out of nowhere. "How are you?"

"Hey, what's up?"

Eddie had not lived through the Spanish Inquisition, but after spending a few minutes with Vada, felt as though she had caught a glimpse of it. Vada had all kinds of questions for Eddie—about her parents, about dragons, about her school. Vada's interest in their relationship—Aldous and Eddie's—was intimidating to say the least. She wanted to know how long they had known each other, what the nature of their friendship was, how they met if Aldous had never been outside of the First Kingdom, those sorts of things.

After trying and failing to answer Vada's questions, Eddie finally broke down and told her the truth. To her genuine surprise, Vada took the news rather well, but Eddie's confession did little to hinder her line of questioning. Eddie wondered if the Kingdoms had detectives, for surely Vada would make a great one if they did.

"So you cannot do majik at all where you come from?" Vada asked. "Wow. That's weird." The thought baffled her yellow-haired friend.

"Nope," Eddie said. "Nothing. I'm just an average American kid. Well, average, but not normal, I guess."

Smiling, Vada replied, "I can see that." Eddie felt her freckled cheeks redden.

After Eddie gave Vada a quick summary of her life story, Vada promised to help Eddie return home, for she knew that Aldous was not the world's greatest suuga, and said as much. Eddie gladly accepted her offer and felt instant relief that she had shared this secret with two people instead of one.

The shrill sound of a whistle cut through their conversation, and when Eddie looked around the gym, she noticed Aldous still jogging. The rest of the joggers had pink and brown mottled skin, and looked rather invigorated after the jog, but not Aldous—he looked as cool as an ice cube. His cheeks weren't flushed or red like the others. His stamina impressed Eddie, and that wasn't easy to do, considering that she hated sports with as much passion (maybe even more) as she hated gym.

Aldous jogged over to them with enthusiasm. "Hey, guys."

Vada said, in disbelief, "I don't know how you do that."

With a shrug, he replied, "I don't know either. I'm a freak. What can I say?"

Vada nodded her head in agreement. "You must be. And Eddie told me. Everything." She pushed his damp arm. "Why didn't you come to me, ya big jerk?"

"Oh, thank the stars," Aldous said, relieved. "Now I won't have to do this by myself."

CHAPTER 6

Za'tari was the last and most interesting course of the day, if for no other reason than Eddie got to hear Aldous gush about his favorite plants and their majikal properties. It struck her as bizarre that Aldous was chosen to be a suuga and not an sujii.

When asked if men could be sujii, Aldous had said that it was fairly rare, but that it wasn't impossible. Simone was a suuga, after all, but one had to be an extraordinary practitioner, worth the extra effort and training.

Aldous explained, "It is easier for a woman to take on the role of a suuga. There have been a few suuga who were able to overcome those barriers throughout history, but for the most part, suuga are men and sujii are women."

"So, no male sujii?"

Aldous shook his head. "Not unheard of, but highly unlikely, I'm afraid."

"Wow. That's pretty harsh, man."

"I know," he said, then paused. "But that's our system, and I already struggle with this stuff, so I'm not going to challenge it."

It seemed like such a shame, though, because Aldous loved plants. That much was obvious from the way he explained the biological makeup of a plant. Eddie had never seen someone so pumped on a stamen and petal before.

"Jesus," she said. "You really love this stuff, huh?"

"I'm just glad we got to sit together. This bit of info may come in handy when we attempt the spell tonight."

Tonight? Somehow she had forgotten about going home. Would things be different? What if she travelled too far back in time? What if she ended up on a planet inhabited by talking sharks or bicycle-riding snakes? Eddie had to admit it: Ashkak's was far more superior to her rinky-dink high school in Milton, and she could have done a lot worse than Aldous Molhata. Would it hurt if she stayed longer? Just a day or two? She then thought about her baby sister and her step-mom. No, Eddie couldn't do that to them, not when things were so screwed up back home.

She had to find a way back. For their sake.

With some difficulty, Eddie tried to recall her little sister's smile while Aldous droned on about the toxic properties of wolfsbane, and noticed that remembering took some effort, which struck her as odd.

"Yo, that is by far the angriest plant I've ever seen." With black and gnarled roots, it spooked Eddie even though it was just a plant. "Damn, man. What the hell is that?"

"Well," Aldous said. "There's a reason why it's called wolfsbane. It turns its head towards the moon when it's full, and I've even heard some of the old folks claim that they've heard a wolfsbane howl before."

"A plant? That plant? With no friggin' mouth? Howls? Like a damned wolf?"

"Hey, I didn't say I heard it or that I believed it. I'm just telling you what has been said to me in the past."

"Were they smoking the wolfsbane when they heard this alleged howling?"

"No," Aldous said, confused. "I don't think you can smoke wolfsbane."

"Ahhh, you can smoke just about any plant."

"How do you know?" Eddie wouldn't dignify his question with a response. "Here, just touch it," Aldous said, gently taking her wrist.

"That's a negative, Ghost Rider. You just said that the plant howls. I'm not touching that damn thing. How do I know it doesn't have hidden teeth?"

"Oh," Aldous said. "So now you believe?"

"I didn't say I believed anything. I'm just asking. How could a plant without a mouth howl? Do pigs here fly? Ya know what? Don't answer that."

"Think about it. The same way you were able to move through worlds, Eddie."

"Majik," they both said at the same time. Eddie groaned and rolled her eyes.

Aldous let go of her wrist slowly and picked up the pot to examine the plant more closely. His touch lingered on her wrist, and even though his hand had felt hypothermic, she wished his odd, cold fingers were still wrapped around her. Aldous continued to point out what others had to say about wolfsbane, but all she could do was watch his lips move. *Were they as cold as his fingers, or would they be warmer*, she wondered. *When did I become such a pervert?*

The closeness of their bodies made her nervous, so Eddie waited for Aldous to return his attention to the chalkboard before scooting her chair away from his.

"Are you bored yet?"

"Oh no, not at all," Eddie replied, hoping Aldous wouldn't mention the space she had just put between them. "I'm good."

"OK. Cool. Now that plant is used for healing burns." Aldous pointed to the chalkboard. "This one for constipation."

Eddie laughed. "Constipation? That hardly seems magical."

Seriously, Aldous replied, "Have you ever been constipated? Sometimes you need a little majik to get things moving."

Eddie laughed again and picked up a mortar and pestle from the table. "OK. Well, I'll be sure to remember that if I ever need the extra help."

"I'm sorry. This is so dreadfully dull, I'm sure. Class will be over shortly, and we can get food and take it up to my room if you'd like."

"No, no," Eddie replied. "It's cool. I never knew just how valuable plants could be, ya know."

After class ended, Aldous's friends said their farewells and returned to the dining hall. In the busy hallway outside, several younger students in pointed hats hurried past Eddie and Aldous, waving their wands and broomsticks in the air, and yelling loudly at one another, which reminded Eddie to ask Aldous if he had a magic broom or wand. She had spotted a broom in his closet earlier that morning while he was browsing for a pair of boots, and assumed that only witches (or in his case, sujii) rode broomsticks.

"Hey," Aldous said. "I know a short-cut."

"Hell yeah, let's do it," Eddie said, with renewed vigor. "This crap sucks."

"OK, follow me." Aldous locked his arm through Eddie's, and together they trudged through the long, crowded hallways. "I hate it when they just stand there like that."

When they entered the dining hall, Eddie immediately spotted Caoilainn, Salvator, and two other boys sitting together. Like a lone carnation in a field of Baby's Breath, Caoilainn was hard to miss. *How is it possible for one person to be so effortlessly captivating?* Back home, girls would have to wear foundation, blush, and eyeliner to recreate even a tenth of Caoilainn's natural beauty. It would take an entire dumpster's worth of cosmetics to cover Eddie's freckles. *Stop being a jealous jerk.*

"Do you want to say hello to the others before we head upstairs?" Aldous asked, turning around so Eddie could hear him over the chatter. But Eddie didn't answer, instead keeping her eyes focused on the group of four who were now laughing and talking loudly with one another. The students were too far away for Eddie to actually hear the conversation, but at some point, she saw Caoilainn shake her head in apparent opposition.

What happened next, Eddie saw it unfold in slow-motion: the two unnamed boys slapping each other on the back, the jeering and pointing at Aldous, and then finally, the unidentified object striking him in the side of the head. The bun, Eddie could see now, smacked his head so hard that she heard the bread split apart upon impact.

Afterwards, the dining hall fell silent, and every head turned towards Eddie and Aldous. No one moved. No one spoke. Eddie grabbed at Aldous's forearm in hopes that he'd stopped walking and looked over at Salvator and Caoilainn. Caoilainn looked down at her plate in horror, and Salvator stood with a look on his face that said, 'don't look at me.'

"Did he just throw that at you?" There was no way to tell who had done it. The bun had been chucked from that side of the dining hall, but since there had been kids in the way, Eddie couldn't say for sure. Aldous looked around the room once more, and then the entire room erupted into boisterous laughter.

"That ugly freak got it in the head!" Eddie heard someone shout. "Yeah, if he weren't such a sorry excuse for a student, he might've seen it coming!" Shouted another. Eddie felt Aldous tense up, and then he pulled his arm out of her reach. She thought he might say something, defend himself from the mockery of others, but he didn't. He just reached over, picked up a plate full of buttered yams, and then placed a loaf of bread under his arm.

Then turning to face Eddie, Aldous said, "Can you get that pitcher?" She was startled by his calm demeanor, but took the container into her hands and followed him as he walked out of the room, anyway. "Thanks."

"Yeah, sure. But don't you want to-." The incident had ignited something awful inside of Eddie, like a volcano getting ready to spew lava made of white, hot rage. "Aldous," Eddie said. "Stop."

"Let's just go."

They climbed the stairs in silence and said nothing for several minutes. Eddie could see from the windows that it was getting dark outside. The servants would soon light the penchant lanterns, and students would walk through the upstairs hall to return to their dorms.

Once Aldous reached his room, he handed the yams and bread to Eddie and placed his hands on his door. The seal was still intact, so there was that at least. He then took the food and decanter from her hands and motioned for her to enter the room.

"Come on. I'm hungry."

Eddie's heart broke for Aldous. "Do you need any help?"

She didn't understand why someone would target him like that, after having shown Eddie only kindness since her arrival, and rarely speaking ill of anyone.

Mister Fluffy hopped down from the bed and greeted them with an enthusiastic tail wag. Aldous placed the food on his large desk and walked over to the closet, then slowly removed his satchel and robe. Eddie didn't know how to make the situation better, so she sat down on the cold floor and patted the enormous animal. Eddie could sense that they were speaking to one another without words, and Mister Fluffy did not look pleased, even while she scratched under his chin and behind his ears.

Of course he wasn't pleased. He was Aldous's lyärgo.

"What did I do today, you ask, Mr. Fox? Well, I learned that I would make a terrible witch because I understood literally nothing today and that Aldous is some super track star runner person," Eddie said. "I don't know if you've ever seen this guy run before, but it's something else. Um, and that he is super knowledgeable when it comes to plants. Ah! And just now, I was reminded that people are freaking jerks. Yeah, I don't see how I could forget that."

Aldous stopped what he was doing and turned to face Eddie.

But she did not look up at him and continued, "Dickheads are everywhere, and they exist to make you feel bad about yourself for no reason. That just because you're different doesn't mean that they have a right to treat you like you're a worthless piece of crap." Eddie was speaking directly to Aldous now but kept her gaze on the fox. "That I couldn't ask for a better friend at the moment, or ever really, because I know what it's like to feel like you don't belong. You wouldn't know anything about that, though, now would you, Mister Fluffy?" Eddie asked. "No, because you're cute and sweet and perfect."

Aldous handed her a plate of warm food and a glass of cranberry juice, then sat down on the floor next to her. The small plate of food looked tantalizing and smelled good.

"Thanks," Eddie said. "But I could have made myself a plate."

"No, you're my guest. And you're welcome. I hope you like sweet potatoes."

"Mmm. I do, but these are yams," Eddie corrected him. "I like them, too, though. Why the hell didn't you say anything to those jerks?" Aldous still had sugar and cream on his cheek and in his hair from the flying pastry. "I mean, if you want me to go down there and say something, I will. Hell, I'll make them wish they had never been born."

"What could I say to them, Edwina?" Aldous asked." I am the headmaster's son. I can't exactly make him look bad, now can I? Let's just forget about it, alright?"

"But you shouldn't let people run you down like that. It's just going to get worse."

"No, it won't," Aldous said. "I'll be out of here by the end of spring. It can't get any worse."

"So you're just going to let them get away with it?" Eddie asked, her mouth full of foods.

"Yes, because I have to. It's what I've done this entire time. Can we just drop it and eat?"

"Wait." Eddie couldn't believe what she was hearing. "This kinda crap has happened before? And no one does anything?"

"Eddie, please," Aldous pleaded.

"Alright, man. It's your call, and I'll respect it, but that's some straight up bull if I ever saw it, and if it happens again, I'm going to say something. I am not the headmaster's son."

Things got pretty awkward after that. Aldous didn't say anything during dinner and refused to meet Eddie's gaze. She was familiar with bullies—she had dealt with them all of her life—and she knew how humiliating it was to be put on display in front of the whole school. The only solution to this problem had been pulled, beaten, and hurled out the door by Aldous. He didn't want to talk about it. He didn't want to admit that things might never change.

Eddie leaned her head back against the wall and thought about her own life and her own experiences with jerks. Until the last year or so, she had been pretty good at dodging whatever crap they thrust at her. While not as blatant or rude as Salvator and his crew of thugs, Eddie knew first-hand what bullying was and what it could lead to, especially for kids who are transgender, gay or lesbian. But Aldous wasn't weird, and he didn't smell bad, and he didn't act smarter than the rest of the kids. Maybe he *was* gay, which wasn't an avenue Eddie had explored and didn't really care to explore, because given her current attraction to Aldous that line of thinking could only lead to a plane of utter existential crisis, and things were already pretty bad. Aldous was at the bottom of the Ashkak's barrel, and Eddie couldn't understand why.

Back home things weren't exactly great either. Eddie knew that if things were back to normal, she would likely be in her room, listening to music and finishing her homework, or making dinner for Sam and putting off returning Alice's calls and texts. In reality, things were really freaking bad back in Milton, West-by-God-Virginia. Her father was gone—living in a rehab center. Her step-mom's finances were in shambles. Her little sister didn't have a father figure in her life. Her relationship with Alice was bad, and probably abusive, and she should have ended things last month when she had the chance.

Eddie finished her food, then sat her plate on the floor next to Mister Fluffy. Things were bad all over, and she didn't know how to fix them, not here at Ashkak's, and not back home. Eddie liked puzzles—she liked fixing things—and she was no stranger to getting her hands dirty, but these were problems that relied on one's emotional resilience, not their mind or might.

In the time it took Eddie to silently assess the situation, Aldous had already gotten up and walked over to the closet.

He must have moved with the stealth of a panther because she hadn't felt or heard him move.

They were supposed to work on the teleportation spell tonight. After Waja Abjou's class, Aldous had acted like a pivotal piece of the puzzle had been found, even though her attempts at moving had been unsuccessful. On top of that, this might be Eddie's last night at Ashkak's. She might never see Aldous again. Knowing this gave her mixed feelings.

Eddie reached over, picked up the plate, and walked over to the desk. Aldous had several used plates on his desk from the past few days, which reminded her of her own griminess.

"Hey Aldous," she said after picking up the plates.

He turned around with an armful of various items. "Hmm?"

"Do you think I could bathe myself tonight? I'm starting to feel like a Chia pet."

"A what?" Aldous asked, puzzled.

Eddie laughed. "Never mind. A shower. I need a shower. Could I take one before we begin? Just in case I have to stick around for a few days?"

"Of course. Gather your things and come with me."

On her way to the bathroom, the hall was dark and eerily quiet. Other than sounds of chatter drifting up the stairwell now and then, things were tranquil in their part of the wing.

After Eddie stepped out of the shower, she felt like a new person. She wasn't a clean freak, but damn, she hadn't taken a shower in three days, and parts of her were starting to smell like an old gym bag. Eddie walked back to Aldous's room feeling like she had landed on cloud nine. Lots of crap at Ashkak's was different—the words, the food, the plants— but a shower was a shower anywhere in the galaxy, and they all held the same restorative power.

When Eddie got back to Aldous's room, she absentmindedly placed her hand on the doorknob, altogether forgetting the seal he'd placed on it after they had gotten back from the dining hall. Suddenly recalling Aldous's afternoon lecture on seals, she felt the cool metal in her fist and braced herself for what she assumed would be a nasty injury. But nothing happened. No lights. No sonic boom. No blowing-your-body-out-of-your-freaking-sneakers impact. Nothing. Just the sound of the door opening and the floor creaking beneath her feet.

She walked into the room.

Turning swiftly to face Eddie, Aldous closed the book in his hands and shot her an unreadable look. The long pause made her feel uncomfortable, so she took the towel from her head and shook it out, in hopes that once she was finished, he would have somewhat averted his gaze. He didn't.

Eddie cleared her throat and said, "Well, that was weird. Maybe someone messed with the seals. Anyway, thanks for letting me borrow the towel."

"Hmm. You're welcome, but I don't think so." Aldous hung the towel on a coat rack next to the closet and returned to what he had been doing, which Eddie could see now was slinging crap from the closet onto his bed. It was then that she noticed the broomstick again.

"Is that your broomstick?" Eddie asked before she could stop herself.

"No," Aldous replied, guarded. "It was my mother's."

Eddie thought about his mother's spell book and her broomstick.

Aldous had been reared in a world of magic and wonder since birth. He had known his place in the world, and what would be required of him at a very young age. Eddie considered this. Their upbringings had been vastly different, even without the element of magic. Eddie's parents had expectations of her, but they were not set in stone, and she had been in-and-out of in-school-suspension since elementary school. Eddie's grades were not bad per se, but she was always late to class, and sometimes argued with her teachers, especially the ones who couldn't see beyond her black clothing. School *was* like prison at times, but she didn't have to live there. Eddie actually got to leave, but not Aldous. He was stuck at this school, stuck being a suuga, stuck being a reluctant life partner of Caoilainn's.

"Hey, Edwina. Is everything OK?"

"Yea, sorry."

Out of the corner of her eye, Eddie could see Aldous monitoring her closely. He had been like this since her return from the showers. Eddie wanted to talk more about the incident in the dining hall but didn't want to piss him off again, so she said nothing, instead of turning her attention to the various objects on his bed. Eddie got the importance of silence and distance, especially if someone didn't want to talk about their problems, so she drew her eyes away from the bed and looked over at him.

Aldous's brilliant green eyes sparkled like jade stones in the low lantern light.

"Are you ready to do this?"

"You mean the spell?" Eddie wasn't sure if she was ready to do anything, confusion now holding her senses hostage, but she consented anyway. "Yea, sure. Are you ready?"

"I've got everything we need. We obviously can't do the first spell my mother mentioned because we don't have all the supplies, but we can try the one from Abjou's class. It's the third spell mentioned in the book, but my mom didn't say whether it worked."

"I guess I am then," Eddie said, cautiously. Because what she really wanted to say was *could this possibly turn my brains to goop and my body into a lifeless bag of flesh and bone*? What happened if the spell worked and she found herself sitting on the yellow chair in the white room? What would she say to the other girls? To her step-mom? What would she say to Aldous right before she left?

"I think I need to sit down for a minute, though," Eddie said. "Oh God."

"Are you ok?" Aldous's voice was as shaky as Eddie felt. "Do you need some water?"

"Yeah, my heart just felt weird for a minute there," Eddie replied, steadying herself on the mattress. "Let me just get something real quick, and I'll be good to go."

Eddie got up from the bed, then walked over to her back-pack, and dug through the small landfill that the backpack was slowly becoming. She pulled out a small orange bottle, opened it, and placed a white pill in her mouth, then searched for something to drink. Eddie hated taking med-ication, but she knew that if she didn't take something, she was going to have a full-blown panic attack, and that wouldn't do, especially not now.

"Are you good now? Shall we try?"

Nodding slowly, Eddie placed the empty glass back on the nightstand, then lifted her backpack up off the bed, and slid the wide straps up her arms.

"Yeah," Eddie said. "Let's get this crap over with."

Aldous gingerly took both of Eddie's hands into his and painted a different symbol in the palm of each hand.

"What's this?" She asked.

The symbols resembled the ones Salvator had drawn in the centers of the diagrams during Abjou's class.

"This symbol," Aldous said, now running his thumb over the dried paint. "Represents time. This one represents space. In order for us to get you back home, we will need to call on both. The paint, I'm afraid, is more of a mixture of water and old, dried sunberries I found in the Za'tari classroom. I have no idea if it will work, but I made you a promise, and I plan on keeping it."

Eddie stared at the deep scarlet symbols on her palms. It was happening. They were going to do it. She was going home.

"OK Miss Burke," Aldous said. "Let's get this crap over with."

For a moment, Eddie said nothing, instead examining Aldous's face with a smile and taking note of his severe cheekbones, slightly gap teeth, and extraordinary green eyes. He had pulled his hair into a tight braid again, Eddie noticed, and now it lay across his chest like an albino snake. She wanted to reach out and touch the braid but decided against it.

Eddie liked him and knew it. She could feel it with every fiber of her being.

It had only taken three days of getting to know Aldous, but they had connected immediately without friction like subway cars. Eddie knew that she would be glad to see her family, but she would miss her new friend, which seemed incredulous, given the short amount of time they had known one another. Eddie smiled up at him. Aldous was a good foot and a half taller than her.

"There's no guarantee that this will work. I hope you know that I will help you as much as I can, though." Aldous squeezed Eddie's hands and returned her smile. "Okay?" He asked.

"I know. Thanks." Eddie wanted to say more, but her tongue felt as heavy as her heart, and couldn't. Some things she would just have to keep to herself.

"Alright, repeat these words after me: mulah andril revole anha. And when you say them, try to say them as clearly and as loud as you can. Shout them if you need to."

Together they repeated the words over and over again until eventually a bright red light engulfed their hands and traveled up their arms. Eddie's body was suddenly jerked up from the ground and suspended in the air like an orange and black balloon. The loud boom that soon followed was momentarily deafening. Eddie stared down at Aldous in horror.

"Aldous, what the hell is happening?!" The painted symbols on her sweaty palms were now cracked and glowing. "My hands are burning!"

"It's alright. We're doing it, I think." Aldous tried his best to remain calm, but his voice betrayed him. Peering down at him with large eyes, Eddie could tell that he was as terrified as she was. "How do you feel?"

"It's different from before. I actually feel like I'm tingling all over, like my body is falling asleep. Hey, I can't see you anymore! Aldous? Aldous?!"

•••

Aldous rubbed his eyes. He couldn't believe what he was seeing or hearing. The stuff they had been practicing in Waja Abjou's class merely skimmed the surface of movement majik. When he and Caoilainn had attempted the spell earlier that day, they had been able to *move* a pencil from the desk to Caoilainn's knapsack, but that was it. Caoilainn wasn't a bad student necessarily, but she was an indifferent one, and Aldous suspected her powers would increase if only she applied herself—of course, he wouldn't tell her that, given the disdain they shared for one another. Aldous had been astonished by their simple achievement.

Before today Aldous had never successfully *moved* anything, but now he could add the words 'pencil' and 'girl' to his spell book. Watching Eddie *move* wasn't like moving the pencil, though. It was painful. At first, her body shot into the air like someone had placed a chain around her neck and yanked with all their might, and then as if to make matters worse, her body became lighter and lighter until she finally faded into nothingness, her voice the last thing to go.

"Thank you," she had said.

Aldous closed his eyes.

What if she had been transported to a lair of hostile, acid-breathing dragons or a lagoon of treacherous mermaids? Monsters moved freely throughout many parts of the kingdom, and some monsters were worse than others, often eating their prey and fashioning jewelry out of bones as a warning for the next unlucky yokel. Aldous knew they had taken a big risk. Every Ashkak's student grows up hearing horror stories of spells gone awry, and Aldous knew just how unsafe a teleportation spell could be.

One thing was for certain though, Aldous would never forgive himself if something happened to the tiny orange-haired girl.

After a short time, Aldous tore apart his room like a bulldozer, opening doors, rummaging through drawers, and emptying large baskets of unfolded laundry onto the already messy floor. But Eddie was gone. Long done. They had done it. The spell had been cast. Case closed. Something didn't feel quite right, though. Aldous should be glad, proud even, that they had been able to do such a thing, but the only thing he felt was regret.

It was hard to explain.

They had spent the weekend together, yet for some reason Aldous found himself wishing it had been much longer. Three days had not been enough. Eddie was fun to be around. Her face was unique and lovely, covered in pixie kisses and surrounded by unruly, orange tendrils. Her manner of speaking was exotic and unique. Aldous could see her face when he closed his eyes. Eddie didn't ask him questions about why he looked so weird, didn't try to shut him up every time he opened his mouth, didn't try to pull away at the mention or feel of his touch. Her sarcasm was refreshing and endearing, even. Before Eddie sudden arrival, Aldous had almost convinced himself that he preferred silence and solitude.

Mister Fluffy jumped up on the wicker chair and shook his head at Aldous.

Idiot boy, did you honestly think she would remain here forever?

Aldous hissed, "No. Of course not." The fox had warned him from the very beginning, and Aldous wasn't a fool. The end goal had always been returning Eddie to her rightful time and place. "I just didn't expect to feel this way. By the stars, Eddie was a nice girl, and I'm sorry to see her leave. Is that alright? Is that so wrong of me?"

I wish it hadn't worked. I wish she were still here. Aldous allowed himself one selfish thought and then fell face-first onto his bed, and into the sheets that now smelled like Eddie's body wash. He took handfuls of the soft fabric with each hand and inhaled.

Gone.

He'd likely never see her face again.

Across the room, the fox sniffed loudly. *You got attached to her. What did I say? I told you from the beginning not to get attached.*

"That's easy for you to say, Fluff," Aldous murmured into the sheets. "You're a fox. I'm a man. She was interesting—and pretty, God, so pretty,—and nice to me, and now I feel absolutely stupid. Does that make you feel better? Is that what you want to hear? Is it stupidity that you want? *I feel stupid.*"

Mister Fluffy sighed and hopped down from the chair. *Boy, you knew her for three days. Three days.*

This annoyed Aldous. He rolled over and sat up. "Yes, and people who have been married for seventy-three years once knew each other for the same length of time. What's your point?"

You know that you will never be allowed to marry. You know that you will never have a wife. Caoilainn made that perfectly clear years ago. Why do you hang onto such rubbish ideas, anyway? I'll never understand the minds of men. Besides, waja are capable of having consorts, and if they choose, they can parent children.

"You're missing the point, Fluff. It's not about the tradition or the ritual. Hell, I don't care about weddings or titles or any of that stuff. Villagers don't have elaborate weddings, nor do they adorn themselves in jewels to symbolize their commitments. They share quarters with one another and sometimes have families and work. It sounds absolutely delightful compared to Ashkak's."

Yes, they work thankless jobs. Their children get sick and die from common ailments. Their husbands cheat on their wives. They starve if their harvests don't produce enough crops to feed their families. They scrimp and save and slave away for their waja. You are naïve, boy. Best to do away with such childish, romantic thoughts. They'll only hurt you in the long run.

"Is it so wrong to want to be a father? To have a family of my own? To be more than just a damned suuga?"

That girl has rubbed off on your more than you know.

Before the fox could launch into another crushing lecture on the impossibility of Aldous's hopes and dreams, he and the boy heard a voice calling from outside their room.

"Do you think," Aldous said, turning to the fox. "Could it be?"

Go find out. Better to have teleported her elsewhere in the building than to have accidentally teleported a dragon into the building. Regardless, it is your problem now.

"Right," Aldous replied, and then following a brief pause, threw open the door and rushed down the hall, following the voice. As he approached the stairwell, he could hear sounds coming from within the broom closet at the end of the long hall. Aldous rushed to the door, fumbled through his pants pocket, and found a ring of various keys. After locating a skeleton key that could unlock every room in their wing, he opened the door and found Eddie sitting in a large woven basket, atop a mass of cleaning rags.

She greeted Aldous with a frown. "Well, crap. It didn't work, magic man. What now?"

Trying his hardest to quash a smile, Aldous extended his hand and lifted Eddie out of the basket. "No, obviously not. And I'm not sure."

Eddie brushed off her pants and smiled up at him. "Well, what the hell do we do next?"

"Come on," Aldous replied. "I still have a few ideas. If you're up for it, that is."

"Man, you should know that I am game for just about anything at this point. I'm just glad that I still have my arms and legs because that crap felt really weird like I imagine that's what water feels like when it evaporates. It was friggin' surreal."

"I agree. You looked like you were being erased right before my eyes."

"I could see and hear you," Eddie continued. "And then everything turned black and quiet. I wonder if that's what it feels like when you die."

"Thankfully you are *not* dead, Miss Burke."

"You can say that again. Let's get the hell out of this closet. It smells like my Aunt Gerdie's house."

"Your aunt's house?"

"Mothballs and vinegar," Eddie said, following Aldous out of the small room.

"That sounds like the makings of a spell."

"Well, Gerdie's house definitely smelled like a den of demons. Let's go."

CHAPTER 7

For the rest of the evening, Aldous and Eddie explored various spell books that Aldous had collected over the years. It was a dangerous thing to do, keeping all of these spell books under one roof because he explained, spell books were living things. Once a suuga or sujii wrote a spell in the book, it was like telling their closest friend a secret, and secrets could be deadly things.

Only a few practitioners in all of existence could read from every spell book, for it was an ability few possessed. But two years after Aldous's mother died, he had discovered a mound of books in his father's study and discovered that he was included in that select few, or so he told Eddie. After accidentally stumbling upon this knowledge, Aldous stole three books from the pile and had kept them hidden ever since. His father never knew, or at least, never mentioned their whereabouts to Aldous, perhaps because he was not supposed to have them, either.

Eddie listened intently to Aldous as he spoke passionately about famous magical feats (and failures) throughout the kingdoms' histories. Aldous was sure that Waja Abjou knew how to teleport, but didn't know the extent of his personal travels, and from the way he had eyed Eddie, they didn't think it was such a good idea to ask him about those travels, either.

Aldous was considerably knowledgeable about enchantments and sorcery, and knew the answer to just about every question Eddie asked. *How could he be such a bad suuga?* she wondered, watching his long, slender fingers turn page after page.

"I just don't understand it," Aldous admitted. "I don't know what could have gone wrong. We did everything the spell book asked," he said, with a hint of defeat in his voice. "My mother was a masterful sujii. I wish I had even a tenth of her abilities. Maybe I am saying the words incorrectly."

Eddie made a sound. "Come on now, I know I wasn't saying them correctly. Besides, we sound different. Our words don't match when we speak. I sound like a hick."

"I'm not entirely sure that really matters. What matters here, I think anyway, is intent. Were you intentionally trying to get back home?"

"I think so," Eddie said. "Yeah, I was definitely doing what you told me, about imagining my house and crap. My sister's face."

Aldous chewed on his bottom lip and closed the book in his hands. "Yeah, something's not right. Could have been the mixture. Let me look at your hands."

Eddie held out her palms. The paint was gone now, but Aldous could still make out the faint shapes and symbols without much difficulty. He traced each shape with the tip of his finger.

"Do they hurt?" Aldous's voice was barely a whisper. "Do they still burn?"

"What?" Eddie asked. "My hands?"

"Yes, the symbols." Aldous released her hands. "It looks like they've been scarred."

Eddie held her hands up next to the candelabra on Aldous's nightstand. "No, they feel fine. Do you think this will go away?"

Aldous couldn't say, because most everything he knew about majik came from books. It would take a powerful healing spell to remove the markings of majik. Furthermore, if someone saw the markings on Eddie's palms, it could mean even more trouble for both of them. They had messed up, and neither of them knew how to correct the mistake.

"Alright. Do you think you have one more in you? Or would you like to go to sleep? Either way works for me. I really don't care." Aldous didn't care—he was just glad to have Eddie back in his room, safe and sound, away from potential horrors that lurked in the Kingdoms' forests and rivers.

"Sure, but only one. Most of this junk goes over my head, anyway."

"One it is then."

The book Aldous now held in his hand looked old and decrepit, with pages falling out the sides, and had the word MONSTERS scrawled across the front, in bold, bronze, cursive letters. From the other books, Eddie gathered that mystical creatures lived in haunted forests, and that cruel pixies often played nasty tricks on travelers, and that sometimes beautiful mermaids lured young children to their horrible deaths. These were not the stories she had been told as a small child. Mermaids were expected to help shipwrecked princes and forfeit their lives to protect them, not skin them alive with knives made from old bones.

"Whoa, whoa, whoa." The etchings in the book were creepy, and Eddie's eyes had landed on a shape-shifter while thumbing through its pages. "Check this out—it's crazy. What the hell is that? Is it like a half-dragon, half-person?"

"Here. Let me see that." Aldous took a seat next to Eddie and leaned his body across her lap to get a better look at the book, lightly brushing against her arm and leg. Neither of them seemed bothered by this. "Ah yes, this species of dragon, in particular, can shift in between beast and man if needed, though I must say I have never encountered such a beast. Thank the stars for that."

"Wait. How does such a creature, ya know?"

"Come about?" Aldous asked, confused by Eddie's euphemism. "You mean, how are they made?"

"Yeah, that. Reproduction or whatever."

"Well, I imagine it's an anomaly. Probably a reluctant pairing if you know what I mean."

"You're talking about rape. Damn, that's horrible. Really terrible." Eddie shook her head, then turned the page. "What about this thing? What's the story behind it? It looks weird as hell too." She said, running her finger across the grotesque etching.

"Ah," Aldous replied, dropping his voice. "Oh. *That.* That *thing* is called a changeling." Eddie thought that if the creature looked anything like the drawing, it would immediately instill panic and fear into the person it approached because it didn't just look like it came from a nightmare, it was *the* nightmare.

"Changelings are fairy children left in place of man babes. They are most often stolen while their parents are asleep."

"Okay. So they come into your room and snatch up the baby, and y'all get a substitute? But why are those super aggro men and women standing around the child with pitchforks and swords? I mean, I get that the baby got stolen, but that seems like overkill. What the hell is a changeling? What does it do?"

"They're mad. They're going to kill the baby. The fairy baby, that is. I have never heard of a man returning from the Wyldewood. Once they are taken from their parents, they do not return."

"What's the Wyldewood? And they kill the fairy baby? That's terrible. How do ya know so much about this stuff? Is it common knowledge?"

"Because," Aldous explained. "They're stories villagers tell each other by the campfire. We grow up hearing about changelings. All of these monsters, really, but changelings are feared by most, if not all, villagers—and waja."

"That's not really fair. It's not the baby's fault that its fairy parents abandoned it for a human child and left it with f-ing whacko farmers. It's not right to kill something just because it's not wanted. You don't believe that. You can't."

"Regardless of how I feel about it, that's just how things have been handled for centuries."

Aldous's indifference made Eddie mad. "Well, I still think it's wrong. And you shouldn't agree with something just because everyone else thinks it's right or acceptable, Aldous. Lots of bad stuff happens because of that kind of thinking."

"I'm not going to argue the morality of such an act, Edwina, because, one, I've never witnessed one, so I don't have a basis for such a belief and am therefore not entitled to one, and two, we'd be here all night and we still have things to discuss. But I will say that I do think it's wrong to hate something simply because it looks different, or because you don't understand it."

"So changelings are killed at birth, but have you ever wondered what an adult changeling would be like? What they would look like? Sound like? Would they be as ugly as that thing in the picture?"

Aldous shrugged in response and eagerly turned the page.

Eddie couldn't get past the absurdity of it all. Monsters were feared in the kingdoms more so than in West Virginia simply because they *did* exist. Sure, back home you grew up thinking that the Moth Man might appear every time you crossed a bridge, so you held your breath and closed your eyes until you were safely across, but here, he might very well show up for dinner, or knock on your door and ask for a cup of sugar. The thought was not a comforting one.

They sat on the floor for god knows how long until they reached the last page. In the time it took to finish the book, Eddie's back started feeling like it belonged to an eighty-year-old woman and not a girl on the verge of turning eighteen. She stood up while Aldous continued to finger through the book and stretched her arms and legs.

She was dog-tired.

Eddie didn't know how Aldous lasted on three-four hours of rest every night, but she knew that if they kept this up, she would turn into a monster befitting the book in his hands. She unrolled a blanket onto the floor, and Aldous cried out in protest.

"Whoa, whoa. No, no. I insist you sleep on the bed tonight. If you feel uncomfortable sharing the bed with me, that's fine. I will gladly sleep on the floor. But you're my guest, and it is likely that this is our last night together in the room."

"Are you sure?" Eddie asked. I really don't mind."

"I am. Tomorrow I plan on asking the headmistress if she can find a bunk for you in the girls' wing. I hope that's all right."

Eddie was exhausted and didn't feel like an argument, so she climbed up into his bed beside Mister Fluffy and curled up next to him.

"Yeah, yeah," she responded, grabbing for a pillow. "Whatever you say."

Aldous got up from the floor and walked over to his desk. For the next few minutes, Eddie watched him search for answers to unasked questions in his mother's books. Sleep was on its way, and no matter how hard she fought it, the thought of closing her eyes was as seductive as a warm blanket on a cold winter's night. Aldous, on the other hand, had mentioned to her that he could go for days without sleep if needed (though he did not recommend it). He didn't look tired at all. It was unbelievable.

Eddie rolled over, pulled the blankets up over her body, and then before drifting off to sleep, propped herself up on one elbow as best she could.

"Aldous?"

"Hmm?" He said, shuffling through papers on his desk. "Do you need another blanket?"

"You win."

Aldous stopped what he was doing to look at her, and asked, puzzled. "What do I win?"

"I just want you to know that I won't say anything to those freaking assholes while I'm here at Ashkak's, not even if they try to start shit with you in front of me. You just take the lead and I'll follow. I'm not happy about it, but this is your gig, not mine, and I won't jeopardize things for you."

"Thank you," Aldous said. "I appreciate that."

"But I just want you to know how much it chaps my ass to see them talk to you like that. You don't deserve it. No one does. If it were up to me—well, it's not, but it's not cool. I'm not OK with it."

"I know it's not. Good night, Miss Burke."

CHAPTER 8

Troubled sleep plagued Eddie that night.

Tossing and turning, horrible visions of destruction and death poisoned her dreams, until something finally tugged at her foot, disturbing the sleep and waking her. Eddie was grateful for this small favor, until she rolled onto her side, and found Aldous sprawled out on the comforter next to her. He was big and took up over two-thirds of the bed with his long limbs. Eddie didn't know how long he'd had been asleep and didn't want to disturb him, because Aldous already slept so little, so she lay as still as she could, breathing as softly as possible.

It was her first time sharing a bed with a boy, other than her cousin Graham, of course, but that had been over ten years ago, and he had peed the bed and was forced to sleep on the floor after that.

This is different. Like way different.

Eddie liked this boy, and this felt intimate in a way that made her uneasy. She adjusted her head to get a better look at his face. A nice face. Eddie liked everything about Aldous- the way his long, bone-white hair lay across his colorless face, his slightly parted lips, his angular profile, and his long, gray eyelashes.

Aldous was achingly beautiful, and the thought made her tremble like the body of a bass guitar. *If you don't calm down right now*, Eddie thought to herself desperately, *your pulse is going to turn this whole damned bed into the San Andreas*

Fault. Mister Fluffy, who rested at the edge of the bed, then lifted his head and glanced at her. At once she put her index finger to her lips and tapped her lips twice.

"Good morning," Aldous said, wiping the sleep from his eyes. "Did you sleep well?"

"I managed to fall asleep, if that's what you mean."

Last night after Aldous had discovered her in the closet, Eddie had been sort of…relieved. Neither of them understood why Eddie was teleported to the broom closet, instead of her home, but there had been an unspoken moment of shared relief when their eyes met.

The thought of going home so soon after discovering this place of wonder, of magic, of mystery, was not a good one. Because it was exciting here. Eddie wasn't trapped in a facility with men and women who had broken their families' hearts. She wasn't sitting in her guidance counselor's office, filling out applications to her local community and state colleges. She wasn't standing in linc at the pharmacy, picking up her psych meds. No, Eddie was sharing a bed with a boy and his animal, and everything was alright.

With her head still on the pillow, Eddie turned toward Aldous and replied, "Did you, Mr. Insomniac?"

Aldous shook his head and said, "No, I'm afraid I didn't get much sleep last night, but thank you for asking. I couldn't get my mind to stop racing. Does that ever happen to you?" He laid his head on the pillow next to hers and stared up at the ceiling, then sighed to himself. "Because now I have a theory. One that I've toyed with since your arrival, really, but now I'm convinced." Aldous turned to her, their faces dangerously close, and said in all seriousness, "I don't think you're going to like it."

What? Now it was time for the girl and the fox to exchange looks.

Aldous pushed himself up and leaned against the oak headboard. "The theory will be hard to swallow, I'm afraid."

"Aldous, I don't understand. What theory? What are you talking about?"

"What if I told you—that you, you were capable of majik?" Eddie stared at him in silence. "What if I told you that I believed you brought yourself here, somehow? It sounds crazy after everything you've told me about your home, I know. I know how this must sound to you. But that's my theory. You did it. Your majik got you here. It had nothing to do with Ashkak's or me. You are the one who brought yourself here, and you will be the one who sends yourself back."

Eddie couldn't bring herself to look at Aldous.

Doesn't he know how insane he sounds?

She was Edwina Burke, an average student at Cabell Midland High, and sure, she had her problems, but she was normal for the most part. She had been diagnosed with anxiety after her mom died, and now and then it would rear its ugly head, and she took meds for it, but she was still normal. Nervous and quick-tempered maybe, but every kid has problems, especially where it concerns friends and school. Besides, Eddie wasn't gifted at anything, other than being good with her hands, making stuff like pottery and jewelry—in fact, she was damn good, brush-your-shoulders-off-good—but that didn't require majik, just a little know-how and guidance from someone more adept.

"Aldous," Eddie said, looking down at her hands. "You do realize how batshit insane that sounds, right? I have never messed around with this stuff before. I have no experience with it."

"It sounds ridiculous to you because majik is lore to you, but to us it is reality. There's no reason to think that you aren't capable of casting a spell or making a simple potion."

"No," Eddie said. "I don't believe it. I'm sorry." Aldous looked so serious, so confident in this assertion that she couldn't help but tear away from his gaze. "There's just no way."

•••

Aldous didn't contradict Eddie. He wasn't the arguing type, but he still stuck by his premonition, because he grew up surrounded by majik, and knew the telltale signs. It didn't matter that Eddie had grown up in West Virginia, that she attended public school (whatever that meant) and not Ashkak's. Everything about Eddie was exotic, from the way she spoke, with her long-drawn-out syllables, to the way she dressed in all black.

Nothing about Edwina Burke was normal, and this pleased Aldous, though he kept this thought to himself. If she had been more like Caoilainn or Vada, the likelihood of them hitting it off right away would have been nil. In his heart of hearts, he was pleased that Eddie was in his bed (a first for him) and that she laughed at his dumb jokes, and wanted to learn about majik. Eddie never told Aldous to shut up or interrupted him. Edwina Burke was too precious a gem, and he didn't want to muck things up by forcing her into accepting his beliefs. Aldous wouldn't do it.

"OK. I won't mention it again," he said, and closed his eyes.

•••

Eddie couldn't move, paralyzed by the fact that Aldous thought she could do majik, and therefore had probably unwittingly brought herself here. She didn't want to move.

What if he thinks I did this on purpose? That I have been lying to him the whole time? What if he thinks I set out to trick him?

Eddie was a lot of things, but a liar she was not.

Last night their plans to send her back home were foiled by a bad enchantment, or maybe a mispronounced word or two, and now Aldous was accusing her of being a witch. Unlike Eddie's white-haired counterpart, her eyes were, and she could see everything.

Is this my fault? All she had wanted to do was to see some art, not be hurled through space and time to land in some foreign kingdom. Eddie was not a West Virginia Yankee in King Arthur's court. She was just a miserable teenager up to no good most of the time, and now she wanted some coffee, and maybe some eggs. One thing was certain, though, Eddie didn't want to hear any of this. She just wanted to—she didn't know what she wanted. Eddie was confused and freaked out, the thought of her in a baggy robe and pointed hat was unsettling.

"Aldous," Eddie began. "This is absurd. Do you know how crazy you sound? I'm just average, man. I'm an average student, and yeah, I'm kind of messed up, I guess," Eddie said. "But I don't know. The only thing I know about magic comes from Wiccan reference books and Harry Potter. Where I come from man controls water, plants, fire, everything, with technology, not by interstellar predictions or magical concoctions. Are you even listening to me?" She asked, waving a hand in front of his face.

Aldous nodded. He was listening to her, but only partially. At some point during Eddie's long-winded lamentation, Aldous's attention had shifted to the shirt she now wore.

His shirt. Eddie was wearing his shirt.

Aldous didn't know why he hadn't noticed before, but it was massive on Eddie, with the hem falling just below her knees. She was practically wearing a tent, but she wore it well. He could see the outline of her body underneath the raggedy shirt.

Eddie was pretty. Real pretty. The freckles on her face mirrored the ones on her hands, arms, legs, and were likely in other places Aldous probably shouldn't think about. He watched Eddie pace back and forth while muttering things to herself. By the stars, she was pretty, and she was in *his* room spouting off some nonsense he didn't quite understand, something about someone named Myrtle and talking snakes. Aldous had to focus, because now was not the time to get caught up in a pretty smile and curls. But it wasn't easy.

Idiot boy, get your head out of the clouds.

Aldous looked at the fox, and then looked back at the girl who was still talking.

"Yes, I was listening. But you're wrong, you are anything but average. How could you even think that?" Aldous asked, turning the tables on her.

At that, Eddie stopped pacing and glanced over at Aldous. Still lying on the bed, his head was now propped up on one fist, and he was looking at her through his glasses. Aldous looked different with glasses, proper and regal, everything that a wizard should be. The square frames fit his angular face nicely, and he was even more fetching with them. Eddie really liked his face.

Now is not the time to be thinking about dumb stuff, Eddie.

"OK. So, say I was able to do majik," she began. "Whatever. What would that even freaking mean? We wouldn't even know where to begin. I thought you guys were chosen as infants or something. I'll be eighteen next week."

"Well, yes, we are paired as young adolescents and begin our training a few years before," Aldous replied. "But my mother used to say that some folks are just born majikal. Their gifts manifest themselves in different ways, and it's not always easy to discern what is a gift and what is not. My hidden gift is, as you have guessed by now, herbalism. I did not choose it, Eddie. It chose me. If I could change it, I would. Things would have been so much easier for me."

"I bet. You must have been crushed when you went to school."

"When my da told me that I was not allowed to become sujii, the world lost its color. My gift is making potions from herbs that Caoilainn collects. While it is not what I desire, it is what I do. I'm good at the ratios and I have a steady hand. If you allow me to help you, perhaps we can discover your gift together, and we can get you back home...whenever you're ready. No rush, of course."

By the time he'd finished, Aldous couldn't tell by the look in Eddie's eyes if he was coming on too strong. There were many things he'd like to show Eddie, to share with her, but he wasn't sure she was ready, or even willing to try. Every time she took a step forward, she would take three steps back. Talking to Eddie about gifts and majik seemed like dangerous territory. Aldous didn't want to upset her.

"I only wish to help you. If you are troubled or bothered by this, say the word and I shall pursue it no further."

Magic. Majik. Eddie knew that majik was real.

She had seen it with her own two eyes, smelled it, touched it.

Eddie knew that majik was real, yet there was a part of her mind that doubted everything, even Aldous's existence. Even though she had spent the past weekend in his room, on his floor, and in his bed, there was still a part of her that believed this was all a dream, that she would eventually wake up. It didn't matter that Eddie had felt the coarse texture of Mister Fluffy's fur many times, that she had tasted the wonderful food from the dining hall, that she had somehow been taken out of Aldous's bedroom and placed in a broom closet.

How Eddie had gotten into the closet, she did not know.

She hadn't walked or ran. She just...arrived. Appeared out of thin air.

Majik had brought her here to Ashkak's—to Aldous.

Eddie peered down at Aldous, in stubborn defiance. "Alright. I'll do it. But under one condition."

Excitedly, he replied, "Anything." He opened his eyes again and sat up.

"Teach me how to talk to animals. With my mind. Like you do with him."

Aldous frowned at her request. "Errr—that might be a problem."

"Why?" Eddie asked. "Can't you teach me how? You know lots of useless stuff."

"Ah, it's not that like, I'm afraid. The lyärgo actually comes to you. It's not really a skill that you learn." Aldous put his hands together and pressed his thumbs against his forehead. The subject was a tricky one. "You see, one day you just hear what the animal is thinking, and the animal is able to do the same. I had the good fortune of having the lyärgo come to me that had been in my family for years. I still have no idea how old this fox is. Mister Fluffy was older than my mother before she passed away."

"OK, so then where do the lyärgo come from?"

"A wildlife sanctuary actually, known to most villagers and waja as *the pujari*. The villagers train them and then waja claim them. They become your lyärgo for life, and will even forfeit their lives if asked."

"Damn," Eddie said. "That sucks."

"I agree. Let's hope it never comes to that. For either of our sakes."

The pujari. While it wasn't what Eddie wanted to hear, it made sense. Most of the time Aldous acted put off by the animal, and the fox was not affectionate or loving towards him, either. Eddie wondered how Mister Fluffy felt about this agreement.

According to Eddie's watch, it was 5:02AM. The sun had not yet risen, and the skies were still as black as coal. Time moved slower here at Ashkak's, or rather, there seemed to be more minutes in a day. Eddie wasn't quite sure how things worked yet. Important things that she took for granted back home, like the rotation of the sun, for example, hadn't been discussed. Her watch meant nothing in the grand scheme of things. A relic from her previous life.

While Aldous thumbed through old, yellow pages of heavy, leather-bound books, Eddie found herself over-analyzing recent events. For the second time now, she had travelled through space and time. It didn't matter that the spell hadn't worked properly. As far as Eddie was concerned, they had identified a piece of the puzzle, a map with which to work, and if Aldous's past determination indicated anything, she would be in her bed soon enough.

For the past few days, Eddie's mind, body, and soul had been pulled in different directions, like scattered pieces of a decaying leaf caught in a wind storm. New truths replaced old assumptions, and she could feel things changing on a molecular level. What if teleportation required leaving a part of you behind every time you travelled? How could something like that be measured? How would she even know?

Aldous is mistaken—he just has to be.

Eddie didn't know the first thing about practicing majik, nor did she truly believe that she would be a good sujii (or suuga, for that matter). Teleportation had been intentional the second time around, but the first had been a fluke, a mistake, and no matter how many times Eddie disagreed with Aldous, his beliefs on the matter were unshaken.

"Hey." Aldous's voice was a welcome distraction from the thoughts racing through her head.

"Yeah," Eddie replied.

"You can take a shower if you'd like. Towel is hanging up on the closet door. You won't find many students up at this hour."

"Mr. Molhata, are you trying to say that I smell bad?"

"What," Aldous said, his shock genuine. "No, I would never say that."

Then motioning to her body, Eddie laughed. "You sure about that? Are you afraid of me getting your sheets all sweaty?"

Without a word, they both looked at the bed, and then back at each other.

Returning his gaze to the book, Aldous said, "I think those sheets are capable of handling a lot more than your sweat."

"I think I'll just brush my teeth instead."

The hall was quiet and dark, save for the few dimly lit lanterns. Now clutching her toothpaste and toothbrush, Eddie rushed down the hall turning twice, and then once, eventually making her way to the girl's room. Unsurprisingly, she found herself alone in the dark room, with only one beeswax candle providing light for the large space. The seemingly glacial water startled her as she splashed it against her heavily freckled skin.

What the hell are you doing? You don't even know him. But it's not like anyone would ever know if you fooled around with him. OK. Now you're answering yourself. Just stop reading into everything he says. He's just being nice is all.

He's nice. He's nice. He's nice.

As Eddie turned to exit the room, something big and purple collided with her, shoving her down onto the concrete floor, so hard that it sent toiletries soaring through the air, and knocking the wind out of her. After that, everything seemed to happen frame by frame—every lantern springing to life when Eddie threw up her arms, the dark figure seizing up immediately, their hands suspended in midair after she'd whispered the word "stop."

Now scrambling away from the dark figure, she struggled to find her voice.

"Please just go away!"

After several minutes of sitting very still with her hands glued to her head, Eddie opened her eyes and peered around the hall.

Nothing. No robed figure. Just silence.

With a forced effort, Eddie stood up and walked back to Aldous's door, pausing to look over her shoulder after every other step. When she entered the room, she found Aldous in the same manner, slumped over a book, with his glasses on the tip of his nose, the door's broken seal now a mere afterthought.

Upon seeing Eddie's frazzled state, Aldous closed the book in his hands and asked, "Is everything alright? Did something happen?"

There was no way of knowing how long Eddie stood there, wide-eyed, mouth agape, struggling to speak, but when she did finally speak, she startled herself.

"Someone knocked me down out there. Someone in a large purple robe."

"Purple? Like Abjou purple or…? Did you see what they looked like?" Aldous replied, his face a sea of concern.

"No. Not Abjou purple, more like an eggplant." Eddie sat down on the bed, trying to collect her scattered thoughts. "The person was big, enormous, like a damn linebacker. Their face was covered by the thing, robe, whatever you want to call it, but I could feel this energy coming from beneath that friggin' hood. And I tell you, I've never felt anything like that in my life. It felt like…anger, like rage on two feet. This sounds crazy, I know."

Aldous regarded Eddie for a moment, then opened his door and peered into the long hall. The lanterns were aglow now, and sounds of life down below were making their way up the stairwell. He closed the door and turned to face Eddie.

"I think we need to be careful," Aldous said. "There's no telling what could be lurking out there. Strange things are afoot these days, and there's no harm in being cautious."

"Oh trust me, I don't plan on being out there again like that. Asshole made me lose my toothbrush, too."

Eddie chose to withhold certain parts of the story on purpose—like lighting the lanterns and the overgrown eggplant's disappearance. Majik terrified her, and she wasn't some freaking experiment. She didn't want to spend every waking hour doing homework and trying to test her newly found powers. Eddie trusted Aldous, she did, but she knew how naturally curious and inquisitive he was—he would have her doing all kinds of crap, and she wasn't ready for that.

"I guess I'll get dressed now," Eddie said rising from the bed. "Yo, Aldous?"

Aldous nodded but said nothing, and Eddie could see that he wasn't with her at the moment. The vacant look on his face wasn't new to her, either. Aldous did this sometimes, disconnecting from everyone and everything, in order to better comprehend something, or work toward solving a problem. Eddie likened it to daydreaming, but not entirely, because it served a purpose.

"Do you want me to just get undressed with you in the room?"

The thought of Eddie undressing caught Aldous attention, however, and he whipped his head around. But before Aldous could give her an answer, a loud knocking rattled the door, startling them both.

"Oh my god, do you think it's returned?"

"I doubt an ogre would knock before entering a room, although there's a first time for everything."

If only it was an ogre. Aldous knew that knock.

He had heard it nearly every week for the past eight years. It sounded when someone overslept. It sounded when someone received a letter. It sounded when boys snuck girls into their dormitories.

Aldous inhaled deeply and then opened the door as delicately as someone opening a can of shaken soda.

"Yes?" He asked.

Fuming, Headmistress Kahlee stood before him, her hands on her wide hips. A tall woman with blue, wire-framed glasses and frizzy black hair, Kahlee met Aldous's gaze with cold, hard eyes. "Well, where is she?"

Aldous carefully stepped to the side, placing Eddie in Kahlee's line of vision. They were both still in their bed-clothes and knew how debaucherous things must appear to this angry woman.

Headmistress Kahlee looked at Eddie from head to toe and smiled a sickly-sweet smile. "Child, you are in great violation of school rules. No doubt you were being led astray by this scoundrel of a boy." Kahlee referred to all boys and men as scoundrels. "Toying with a young girl's heart, knowing fully aware that he is also in violation. Tsk tsk. Well no matter, get dressed and gather your things. I shall take you to the West Wing and we can find you a room. Aldous, really, this is no way to treat a friend of your family. You should be ashamed of yourself."

Aldous looked at Eddie and shook his head, feigning shame and guilt.

"You're right," he said, shrugging his shoulders. "I'm a mighty bad seed. I don't know what I was thinking. I just get so lonely up here sometimes, and I wanted to heat things up a little, if you get my drift." The emphasis on 'heat things up' made Eddie nearly choke.

"Oh, I get your drift all right. All men are the same."

Eddie didn't fully understand what was going on, but somehow this headmistress individual had accepted the poorly spun story Aldous had been telling everyone, and she was expected to play along.

The tall woman eyed Aldous and said to Eddie, "And we will get you proper nightclothes. I'll be waiting for you out here. Hurry up, child, you will want to catch breakfast before your first class. And Aldous, your father would like to see you this afternoon at some point, perhaps after second tea." Kahlee took a step back through the doorway and closed the door, never taking her eyes off of Aldous.

Aldous let out a long sigh, then fell back on the bed, and closed his eyes. "Gah. That's a nasty woman. I'm done for."

Eddie stared at him. "Done for? Why? It sounds like everyone has bought that dumb-ass slayer bit."

Without looking opening his eyes, Aldous replied, "My da wants to see me. No doubt to ream me about you and he'll expect the truth. He knows that we don't have any slayer friends in the Second Kingdom. Stars above, I hate talking to him. I haven't spoken to him in weeks. And the last time, things did not go well. We don't get along."

Eddie sat down next to Aldous and placed her hand on his, forcing him to open his eyes. She smiled warmly at him.

"Oh, come on," she said. "We've made it this far. I think you'll do fine. Just tell him exactly what happened. Tell him how I unknowingly brought myself here and how I'm trying to get back. You did nothing wrong here, dude."

"You know, you're the nicest person I've ever met. How are you like this?" Aldous asked, now leaning back on his elbows. "I'm glad that you ended up in my room instead of someone else's."

"I'm not that nice. I offered to beat up Salvator, remember? And yeah, me too."

For the next few minutes, the two friends sat on the bed, their hands still interlocked. Aldous had mentioned his father a few times before, but it had never gone any further than "he thinks I'm a disappointment." With any luck, the news of her arrival would be met with curiosity, not criticism—probably not, she knew how dads were, but she could hope.

When Aldous finally turned onto his side, Eddie got up from the bed & located an undershirt. She looked down at her chest. *I mean, I really don't have anything to be embarrassed about. I'm as flat as he is.* Eddie removed her shirt, and slipped a t-shirt over her head, then pulled on a pair of clean leggings.

"Do you reckon she'll ask me to find a room before breakfast?" Eddie asked, now lacing her boots.

Aldous got up from the bed and fashioned his hair into a bun using loose strands. Despite his unusual features, Eddie couldn't take her eyes off of him.

"I'm not sure," Aldous answered. "I should hope not. Breakfast is more important than finding a bed right after you wake up. I mean, you've already slept."

Eddie cast a glance around the room one more time after slipping on her backpack.

She would miss the fox.

She would miss Aldous and the conversations they shared over tea.

Eddie knew that her time here would still be largely spent with Aldous, but the thought still freaked her out. She also didn't like meeting new people, and the thought of being surrounded by high school girls was unnerving, to say the least.

"Aldous, I—." Eddie wanted badly to tell him just how cool he was, how she didn't want to leave him, and how if Salvator opened his big flipping mouth, she was going to knock him into next Sunday, but she didn't.

She couldn't.

"Hmm?" Aldous asked, his mind elsewhere again.

"Your hair," Eddie replied with a grin. "It looks nice like that. You can see your face. I like it. You have a good face." Eddie shifted the backpack on her shoulders and opened the door. "Well, I guess I'll see you later. Wish me luck. I'm gonna to need it."

The headmistress was standing with her hand on her hip and scowled at Aldous when Eddie opened the door. Eddie turned around and flashed a peace sign, then started down the long corridor with the headmistress.

Aldous sat on the bed and played Eddie's words over and over again in his head.

A compliment.He had received a compliment from a girl. *She said I have a good face. That's a first.*

Other than encouraging things Simone and Vada said to him about sorcery and track, Aldous never received them, especially about his looks. Aldous knew that he looked weird. No matter how much he ate, he had always been gangly and bony. His features were unlike either parent and growing up, he had endured relentless teasing for this.

He walked over to the mirror on his wall.

He looked at his face.

How can one be unremarkable yet so bizarre? Who had ever heard of a child starting out with white hair? Wasn't that supposed to happen after you lived a long, fulfilling life? Yes, most suuga had long, white hair, but they were generally older than the forests, and had received that hair by assisting brave heroes slaying monsters, by performing death-defying acts, and of course, old age. Aldous was nineteen-years-old, though. He never even had a chance.

Aldous, don't let it go to your head.

The tall boy didn't acknowledge the fox's comment. Aldous had waited for this moment all his life. He needed it. He needed her.

After Aldous discovered that Caoilainn was not interested in him *that way*, he had been forced to accept the harsh reality that he would spend the rest of his life alone, even with a waja. A couple of years ago during a lighting of the Great Fires, Caoilainn had made it abundantly clear that she was interested in someone else. Her words were not malicious, but the news spread faster than a virus, infecting each student in its path. Aldous's failures had become a topic again.

After that, he cut himself off from everyone, minimizing his interactions with Caoilainn, and choosing instead to focus on his running and his studies. Until Eddie had popped into existence, Aldous had been a very lonely young man.

"You're right, Fluff," Aldous responded. "I won't."

Aldous got dressed, then walked over to his dresser, and retrieved a long, wine-colored ribbon. He released his bun and wove the silky fabric in and out of a long braid—something he hadn't done in quite a while due to boys on the track team harassing him for it.

Don't read into it. Aldous.

"I'm not." Aldous smiled, drew back the drapes, and looked into the valley below.

CHAPTER 9

When Aldous walked into Waja Abjou's classroom only to find Salvator and Eddie laughing with one another, he was hit with the familiar pang of betrayal. How could she go from wanting to punch the guy last night to laughing and sharing a desk with him a few hours later? *It doesn't make any sense. Eddie doesn't make any sense. Girls don't make any sense.*

Aldous took his seat and said nothing, altogether ignoring the girl sitting next to him. He wouldn't be the first to speak. He never was. Things had been awkward between the two of them since the fire rites. Simone and Vada had encouraged Aldous to work through things, so that when the time came to light the Great Fires again, they would be prepared to say farewell to Ashkak's as students, and hello to their new village as waja. But seeing as how Caoilainn wanted him dead, Aldous ignored their pleas and advice, instead allowing the hole inside to grow and blacken. He had no idea how this set-up was going to work for the next seventy-five years. Someone was bound to snap.

"It looks as if your friend and Salvator are getting along nicely," Caoilainn said, her voice an octave lower than usual.

Aldous didn't want to turn his head, but he didn't like her tone, so he did. Eddie was sitting next to Salvator, her eyes closed and her hands over her mouth, no doubt laughing at something stupid he'd just said.

Aldous turned back around and said, "Yeah, I guess so."

Aldous couldn't avoid the truth any longer. Salvator had stolen Caoilainn, and now he had his sights set on Eddie. *Vulture.* Besides, who in their right mind wouldn't get along with Salvator? For one, he was the most attractive man Aldous had ever laid eyes on. Two, he was a first-rate archer, and excelled at painting, and possessed other artistic abilities. And three, every movement spell he cast was successful. Or was that four? Aldous tried to bury the acidic jealousy now seeping into his thoughts.

What is wrong with me?

Aldous had no right to be jealous. They were just friends and had only known each other for a few days. But Aldous couldn't help himself. She was his secret, dammit, and he'd wish they'd kept it that way. If Eddie found out Salvator was a talented artist as well, they would get along even more. Aldous swallowed. The thought made him feel even more sour.

I hate feeling this way. Why am I like this?

Aldous glanced at Eddie once more before Waja Abjou entered the room. She had taken her hat off again, and allowed her curls to fall this way and that way like a big, orange fern. He wondered if her hair was as soft as it looked.

Have I always been such a lecher?

•••

Salvator was a sociopath.

He had to be.

When Eddie walked into Abjou's room that morning, Salvator had greeted her warmly and acted like nothing had happened the day before. Even though it was common knowledge that Aldous had housed Eddie in his room, Salvator did not seem to understand the bonds of friendship.

At first, Eddie had been determined to find a seat away from the bun-throwing son of a bitch, but once the room filled up with students and everyone took their seat, the only place left was the one next to his. The events from the previous day had left a bad taste in Eddie's mouth. She hated bullies, and she couldn't stand the thought of someone attacking Aldous like that in front of the whole school.

Salvator didn't mention it, though, instead talking to Eddie as if they'd known each other their entire lives, and no matter what she did, Eddie found herself laughing at his jokes.

When Aldous walked into the room, Eddie had tried to make eye contact with him, as if to send out an SOS, but if he saw her trying to get his attention, she had missed it. Eddie did not want him getting the wrong idea about Salvator, though. They were not friends. She was not cool with him.

"Edwina." Salvator whispered. "I don't believe that you are from here."

Eddie nodding in agreement, replied, "That's right. I'm from the Second Kingdom."

"No. I don't think so."

She turned toward him. "What are you talking about? Yes, I am."

"No," Salvator replied. "Nobody from the other kingdoms would dare refer to themselves using the First Kingdom's hierarchical ranking. Not unless they agreed with how the First Kingdom looks down on the other kingdoms. I don't believe you."

Eddie didn't know how to respond to that. Back when she and Aldous had discussed the layout of the kingdoms, he had mentioned something along those lines. Eddie had never been a gifted liar and knew that she wouldn't be able to answer any of Salvator's questions about her alleged home if asked.

They regarded one another.

"I honestly don't know what to say to you," Eddie finally said.

"You don't have to say anything. Just listen. I am not from the First Kingdom either."

"OK. Wait, what?"

"You see," Salvator said. "One day, I was putting the finishing touches on a painting, and the next thing I knew, I was on the ground. At first, I thought someone had hit me over the head because I was very disoriented and surrounded by darkness, but then once my sight cleared, I realized that I was no longer in Naples."

"Nah-pol-ee?" Eddie paused. "Where's that?"

"Italia."

"Ital-ee-ah? Do you mean Italy? Do you mean Nay-puls, Italy?"

"Sì."

Two minutes and thirty-seven seconds.

That's how long it too Eddie to process the information just given to her. Salvator was not from the first, second, third, or fourth kingdom. He was from Europe, and more specifically, Italy. Eddie had never been to Italy—hell, she didn't even like Italian food—but she knew where it was. They were from the same planet.

Eddie could barely contain her excitement. "Holy crap, dude!"

Like a fireworks display on the fourth of July, her sudden exclamation startled everyone in the class, including Abjou who was standing at the chalkboard. Aldous gave her an unreadable look, while Caoilainn gave her a very readable look. Both she and Salvator turned their gazes towards the books in front of them and then lowered their voices.

"Sorry. But how? How did you get here?"

"At first it was all very confusing. I had a difficult time navigating my way through the darkness because I did not have a white guiding light." Salvator motioned toward Aldous with his chin.

"Do ya know how to get back?"

"I'm afraid I don't," Salvator replied. "But even if I did, I would not return."

During their conversation, Eddie learned that Salvator was sixteen-years-old when he had left Italy in 1631. There he had been training as a painter, and Eddie discovered, dabbled in all sorts of dark majik. One night, after repairing several paint brushes by hand, Salvator continued work on a nearly finished painting. That was the last thing he could remember before being heaved through space and time.

When Salvator first arrived at Ashkak's, he couldn't speak, read, or write the language. Finding a way to communicate with students took quick thinking and plenty of errors. Most students avoided eye contact when he asked them questions. All it took was two days of thirst and hunger to aggressively recall an enchantment he'd once read in his mentor's grimoire. The enchantment he cast over the school allowed him to speak and read the primary language used by most students. It had been an enchantment that altered the appearance of words heard and spoken by himself and others. Then following looks of suspicion, he cast another enchantment, one that would modify the memories of every person he encountered. This was how he knew Eddie was not from the first or second kingdom. Even if someone hadn't met Salvator before, they *felt* as if they had seen him somewhere, perhaps in the marketplace of the nearby town of Chimla, or while at the annual fire rites.

Eddie wondered if this spelled had enabled her to understand what others were saying.

"Did they know you were a witch back in Italy? I mean, weren't witches hunted and burned and stuff?"

"Yes, which is why I'm not eager to return. I've been here for three years now, and when the time comes, I'll *move* elsewhere, but not until I absolutely have to. I've got a few months to figure everything out."

Salvator and Eddie were not from the same country or the same time period, but they had both *moved* to Ashkak's without actively trying to do so. If there was a shared connection or link, Eddie was determined to find it, regardless of whether Salvator wanted to stay. Majik had brought her here—she was sure of it. Now she just had to figure out how it worked, and if it could work for her as it had for Salvator.

"It is a different kind of majik here, Eddie. Be careful."

After class, Eddie looked for Aldous in the hallway, but by the time she made into the hallway, both he and Vada were too far ahead for her to call out to him without making a scene. When Salvator touched her shoulder a few seconds later and then offered to walk her to gym, she was relieved. She didn't understand why Aldous had left her behind. Had she done something to piss him off? Was it because she sat next to Salvator? It's not like she had a choice. It was the only seat left in the room. Eddie would talk to him during gym, and hopefully they would sort everything out.

Things didn't go according to Eddie's plan.

Since the track team used an outside track to train, Eddie didn't have a chance to talk to Aldous until lunch, so she and Vada walked to the dining hall instead, to wait for him to join them. On the way, Vada said that Aldous was feeling a little "out of sorts" today and needed time to shower and recover, but when they entered the dining hall, Caoilainn and Aldous were already sitting together. When Eddie sat down next to Aldous, she could feel Caoilainn's eyes on her. She returned the red-haired girl's glare.

If Caoilainn's eyes had been daggers, Eddie would have been dead on contact.

"Hey." Eddie finally said. "What's up?"

Aldous replied, "Hey."

"Look, I was wondering if maybe later tonight we could get together."

"I don't know. Maybe."

Maybe? This was not the Aldous from last night or this morning. When Eddie had left with Headmistress Kahlee, he was smiling, and they were on good terms, but now, she was getting bad vibes. She didn't want to badger him, but she needed to tell him about Salvator.

After Vada informed everyone that Eddie was her new bunk-mate, Aldous excused himself from the table, and Simone took his place. No one else seemed bothered by Aldous's behavior. But how could that be? They sat together for nearly twenty minutes, and he had said less than ten words.

"Hey Aldous, wait up," Eddie shouted, with her backpack in her hands, rushing to meet him. "Jeez. You walk too fast."

At the sound of her voice, Aldous stopped in the hallway, with his shoulders slightly slumped forward. "Yeah?"

"Are you okay?" Eddie asked. "Are you sick? Or did something happen again?"

"No, I'm sorry," Aldous replied. "I just feel weird right now."

"Well, the day is halfway over, and I would really like to see you this evening if that's cool?"

Aldous straightened up like a flower placed in the sun. "Really?"

"Are you serious? You're like my favorite person here. Anyway, I was wondering if we could go over some stuff in your dorm. I've got a lot of stuff that I need to tell you. It's really important."

"Of course we can," he said. "You don't really need to ask. I'm always available."

Eddie's face brightened. "Really? Awesome. And Aldous?"

"Yes?" He asked, finally meeting her eyes.

Eddie took his braid in her hand and caressed it like a small kitten. "I like the ribbon. Your hair looks like a candy cane."

By the time Eddie made it to the haunted halls, it was nearly six o'clock. The stairs were still bustling with students, and one of them had even contributed to her tardiness. First-years could not be trusted with giving directions. Her head now hurt from all the running, and since she had gone the entire day without smoking, everything seemed to be getting to her. The promise of seeing her friend's face was the only thing that seemed to help.

To her surprise, Aldous was waiting for her and swung open the door like a jack-in-the-box when he heard the sound of footsteps.

"Oh stars above, please come in. Did you run up here?"

"Good god. What happened to you?" Disheveled and concerned, Aldous looked as bad as she felt. "And yeah, I did. The stairs by the girls' dorms are a bitch. But don't worry about me. Why do you look like this?"

"I just got back from a meeting with my da." Aldous replied.

"And? What did he say? Is everything OK?"

"No. Things are not OK. He'd like to meet you," Aldous said, breathlessly. "Tomorrow."

"What? Are you serious?" Eddie complained. "Tomorrow? Jesus Christ."

"I know. I'm sorry. It's so soon. I thought we'd have a few more days to prepare for it. But he is a horrible man, and I don't want him doing anything to jeopardize your stay or your return."

Eddie didn't know what to say. They both knew that their lies would eventually catch up to them, but Aldous's father knew they were lying, and Eddie would have to tell him the truth. There was no alternative option.

"But if you don't want to meet him, we'll have to find you a way home *tonight*. I won't force you to do that. To meet him, that is. My da is just a very persistent man, and I know he won't take no for an answer."

"Yes. Of course I'll meet him tomorrow." Eddie said, with a rueful smile. "But first, we gotta figure out what the hell we're going to say to him. I'm not good when I'm put on the spot." Aldous took a seat on his bed. He looked tired, dead tired. Eddie needed to talk to him about Salvator, and she wanted to try last night's enchantment again, but if he were as exhausted as he looked, she wouldn't bother. "Are you feeling alright?" She placed her hand on his cool forehead. "I don't know, man, but you look really out of it. We can do this another time. I can come back tomorrow evening if you're not feeling up to it."

"No," Aldous said, placing his hand on her wrist. "Please, don't go. We can do whatever you want. I feel fine. Really."

Eddie removed her hand from his head, and then placed it on her hip. "Alright, if you say so. Would you be up for teleporting again? I know we don't have any more of that sunberry stuff, but I went ahead and drew those symbols and stuff on the palms of my hands with a red sharpie. Who knows? It may work."

But Aldous didn't look at her hands, in fact, he never took his eyes off of her face, and for a moment, looked as if he wanted to say something, but then thought better of it.

"Pretty please? With sugar on top?"

Aldous nodded and said, "I see."

He knew it was wrong, but Aldous didn't want to help Eddie, not tonight, not after meeting with his father. Every meeting was an arrant reminder of how just alone Aldous was in the world, and he wasn't ready to see this girl go home, not yet. His father would bombard her with questions tomorrow, and Aldous would have to allow it. He had no say, no voice whatsoever when it came to his father. Still, he selfishly wanted to get to know Eddie better, and he couldn't do that if she left tonight. If intent were the key to sending her home, the enchantment would likely fail; this made Aldous feel even worse.

"Alright," Aldous agreed. "Let's do it."

Eddie spit into the palms of her hands then rubbed them together and placed them in front of her. Aldous arched his left eyebrow at this.

"What? I don't know. Spit and sharpie is kinda like paint."

Aldous couldn't argue with that. Neither of them knew how movement majik worked, and Eddie was the one who had moved twice already, not Aldous.

Aldous placed his palms against Eddie's and replied, "Repeat these words after me: mulah andril revole anha."

For several minutes they both chanted the words over and over again, pressing their hands together as if trying to absorb the other person, but nothing happened.

"Crap. It's not working."

Aldous was the first to drop his hands. "I just don't understand. Words are powerful, and if I've learned anything from this forsaken university, it's that words alone can make or break a spell. A lack of sunberry juice and twigs shouldn't be what's holding us back. Let me look at the other two spells."

While Aldous went to retrieve his mother's book, Eddie continued to repeat the phrase to herself, determined to make *something* happen. If Salvator could move in and out of places with ease, surely she could, too. Movement majik was real. Eddie just needed a better understanding of how it was practiced.

She repeated the phrase once again, and to her surprise, something behind her stirred. Her backpack had moved from the floor to the bed, and she had done it by herself. The spell had not worked as intended, but it had worked. If Eddie could move things by herself, surely she could find her way back home.

"Aldous," she said, looking down at the symbols on her hands. Small spiraling flames danced in her palms, and eventually spread up her hands and arms like a house fire. The blue fire didn't hurt, in fact, she couldn't feel it, but when Aldous turned around and yelled, his reaction startled her, and she stumbled back onto the bed.

"Edwina, your hands!"

Aldous moved so fast that Eddie barely had time to register what was happening. At once, the fire consuming her arms was extinguished by a large blanket, and then Aldous was kneeling on the floor next to her.

"Are you hurt?"

Eddie removed the blanket from her arms and examined her limbs. Nothing had changed. The markings on her hands were slightly faded, but still there, and her shirt was intact. The fire had not affected her clothes or body. Aldous put his head on the bed and let out a sigh of relief.

"What was that," Eddie quavered.

"I don't know. I've never heard of anything like that happening. What did you do?"

"Do? Nothing." Eddie didn't like the sound of Aldous's accusation.

"Are you serious? Your arms were on fire. I could hear the flames crackling."

"Yes, I definitely was." Eddie shivered at the memory.

Aldous lifted his head and took Eddie's hand into his. "But nothing happened to your body." He turned it over and traced the symbols with his finger. "What is happening?"

"I'm not sure. But uh," Eddie said. "I moved something."

"What do you mean?"

Eddie pointed to the backpack on the bed. "That was on the floor."

Aldous regarded the backpack. "You moved your backpack?" Eddie nodded. "Holy cow! You moved your backpack! Stars, we did it. I mean, you did it. How do you feel? Do you feel strange? Disoriented? Sleepy?" Aldous asked. "Anything? Do you believe in it now? Majik?"

"Hey, calm down," Eddie said, startled by Aldous's sudden movements. "You're shaking the bed."

By this point, Eddie didn't think of majik in terms of belief. There were facts and then there were falsities. The facts before her were reasonably straight forward. Majik existed on Earth. Salvator was from Italy and had traveled to Ashkak's by way of teleportation. Eddie was also from Earth and had traveled to Ashkak's by way of teleportation. There was no alternative: Majik was real, and that was the truth.

"I need to tell you something."

Aldous got up from the floor. "OK."

"Actually, we need to talk about a lot of stuff. I guess I should start off with the other night when that eggplant dude tackled me. Some things happened out there that I didn't tell you."

"Like what?" Aldous asked.

"I'm not sure, but I think I made it disappear."

"It? Oh, you mean the eggplant person," Aldous clarified. "How?"

"I'm not sure," Eddie replied. "One moment I was on the floor, and it was standing right next to me, and then I said something about it leaving me alone, and it just vanished."

"Vanished," Aldous said. "Are you telling me that you *moved* it?"

"Possibly? I mean told it to stop, and it froze, like a statue or something."

Aldous considered Eddie.

His new friend was practicing majik without intentionally doing so and had done it several times now. Most students come to Ashkak's aware of their potential, but are unable to cast enchantments without assistance, because it usually requires years of training. This scared Aldous. Unlike Eddie, he knew that strands of majik were constantly being woven in and out of the universe, crisscrossing one another, like a huge, colorful rug. Majik was as essential to his life at Ashkak's like food or water, but Eddie had lived her entire life thinking majik was nothing more than folly.

Aldous picked up her backpack and shook it violently.

Eddie snatched it from him and said, "Hey, that's my stuff in there. What's your malfunction?"

"Let's see," Aldous responded. "You moved into my room. You controlled the movements of another and then moved them elsewhere. You moved into the closet. And now you're moving objects without my help. In fact, I don't believe I've helped you at all." He scratched his head. "You don't need my help, and I'm not sure those symbols are even necessary, especially after your hands caught on fire." Aldous motioned to the marker remnants on her hands. "It is quite possible that you are doing all of this on your own."

"How is that even possible, though?" Eddie asked.

"Look, we already know that movement majik is a certain type of majik practiced by a few waja. Enchantments and symbols can be helpful, yes, but depending upon the waja, they are not always necessary. I have never met anyone capable of practicing majik without the use of an aid, however. You are the first. You are certainly the first *mover* I've ever met."

"What the hell is a mover?"

"A mover," Aldous repeated. "Simply put, a mover is a majik user who can manipulate movement."

"What? You've lost me again."

There were so many new terms Eddie had to learn, and she struggled with keeping them straight.

"So," Aldous continued, walking over to his bookshelf. "You said that you fell asleep on a chair, and when you came to, you were on my floor."

"Uh, yea, but I didn't become tired this time. Nothing happened."

"Except for your arms catching on fire, that is." Aldous pointed out.

"Yes," Eddie admitted. "I suppose that is worth mentioning."

"What about when you stepped out to brush your teeth?" Aldous hesitated, then turned around, now with a book in his hands. "Did anything else happen?"

"No." Eddie shook her head and walked over to meet him. "Nothing, unless you call being scared out of my wits 'anything.'"

"Nothing? So that leads me to believe that the chair, or painting, somehow acted as a gateway for you to move through it. Don't you remember that bit we read about moving through an object? A mover can move objects with their minds or move through those objects. Other than the stuff I've read in books, and Abjou's lectures in class, movement isn't a form of majik that's encouraged."

"Then why do y'all have a class on teleportation?" Eddie asked.

None of their rules made a lick of sense to her.

"Because teleporting is not the same as *moving*. Think of it like this: you have a hand, and you have five fingers." Aldous held out his hand and wiggled each finger individually. "The hand represents movement majik as a whole, and the fingers each represent a different component of movement majik. Teleportation is one component, and therefore not as threatening or damning as movement majik itself."

"The whole is greater than the sum of its parts?"

"Yes. Exactly. We don't really talk about *moving*."

Eddie blew out some air and then rubbed her chin. Before arriving at Ashkak's, she had never messed around with majik, unless playing with a Ouija board and having a séance counted, and she wasn't sure they did—a Ouija board was a toy and speaking to the dead with candles had proved ineffective.

"I am not the first mover you've met," Eddie said, contradicting Aldous's earlier statements.

Aldous adjusted his glasses. "Huh? What do you mean?"

"Salvator," Eddie said.

Aldous wasn't going to like what she had to say, but Eddie needed to say it anyway.

"What?" Aldous's confusion was palpable. "Salvator?"

"Yeah, he told me earlier today. I know he's not exactly your favorite person in the world, and I hate to bring it up like this, after everything that has happened between you two."

"He could be lying, just to get information out of you."

"I don't think so," Eddie replied. "We are from the same place."

"Of course you are." The venom in Aldous' voice could have stopped a small rodent's heart.

"Are you mad at me? I wanted to tell you earlier, but I couldn't find you after gym, and things were so awkward at lunch that I didn't want to bring it up with Caoilainn sitting there. She was giving me dirty looks the entire time."

For the next few minutes, Aldous stood as still as a forest during wintertime. Eddie knew he was mad. It was a dumb thing to ask, and probably wasn't the best timing given all of the crap with his dad, but she needed to get it off her chest.

"I wasn't keeping it a secret if that's what you're thinking. I literally could not find you at all today. You disappeared after lunch."

"Do you trust him now?" Aldous asked, his voice soft and low.

"Are you freaking kidding me? Of course not. Just because we're from the same planet doesn't mean that I want to hang out with him or try to get to know him. Even if he wasn't the one who threw that stuff at you, his crew did, and I am not OK with it."

Aldous opened his eyes and looked at Eddie through his lenses. "How did he get here? And how am I just finding out about this?"

Eddie didn't realize she was holding her breath, and when she opened her mouth to speak, exhaled loudly. "If I say majik, are you going to kill me?"

"Movement majik. From West Virginia?"

"Yes and no. He is a witch from a place called Italy."

"He practiced majik back home, but you didn't."

"I didn't," Eddie replied. "But he swears up and down to have practiced it in the past. It makes sense after everything he's told me."

"And what did he tell you?"

Now feeling far less intimidated by the discussion at hand, Eddie launched into everything Salvator had told her during Abjou's class—the paintbrush, the various enchantments he'd cast in order to communicate and modify the memories of everyone, everything.

"And you believe him?"

"I'm not sure he's telling me the whole story, but I do think he's telling me enough to validate some of his claims. I think he's from Italy and I think he's a mover, but other than that, I don't know what to believe. He might be telling me the truth, or he might be a time-traveling serial killer who preys on people and then erases everyone's mind. Actually, that's a scary thought. Forget I said anything."

"I am not going to stand here and lie to you," Aldous said, trying his best to keep his voice steady. "I don't like that man, and it's unlikely that I ever will—unless something radically changes, or he erases my memories, I guess. I'll take your word for it, and I will just try to avoid him at all costs."

"If you want me to do the same, I will."

"No, I'm not asking you to do that. You're both from the same place, and he might be able to help with getting you home. If he talks to you, you should probably talk to him."

"But Aldous, I really don't mind."

"Just don't get too close to him," Aldous said. "Please."

For the next hour or so, Eddie and Aldous sat at opposite ends of the room, going through a stack of books, looking for anything that pertained to movement majik. Because each book was written in a different language, Eddie couldn't understand a word of them, and instead used her time to mark any pages containing symbols and diagrams for future use.

"What are you doing?" Eddie asked, after closing the last book in the stack. "It looks a helluva lot funner than what I've been doing."

Aldous emptied a leather pouch onto his desk and signaled for Eddie to come over with a nod of his head. Several stones glittered in the lamplight on the wooden table top that Eddie soon identified as azure, turquoise, amber, and onyx.

"Damn, these are beautiful." Eddie loved gemstones. "God."

"I know. They were my mother's. Go on, I know you want to touch them."

Eddie scooped the jewels into her palm and ran her thumb and forefingers across their smooth surface.

"Like I said, they were my mother's, and I'm sure that I can make a simple talisman out of them if I follow the instructions from her book. I'm not one for crafts, but I'm sure I can throw something together."

After several minutes of watching ridges and peaks form in the valley that was normally Aldous's forehead, Eddie offered her assistance. "May I?" He handed her a gem and a piece of wire, then watched in admiration while she effortlessly set the stone inside of the wire and twisted it to perfection.

"Now give me that band."

Aldous handed her a leather string, and within seconds, Eddie attached the metal clasp and was swinging it back and forth like a pendulum. Now pleased with her work, she handed it back to Aldous and said, "There. All done. It's a lovely necklace."

"It's a talisman, actually, and with a simple enchantment, it should turn into a strong charm. Theoretically, the person wearing it should be able to use it to move themselves to wherever its mate is—in theory, anyway," Aldous said, now holding a similar stone in his other hand. "These gemstones were my mother's, but I'm afraid I didn't take care of them. This one is really bad. Once the stone fell out, I just sort of twisted it back in there. It looks really awful, I know."

It did look awful. Aldous's attempt at resetting the stone was pitiful. Aldous was pitiful.

Eddie took the band and the stone in her hands and quickly fixed the minor aberration. "There ya go," she said and grinned. "Good as new!"

"Thank you for fixing them both. Here," he said, handing her one of the talismans. "You take one, and I'll keep this one." Aldous placed the band around his neck and then continued, "Please keep yours on whenever you can, and I shall do the same. Now that you're in a different part of the school, it'll be harder for us to speak to one another, and we have no idea if we've seen the last of the eggplant people. From the sound of it, they could be dangerous, and if they know that you, an outsider, can do majik, there's no telling what might happen. If you can move using random pieces of this and that, surely you could move to wherever I am if you're in danger." Eddie turned the encased stone over in her hands.

The resplendent gemstone was black and flawless, just like a pair of earrings Eddie had sitting in her jewelry box at home. *Home.* The word hit her in the gut like a softball. She hadn't thought about going home all day. Had it crossed her mind yesterday? Eddie couldn't remember.

Until this moment, everything at Ashkak's had been exciting and new. Throughout her short stay, Eddie had met several new people and seemed to be discovering new things about herself on a daily basis. Despite the many similarities, life at Ashkak's was undeniably far more interesting than life back home. Staying with Aldous for a few more days wouldn't hurt. Besides, the more she learned about movement majik, the more dangerous it sounded, and there was no way of knowing where she might end up if she did *move* out of Ashkak's.

"Hey, would you care for some tea before you head back?" Aldous's voice was a whip, cracking through the trance Eddie had fallen into. "I have enough for two cups."

"Is it caffeinated? I can't be wired all night, or I won't be able to fall asleep."

"No, I don't think so. It's just herbs."

The tea was delicious and unlike anything Eddie had ever tasted. The herbs used in the tea, Aldous explained, were supposed to have a calming effect on the drinker, so Eddie drank slowly and deliberately. It wasn't until the last drop of tea was gone that she noticed Aldous staring down at her chest. Eddie's face flushed, and she clutched at the necklace.

Aldous moved his eyes to her face and apologized. "Oh, sorry. It's just that I've never seen someone work with such grace and elegance. Your hands. You are truly a gifted artisan."

"Yeah," she asked, examining her hands. "You should see me work a pottery wheel."

"I bet you're really good with your hands. I mean—"

As soon as Aldous said it, Eddie's freckled face turned a light rouge color, and he began stammering about 'getting the wrong idea' and 'always saying the wrong things at the wrong time.'

"Alright, well," Eddie replied with a forced smile. "It's late. I better get going. Kahlee is a nightmare, and I don't want to cross her." Besides Eddie was sure her face was still the color of a pomegranate. In contrast with her outward appearance and often tough demeanor, it didn't take much to embarrass Eddie

"No, I get that. She truly is a nightmare. Oh, one thing, real quick before you go—I was wondering, if you'd like, I could take you to the pujari where all the lyärgo live," Aldous said, opening the door for Eddie. "Maybe this weekend, if you're not busy?"

Eddie turned around and said, "Oh my god. Are you kidding me? That sounds freaking awesome. Yes, a thousand times yes."

Eddie's unexpected enthusiasm was met with a big smile. "Great," Aldous said.

"It's a date then."

"What's a date?" Aldous asked, his forehead all ridges and peaks again.

Eddie bit her lip and wondered how could someone with such flawless skin and eyes *that green* could be single. Didn't Caoilainn know what she was missing?

Kissing Aldous wasn't something Eddie had considered with any real conviction, not really, but she did it anyway. Standing on her tip-toes, Eddie pulled Aldous's face towards hers and kissed the corner of his mouth and cheek. It wasn't a sexy or graceful kiss by any stretch of the terms, but the impact it had was all the same.

They stared at one another until Eddie finally said, "It's just when two people hang out and do something together. I'll see you tomorrow."

The kiss left Aldous speechless.

He didn't remember saying goodbye to Eddie.

Hell, he didn't remember closing the door or getting into his bed.

He couldn't get over the feeling of her lips against his skin, and how quickly the sensation had spread to different parts of his body. Eddie had awakened something in him, something he had assumed would sleep forever. Aldous rolled onto his side, and replayed the moment over and over again in his mind, intentionally shutting out the fox's loud warnings.

Aldous had received his first kiss.

It had taken nineteen years of voluntary isolation, rejection, and copious amounts of carefully curated self-doubt, but he knew with certainty that he was in love with the person who had given it to him. Aldous was in love with Eddie.

Chapter 9

CHAPTER 10

Early the next morning, Eddie climbed down the solid oak ladder and stretched her limbs. For the first time arriving, she had gotten a good night's sleep. The linens were soft, and the bed was firm, and now that she shared a room with Vada, ducking under and sneaking around were things of the past. Her anxiety wasn't nearly as high as it had been when she first *moved* into Aldous's dorm room, because Eddie could actually walk to the bathroom to brush her teeth without causing a scene or bringing attention to herself because everyone had accepted Aldous's story. Things weren't necessarily *normal* in Eddie's life, but at least they were uneventful.

The room she and Vada shared wasn't nearly as spacious as Aldous's, but it was tidier and smelled better. Vada did not strike Eddie as the type who would sneak into the kitchen during the middle of the night only to let the untouched food spoil in a corner of the room the day after. When the headmistress had informed Eddie she could stay with Vada for the next few weeks, it initially made Eddie nervous because Vada was Aldous's best friend, and while Eddie trusted his judgment, rooming with Vada could blow up in their faces. Eddie didn't know if she was a bad roommate, or if she had weird behaviors. What if Vada ended up hating her after everything and decided to tell Aldous just how horrible of a person she was?

But after talking with Vada for a couple of hours last night, Eddie felt more comfortable with the arrangement and decided to give it a chance. Of course, Eddie didn't mention kissing Aldous to Vada because she didn't know if it would upset him, and because talking about it meant that it had actually happened.

Eddie had kissed a boy and enjoyed it. The implications of her actions could destroy the identity she had spent eighteen years creating. Why did it matter anyway? Could a person's identity change…just like that? No one could accuse her of lying about being a lesbian. No one had seen it. No one could take her sexuality away from her, except for maybe Aldous, because her body had responded to his in a way that was familiar and good.

If kissing his cheek made her body feel like it was on fire, she couldn't help but wonder what kissing his mouth would do to her.

Hell, sleeping with him might set the whole damned school on fire. *No. Absolutely not.*

Eddie shuddered at the thought. *What is wrong with me? When exactly did this happen? Why am I like this all of a sudden? Why am I so boy-crazy?*

Just thinking about sleeping with Aldous felt wicked and dangerous, but she couldn't stop herself, not after last night. Aldous hadn't pulled away or put up a hand in protest; in fact, he just stood there afterward and watched her walk away, without even saying goodbye.

Eddie closed her eyes and thought about running her hands through his long white hair. It was a forbidden thought, one that felt off-limits to her, and filled her with guilt as soon as it entered her mind. If she were going to make it through her stay at Ashkak's, she would have to hide these thoughts and hope to god that she could ignore them before they drove her to do something she might regret.

Accidentally *moving* into Aldous's dorm did not help matters, either.

Eddie didn't know when or how it happened, only that it *had* happened before she could react. After her fingers and arms began tingling like before, her eyes shot open, only to see a dim purple light emitting from the talisman around her neck, a light that traveled down her arms and eventually engulfed her entire body before she had time to stop it.

When Eddie emerged from a crouched position in Aldous's room, she could see Mister Fluffy positioned next to Aldous in a defensive stance. The intrusion, however unintentional, was still an intrusion, so Eddie was not surprised when her sudden appearance was met with a cold stare. She didn't want to wake Aldous, and placed a finger on her lips in hopes of silencing the animal. It had worked in the past, and besides the lyärgo knew Eddie was defenseless. Her gesture did little to affect the cold stare, but the fox did not growl or advance toward her. Eddie took this as a sign and walked over to where Aldous slept. Without lanterns and candles, Aldous's room was more like a coffin than a dorm room.

Seeing Aldous half-clothed on his bed, sprawled out like some hedonistic Greek god, felt like an invasion of his privacy, but Eddie couldn't bring herself to look away. She told herself it was more curiosity than perversion—that's what she told herself, anyway.

Tip-toeing closer to his bed, Eddie toyed with the idea of climbing in next to Aldous, but changed her mind after he twitched in his sleep and rolled over to one side, revealing that his shirt was not the only thing missing.

She froze. *Damn. I really am a pervert. I have to get out of here.*

Eddie knew it would take twenty minutes at the very least, to get back to her dorm, and that was without getting lost, or hiding if she saw someone. She shook head and wrapped her arms tightly around her chest.

Aw hell. No. Dammit.

"Hello?" A quiet voice broke through the dead silence.

Eddie scrunched up her nose and bit the inside of her mouth. *Dammit.* "Hey, it's just me."

"Eddie?" Aldous shot up urgently. "Has something happened?"

Eddie averted her gaze, knowing that even in the dark, he was completely naked.

Erratically waving her hands in the air, she stammered, "No. No. No. Calm down. I just woke up and thought about you. That's it. For a second. A literal second. And here I am. I am so sorry for coming into your room like this, man. I didn't mean for it to happen. It will never happen again."

"Oh, that's a relief, and you don't have to apologize. You can come in here whenever you like. It's not a big deal. What are you wearing?"

"Oh, okay," Eddie said, shyly grabbing a small handful of her short Pepto-Bismol colored nightgown. "Yeah, this ugly thing is Vada's; though I suspect she hasn't been able to wear it since she was in grade school. But at least *I'm* wearing something."

Aldous looked down at his bare chest and pulled at the white sheets surrounding him. "Sorry about that. I wasn't expecting guests."

"Do you normally sleep like that?"

"Sometimes," he replied.

"Jesus, I don't see how. It's freezing in here."

"It's not that bad. Stuff like that doesn't really bother me."

"Ya know," Eddie said. "You're so white that I can barely see you in those sheets. I bet if you went outside like that in the snow, you'd disappear."

"What? Go outside like this? Oh, you mean naked. Is that a theory or a suggestion? Are you that eager to see me undressed?"

Eddie laughed. "What? No!"

"You sure? Because I mean, I can make that happen right now." Aldous slightly shifted the sheet.

"Ok, no," Eddie protested and grabbed at the sheet. "You're being extreme. I think we need to have a discussion about boundaries."

Aldous reached for her elbow and pulled her towards him. "What happened here?" He asked, feeling the scars on Eddie's forearm. "Those are some serious scars."

Frick. Eddie pulled her arm out of his grip but didn't get up from the bed. "It's nothing. Don't worry about it."

"Are you sure? Because that doesn't feel like nothing to me. Did you do that to yourself?"

The gashes on Eddie's arms were fully healed, and she hadn't cut herself in over six months. "I don't really want to talk about it," Eddie replied. The scars were secrets, secrets Eddie didn't share with just anyone, secrets she'd never meant to share with this boy.

The deepest gash, the one Aldous felt first, was also the oldest. Only two people knew about Eddie's cutting and the one time she had tried killing herself, but it *was* common knowledge back home that she was an emotionally fragile, screwed up girl. Nobody asked about her wearing long sleeves in the summer and her outright refusal to wear a bathing suit. If anyone suspected something, they didn't mention it.

Eddie didn't like talking about her problems, and rarely did it unless the person was her therapist, and even then, she hesitated. No one wanted to hear about her mom's death, or how her dad had screwed everyone over, or how she couldn't wait to move out of Milton. Those were her problems, not everybody's else's. Besides, talking often led to feelings, feelings. Eddie tried her best to bury.

"You're very special to me," Aldous said. "I want you to know that."

"Ugh. You don't even know me. How can you say that?"

Aldous wasn't trying to pry, but he couldn't hide his concern. "How long do I need to know you before I can form an opinion?" He asked, not giving up.

"I don't know. More than a few days."

Aldous let go of the sheet and pulled Eddie into an embrace. "I've known you for five days. That's more than a few. It's technically several."

"A few, several," she replied. If Aldous was trying to be cute, it wasn't working. "What-the-hell-ever. Ya know what I mean."

"Is time that big of a deal, anyway? Does it really matter if I've known you for a few days or a few months? I know how being around you makes me feel. That has to count for something, right?"

Eddie didn't answer Aldous, because in the short amount of time she had known him, weird, foreign feelings had formed somewhere inside of her. She didn't want to acknowledge the truth in his statement, especially since he had called her 'special.' Accepting compliments didn't come easy for Eddie.

When Eddie looked up at Aldous's face, her eyes settled on his lips. She wanted to kiss him, but she wanted it to be a proper kiss. No more half cheek-half mouth kisses. He was still shirtless and had a sheet tucked in around his bottom half, so it was a relief when he kissed her forehead instead. Eddie leaned her head against his bare chest and closed her eyes.

The *moving*, the talking, and the desire to be with Aldous had made Eddie sleepy again. She got up from the bed.

"I'd better go. If not, I'll just end up falling asleep on your bed."

"What's wrong with that?" Eddie waited for him to laugh or otherwise indicate that he was joking, but he didn't.

"Our discussion on boundaries needs to happen sooner than later. If you think I'm getting into bed with you while you're naked, you're crazy. We haven't known each other that long."

The lie tugged at her words as soon as Eddie said them.

Including Alice, Eddie had messed around with five girls —two of them she had known for less than a day. Church camp, she had come to find out, was good for that. In all honesty, the thought of sleeping with Aldous intimidated her, and it was entirely possible that she was misreading things.

Friends could think of one another as special, right? They could even kiss each other on the forehead. Besides Eddie usually made the first move when it came to this kind of stuff, but things felt different with Aldous, so she decided to wait and see how things panned out before making an ass out of herself.

The icy cold, hardwood floor felt like pins underneath Eddie's bare feet as she walked over to his bedroom door.

"Hey, wait. Why don't you try *moving* back into your room," Aldous said, getting up from his bed, wrapped in a sheet.

"But how?" Eddie let go of the doorknob. "Dude," she said. "What could I possibly use to *move* back? To act as a gateway, or whatever. I didn't bring anything with me."

"Hold on," Aldous replied, scooting across the floor to his closet. "I might have something." Wrapped up in the sheet, Aldous looked like a ghost. *Aldous the friendly wizard.* Eddie chuckled but kept the comment to herself. It was just another reference he wouldn't get.

A few minutes later Aldous emerged holding a maroon cardigan. "This is Vada's. You should be able to *move* using it as a guide." He tossed it to her as best he could. Wrapped up like a hot dog tended to obstruct one's throw, however. Eddie caught the sweater in midair and slipped it on her shoulders. It was enormous and scratchy. She held up the sleeves and laughed. Would she ever not be the size of a child?

Aldous adjusted the knitted maroon collar and bent his head towards Eddie's.

He's going to kiss me. She closed her eyes, held her breath, and waited for the connection. But before his lips could meet hers, light surrounded them briefly, and Eddie soon found herself curled up on her dorm room floor.

"Damn it." She laughed to herself. *Of course. Why is this so hard?*

The dorm room was dark, which meant that Vada was still asleep.

Just what the hell time is it? Why does time move so slowly around here?

Moving in and out of Aldous's room had left her with a terrible headache, so Eddie took the talisman off her neck and placed it on the vanity, then carefully climbed up the bunk bed ladder. For the next few minutes, she stared at the wall.

Her head and heart ached.

No one ever saw Eddie's scars. She took every precaution to hide them from the outside world.

She *was* ashamed of them.

The last time she wore a swimsuit in public was in the ninth grade.

They looked horrible, they were embarrassing, and they were a constant reminder of her ex-girlfriend, Cheryl. *Who needs a tattoo of your girlfriend's name when you have the constant reminder of two slit wrists, am I right?* Eddie rolled over onto her side. What a dumb ass she had been back then.

The relationship had lasted seven months, but love-struck, dumb ass Eddie had been sure that it would last forever. Looking back on those seven months, Eddie now knew that it hadn't been love necessarily, but it had been something special to her. Cheryl and Eddie would talk about prospective colleges, and how they would live together after high school. Cheryl would be Eddie's ticket out of Milton, West Virginia.

Everything had seemed perfect back then.

It was the first time Eddie felt noticed and wanted by another person, but things didn't work out because Eddie wasn't the only girl her girlfriend had noticed and wanted. Cheryl had broken up with her for a sophomore and stopped talking to her altogether after they hooked up. Cheryl wouldn't return Eddie's calls or texts and actively avoided her at school. Her new girlfriend spread nasty rumors about Eddie and would sometimes text her from Cheryl's phone, harassing her viciously.

By that point, Eddie had just wanted to be left alone.

The whole ordeal had crushed Eddie's hopes and dreams.

How she made it through the rest of ninth grade, she did not know.

She blinked away a few tears and rolled over onto her back.

How was it possible to attract nothing *but* skeazy cheats? It had to be a personal flaw, surely. It had to be Eddie, didn't it? Aldous wasn't a loser though, and he didn't shy away from her touch. She was almost positive that he was trying to kiss her before she *moved*. Even if it led to nothing but heartbreak, deep inside Eddie hoped for something more than just friendly affection.

After a few minutes of wrestling with her thoughts, Eddie closed her eyes and pictured Aldous's face, bare chest, and legs in gym class, then did what she had been doing for years to help put herself to bed.

•••

No matter what he did, Aldous couldn't get back to sleep.

He couldn't shake the feeling that something was very wrong with his new friend.

Eddie's skinny arms were covered in scars, and not just any old scars, but scars that she purposely put on her body —scars on each arm that stopped at her wrists, the area that held the most scar tissue. Why hadn't he noticed it before? Eddie didn't want to talk about it either, and Aldous respected that, but she had tried killing herself some at one point, and this worried him. He had thought about it in the past, twice, actually, but had never gone through with it. But Eddie? He groaned. Eddie was a nice, kind person, and he couldn't imagine why she would want to do that. Aldous didn't know how to help her either, and that's what bothered him most of all. She had shut him down immediately.

Aldous knew he was a black cloud in an otherwise clear sky, but Eddie didn't seem to care.

Stars, I don't want her to go back. I want her to stay. I want her to stay here with me.

Aldous tossed and turned in his bed until finally deciding to get up.

I have to show her that life here would be better. Life here with me. But how?

Aldous decided he would go for a jog.

He needed to clear his mind.

If he really tried, he could get in nine or ten miles before class began.

He jumped out of bed, hastily threw on a pair of black shorts and old running shoes, then he and the lyärgo swiftly made their way to the dirt track.

•••

Simone and Vada were already dressed and waiting for Eddie when she got up later that morning. After showering and brushing her teeth, Vada gave Eddie permission to wear "whatever she could find" in her dresser and closet. Eddie was considerably smaller in stature and weight so she assumed finding anything would be a challenge, but was pleasantly surprised by a gray sweater she found hanging in the back of the closet. The torso was long, but the sleeves were acceptable, and when paired with some black leggings, she discovered, it didn't look half bad.

Eddie walked over to the dresser and looked out the window above it. Outside she could see someone running in the distance. From this story, the runner looked more like a shooting star in the night's sky, with their long white hair and slender white build. Unless someone's grandfather got up and decided to go for a jog at this hour, the runner could be only one person—Aldous.

Upon closer inspection, Eddie could see that both he and Mister Fluffy were outside jogging. *Odd.* It was the first time she witnessed the animal outside of the school. Eddie banged on the window several times, trying to get their attention, but they were too high up for the noise to register, so she hurriedly threw on the rest of her clothes and snatched the talisman off the vanity, and then rushed out the door.

At breakfast, large woven baskets of hot biscuits were passed around by greedy little hands, while half-eaten jars of lavender jam and peach preserves occupied the centers of the messy tables. Like small, rowdy beasts, ravenous children shoved one another and grabbed at the decanters of warm sheep's milk and silver dishes of fresh butter.

More wedding food. Eddie had never been so hungry in her life.

She procured a seat next to a very silent Caoilainn, then gratefully took a plate from Vada's hand. By the time Eddie finished putting pieces of fruit and biscuits on her plate, Aldous had already walked through the door, wearing only a pair of shorts and an enormous towel draped around his neck and torso. He was so tall and thin, so painfully thin, Eddie didn't know where all of his food went. Then without saying anything, Aldous deliberately took a seat next to Eddie and reached for a plate—and for several minutes, Vada and Simone stared at him in disbelief. He loaded his plate with biscuits and pieces of cheese and asked Eddie to pass him the glass pitcher of milk. After eating in silence, Aldous acknowledged all of his friends staring at him.

With a mouthful of fruit, he asked, "What? What is it?"

Eddie was the first to speak. "Um. It is freezing outside, dude. Aren't you cold? You're literally covered in sweat."

Aldous looked down at himself and acknowledged his lack of clothing with a grunt. "I guess I am, huh?"

"It's pretty gross actually," Eddie said, scooting away from him. "You can see the sweat. It looks like you took a shower and forgot to dry off. And you smell."

Aldous laughed in response and then threw an arm around Eddie. "Oh yeah?"

"Ew! Get the hell off of me. You're soaking wet. It's disgusting!" Eddie said, pushing him away. It was the first time Aldous had shown affection toward her in front of others. Eddie usually hated PDA, but something about this felt different.

Aldous laughed again and got up. "I'll see you girls later."

After Aldous got up and left the hall, Simone, Vada, and Caoilainn turned their eyes to Eddie. She lifted a piece of toast and took a bite before noticing their stares. "What? What's wrong?" Eddie asked.

"Nothing," Vada replied. "It's just that I've just never seen anything like that in my life. I've never seen him show outward affection toward anyone other than his little sister. And I have never seen him without a shirt." Simone and Caoilainn nodded in agreement. "Aldous is hands down the most socially awkward person I have ever met. And he was flirting with you. I just—I don't know what to think anymore."

Eddie said nothing.

Given the number of times she had seen Aldous without a shirt, this bit of information struck Eddie as odd. He never seemed uncomfortable or put off by her presence. They had bypassed the awkward stages of getting to know one another with ease almost immediately and went straight into a friendship. Their connection had been instant. Eddie regarded this. Had her attraction to Aldous been instant as well? She couldn't remember, but it certainly seemed like it had been.

You do not believe in love at first sight, she reminded herself. *Besides, you have a girlfriend back home, you freaking asshole.*

But she didn't miss Alice. Until this point, Alice had been an afterthought, something to feel guilty about. Because no matter how hard she tried, she did feel guilty and ashamed for liking Aldous. She was forsaking her identity. When Eddie had put things on hold with Alice, it was with the intention of working through things, and eventually getting back together, but then Aldous had come into the picture, and thrown a wrench into everything. What if she was wrong, though? What if he didn't return her feelings? What if she was misinterpreting his actions? What if he was confused and just looking for someone to replace Caoilainn for the time being? It wouldn't necessarily be the end of the world if that was the case, but something about the idea pissed Eddie off.

She sighed and took a drink of milk. *Screw this.*

Things were complicated at the moment, and she knew that after last night, ignoring her feelings for Aldous would only make matters worse. She needed to just get it over with, and let go of the possibility that she was wrong, that he didn't *like her like that*.

Besides, it's not like Eddie wasn't used to rejection.

Straight girls had no problem with shutting Eddie down. This felt different, though. Everything about this was different.

For the good part of the day, Eddie ignored Aldous.

Her anxiety was at an all-time high, and being around people seemed to exacerbate the symptoms. Most people usually took Eddie's avoidance personally, but it wasn't about them—it was about her. She needed to be alone. She needed to get her mind off of things. At the moment, both halves of her heart were in different places, on different planets maybe, and she needed to contemplate this. Being around Aldous would only further muddle things, especially since she couldn't keep her eyes off of him.

Back in her dorm, Eddie sat on her bed reading notes she had taken from the day's lectures. During class, Waja Abjou briefly mentioned *moving* but quickly brushed it aside, because, he reiterated, it was an unlikely skill to have, especially if one hadn't already discovered they were capable of doing it. It wasn't like *just anyone* could *move* through majikal objects. It was a gift. After Abjou's tangent, Eddie and Salvator looked at one another, and then met Aldous's eyes. The secret they shared with one another felt more significant than the classroom.

Studying proved useless.

No matter what Eddie did, she couldn't focus on the diagrams before her. She looked at the talisman hanging on her bedpost and knew with certainty that if she put it on, she would find Aldous immediately. How could he be the first and last person she wanted to see at the moment?

To her right, bright purple lights surrounded the doorframe, and Vada opened the door seconds later. Wearing her usual smile, Vada greeted Eddie and then set her satchel down on the vanity next to the bed. Taking notice of the talisman hanging from the bedpost, Vada lifted the stone up and examined it. "Cute. And useful. I assume this is a charm that Aldous gave you?"

Eddie nodded then fell back on the bed.

"Yeah," she said. "We're both supposed to wear the necklaces in case one of us gets in over our heads. I don't know. Sounded like a good idea at the time. Now I'm…not so sure."

Vada regarded Eddie. "Are you ill?"

Eddie shook her head and said, "Nope."

"Tired?" Eddie shook her head again. "Do you want to talk about it?"

After the third head-shake, Vada climbed up the ladder. "Look, I can't imagine what you're going through at the moment. I've never been permanently separated from my family and friends. I know that it must be difficult for you, but you have my ear always if you need to talk."

Eddie rolled over and looked up at Vada. "It's not my family," Eddie began. "Being here has made life more complicated. I've never been so confused in all my life. Everything is just getting to be too much."

"Majik certainly has a way of doing that. Complicating things, I mean. But hey, Aldous told me that you are more open to the idea of learning spells and such. And that's good, yeah?"

"I guess," Eddie said. "But practicing majik is definitely one of the things that's bothering me. I mean, I've never done anything remotely majikal, and now all of a sudden I'm *moving* into and out of existence using flippin' jewelry. It makes no sense. I feel like I don't even know who I am anymore. And Aldous is being so nice and helpful about it. He's really not helping things. *At all.*"

"Wait a minute. Is he confusing you?" Vada asked, peering down at Eddie.

"Yes." Eddie nodded, then desperately looked into Vada's kind eyes. "Yes. It sucks. I have no idea who I am anymore. Everything I've known up until this moment has been wrong. I don't know how to go forward from here." Eddie sat up and took the talisman in her hand briefly, then dropped it.

Vada studied her carefully and said, "Perhaps it is not false or wrong, but incomplete. I assume we are talking specifically about Aldous now." Eddie nodded and rolled over. "You have not told him? Any of this?" Vada asked.

Eddie shook her head. "Uh, negative. How can I? I have a girlfriend back home, and he'll think I'm a snake if he founds out how I feel about him. There's no way to explain this to him in a way that won't make him feel bad or guilty. And who is to say that Aldous wants to be with me anyway? I'm not Caoilainn, and she's his Waja." Vada waited patiently while Eddie got everything off her chest. "I've known him for less than a week, and she's supposed to spend the rest of her life working alongside him in a quaint little village nestled on top of a mountain or some crap. Who knows how long I'll be here?" Eddie asked. "I could leave tomorrow for all I know. It's stupid. All of it."

After Eddie finished, Vada spoke up. "Eddie, it is a pretty thought, the thought of being with someone until they're old and withered, but not everyone gets that chance. Sometimes disease takes them. Sometimes they die for no apparent reason. Sometimes the two separate and never speak to one another again. But I'm sure that no matter how long you're here, Aldous will cherish that time spent with you. My recommendation is to tell him how you feel. He might not share your feelings, but that's not the end of the world, now is it?"

Eddie was not a fan of uncertainty, which is why she almost always plunged head-first into situations without considering repercussions or the consequences of her actions. Such pigheadedness largely contributed to her overall anxiety. For Eddie, making bad decisions came as easily as breathing or drinking a glass of water.

"Just be honest with him," Vada said, now peering down at Eddie. "Everything will work out for the best."

Vada left the room shortly after climbing down from the bed.

Eddie sat up. A decision had to be made. She placed the talisman around her neck and thought about Aldous. Within seconds, a faint red light grew from her fingertips and spread to other parts of her body.

Aldous was crouched down in his mother's garden when Eddie suddenly appeared. Startled, he fell back onto his backside when she landed directly on top of him.

"Jesus! Sorry about that!" Eddie said, straddling his chest. "I had no idea where this thing would actually take me."

Aldous was not in his usual brown robe, Eddie observed, but had donned a simple black smock and dirty white gloves.

"Well, it seems that you found me, regardless." Strands of white hair lay across in his face as he looked up at her. "IIow are you?" He asked.

"Oh, I'm better," Eddie replied. "I'm okay now. I wasn't really feeling all that good earlier today. Sorry about class."

"It's alright," Aldous said. "I imagine everything is pretty overwhelming at the moment."

"Yeah, you could say that. I just needed some time to myself."

"I understand. Are you planning on getting up, or should I make myself comfortable?"

"Oh crap," Eddie exclaimed. "Sorry!"

"It's OK," Aldous said, placing his hands behind his head. "I don't know. I could get used to the view."

Eddie hit his shoulder with the palm of her hand. "What is wrong with you?"

"Lots of things. Now help me up."

After Aldous accepted Eddie's hand, he brushed himself off. Every inch of his body seemed to be covered in dirt. Now feeling bad that she had interrupted Aldous's gardening, Eddie bent down and gathered what he had dropped.

It wasn't until the sun set that Aldous paused and wiped his brow, smearing dirt across his forehead and cheek. Eddie wasn't quite sure how to explain it, but Aldous blended in with the scenery when he was outside. Ashkak's amplified his differences, whereas being outside minimized them. The striking difference was as evident to Eddie as night and day.

Eddie took the gloves off her hands and handed them back to Aldous, taking note that the wheelbarrow was now full of weeds and flowers.

"Hey, it looks like you pulled out some flowers, too."

Aldous shook both of his gloves and smock, then draped them over one arm. "That's for tea, actually," he replied, pushing hair out of his face.

Grabbing a handful of the tiny orange flowers, Eddie asked, "Wait. Do you make the tea we drink?"

Aldous nodded, then dug through the weeds and uncovered a burlap sack. "It's too late for tea now, but I can make you a quick sachet to take back to your dorm."

"Damn. What time is it?" Eddie thought about the terrible decision she had made earlier that afternoon and was eager to discuss it with Aldous. "Time moves so slow here," Eddie said.

Shoving handfuls of weeds into the burlap sack, he replied, "You're meeting my father tonight, remember?"

"Oh crap, right." The discussion would have to wait. Meeting his father would require every milligram of Xanax and every ounce of energy that Eddie could spare. She wasn't built for rejection *and* an interrogation on the same day. "No, no. Of course I remember. How could I forget? Can I wash my face at least?" Eddie said, looking at Aldous through her lashes. "You could also use a scrub."

Reaching up, Eddie ran her finger gently across his forehead, and for a moment the two of them said nothing, instead staring at one another in silence, filling the cold air with their hot breath. Eddie could smell Aldous from where she stood. While the wind cheerfully played with his hair, a dizzying array of scents flooded her nostrils—the broken earth beneath their boots, the now decaying flowers in the cart, the uprooted grass, all of it smelled ancient. Not musty or weird like her Mamaw's basement, but old, like it had always been there, and would always be there. Eddie glanced up at Aldous again, not fully understanding what any of this meant.

Aldous swallowed. "Let's go back to my dorm."

With their hands now interlocked, Aldous led Eddie to an enormous iron door, that he explained, protected the gardens from large animals, vandals, and curious children. Aldous dropped the burlap sack onto the ground, then placed his hands on the door, and said a few words under his breath. Eddie took a step back in awe when vines began to cover the door.

Once inside the building, children with tall, pointed hats rushed past them, pushing against one another like livestock in a corral. When they finally reached Aldous's door, he didn't try to break the seal, instead instructing Eddie to do it.

"Go ahead. You try it."

"What? Are you sure?" Eddie asked, uneasy.

"If I'm right, nothing will happen."

"Well, crap. For my sake, I hope you're right."

Eddie turned the doorknob with ease, and Aldous pushed the door open.

What Eddie saw amazed her. The room was spotless. Everything was in its rightful place. The books were put away, and Aldous's desk was orderly. The fox was asleep on the wicker chair, and the bed was made.

"Wow Aldous, you cleaned," she said, looking around the room No more dirty dishes or old loaves of bread. No crumbled up pieces of paper spilling out of his wastebasket. The room was cleaner (and a lot nicer) than her new quarters.

"Well, you never know when you'll have unexpected company," he replied, laying the flowers down on the clean desk. Eddie dropped her eyes and shyly looked away, then followed him to the desk.

Aldous opened a drawer and took out a mortar and pestle. She watched him clean the flowers and crush them and set them out to dry. It was a fascinating yet simple process. Eddie wondered if he made potions using a similar method.

After Aldous finished washing the herbs, he handed her piece of terrycloth and a pitcher of cold water. While spot bathing her neck, Eddie noticed out of the corner of her eye that Aldous was watching her. They made eye contact, and for a second, Eddie thought he might look away, but he didn't. He just watched the rag go up and down her neck as intently as a cat watching a mouse.

I can't do this. It's insane, Eddie thought to herself, now wiping her brow. *I should just ask him how he feels about me and get it the hell over with. I can't do this much longer.* But she didn't.

"So, why did you have me break the seal on your door?" Eddie asked instead, sitting down on his bed.

Aldous replied with a grin, "Just trying to see what you might be capable of doing. Oh, the tea should be finished drying tomorrow. I'll bring you a small bag when it's ready."

Eddie laughed. "I'm capable of doing plenty of things without majik, Aldous. Have you ever considered this?"

"Oh, I bet you are," Aldous said, smirking.

CHAPTER 11

Meeting Aldous' father wasn't nearly as bad as Eddie had thought it would be. After supper, the two of them walked to the south wing but spoke very little while doing so. Eddie could tell that Aldous was nervous, maybe even more nervous than she was. He hadn't bothered changing his clothes or washing his face, and his hair hung lifelessly from his head. It looked like he was trying to hide his face to Eddie.

When they finally reached the door, Aldous motioned for Eddie to stop and knock. The door had a powerful seal on it and would likely not be broken by Aldous's 'cheap tricks,' or so he claimed.

Aldous's father invited them in, and they soon found themselves standing in front of a short, black-bearded, balding man, and a tall, lanky young lady. The girl looked no older than fourteen. The man with a sharp look across his face sat in silence, holding a large, bejeweled goblet. He looked ridiculous to Eddie, but she quickly subdued the thought in case he could read minds.

Damned suuga.

But the little man *did* look important and powerful. On each stubby finger, he wore multiple rings—tawdry jewelry, really—thick golden bands with several jewels set in each one. He was finishing up his dinner from the looks of the room. Sitting next to him was a half-eaten carcass of a chicken and a pile of bones sucked clean.

Eddie shuddered. *Disgusting.* One of the many reasons why she didn't eat meat was because bones freaked her out.

The young lady sitting next to Aldous's father was beautiful by conventional standards. She had long, fine, black hair and olive skin. Her heavy-lidded, prominent eyes were green like Aldous's, the same exact color actually, and just as fearsome.

This must be Astrid, thought Eddie, looking at her gorgeous gown.

Eddie glanced at Aldous who was now standing in front of his sister. The two siblings were as similar as fire and ice, but Eddie observed, equally striking in their own way.

While his father loudly sucked the fat off of each finger, Aldous spoke. "Father, this is Edwina Burke," he said. "Edwina, this is my sister, Astrid, and my father, the High Suuga and Headmaster of Ashkak's, Waja Molhata of the First Kingdom."

Astrid sat her cup on the table and stood to greet Eddie. Even though Eddie would technically be a woman in a few days, this girl towered over her. Astrid leaned in toward Eddie and hugged her, her long gown clinging to her body much like Eddie's did.

Shapeless just like me. Welcome to the club, kid. It doesn't get better.

Astrid wore a white muslin dress that had a golden embroidered trim along the collar, with cerise-colored jewels placed in the embroidery, that formed little flowers along the neckline. Her dress was a work of art. Over Astrid's shoulders, she wore a light wool shawl and simple brown loafers on her feet. It was hard to imagine this pleasant girl being the all-powerful sujii that Aldous claimed she was.

"My child," his father said. "If what Aldous says is true, I will do what I can to help you. Come here. Have a seat." Waja Molhata reached for a rag on the table and wiped his fingers off, then patted the seat next to him. "Don't be shy." Aldous said nothing and took a seat next to his sister. "Now sweet girl," his father said. "Tell me how you got here."

"Well, sir," Eddie said. Surely they didn't expect her to remember that long title of his. "I ended up on your son's floor in the middle of the night. I'm not entirely sure how I got here, but it's possible Aldous had a hand in it." Eddie smiled at her friend.

"Aldous?" Waja Molhata laughed to himself. "That would be a first. Are you certain you did not bring yourself? My dear son likes to play in the dirt. *Movement* majik requires a strong mind and body." He glanced at Aldous. "No, that seems highly unlikely, child."

In seconds, the Hugh Suuga's words sparked a fire deep within Eddie's chest, and she could feel the flames spreading throughout her body. It was easy to see why Aldous thought so little of himself. She swallowed. She would have to choose her response carefully.

Eddie straightened her back and held his gaze with a smile. "Sir, with all due respect, don't you need herbs to make potions, and potions to aid in enchantments? I'm not sure why I'm here or what brought me here, but I do think that majik was involved, and I am just an average girl," Eddie said. "I have a difficult time following what is said in class, and when Aldous tries explaining things to me, he might as well be speaking Chinese. I seriously doubt I had a hand in any of this." Eddie held up the backs of her hands and showed them to Molhata. "See? Just your average hands."

Molhata looked at his son, then looked back at Eddie. "I see. Tell me, do they practice majik where you're from?" He asked.

Eddie didn't know how to respond to his question. A few girls back home claimed to practice witchcraft, and she had seen satanic graffiti on bathroom stalls at school, but she had never seen anyone levitate or put a hex on someone. Mostly they talked about 'being one with nature' and casting love spells with candles. No one had any *real* power, or did they? After her conversations with Salvator, Eddie wasn't so sure.

"I suppose they do, but I have never seen anyone teleport or turn into a cat, if that's what you're asking," Eddie replied. "Majik is different back home."

"How so?" Waja Molhata asked, his curiosity unwavering.

"See, where I'm from, they burned y'all at the stake, and it's still unclear if any of them people actually practiced magic. Nah, most witches were old ladies, widows and spinsters, who owned land, and the people wanted the land, so they accused them of bewitching people. Straight up stole it," Eddie said. "Lots of cats were drowned, too. Really heavy stuff."

The High Suuga propped his feet up on the table and said, "How peculiar. That is different. What do you think of majik now, after being here for a few days?"

"Uh," Eddie said. "I think it's cool how y'all use seals instead of locks. And I really like how Aldous can move junk with the wave of his hand. It seems to come in handy from time to time." Eddie looked over at Aldous. His eyes were still glued to the floor.

"Here. Take this." Molhata handed her the plate of greasy chicken bones. "See if you are capable of *moving* this into the kitchen. I'm fascinated by *movement* majik."

Aldous shifted uneasily in his seat and glanced over at Eddie through his hair. His father was being disrespectful in more ways than he knew, but if Eddie was bothered by this gesture, Aldous couldn't tell. She graciously accepted the plate and nodded.

"Alright. Sure. Let's do the damn thing." Eddie knew that Molhata would have the final say anyway, and that the sooner she showed him what she was capable of doing, the better. Besides, she and Aldous needed to get the hell out of the room ASAP.

Eddie soon discovered that, with an audience, it was overwhelmingly difficult to *move*. With her eyes closed, she gripped onto the plate with both hands and focused all of her energy on *moving*. Aldous's father had pissed Eddie off, and she could think of nothing other than how he'd dismissed Aldous's potential. Her anger made it difficult to focus on *moving*. Then after several minutes of deafening silence and aggressive concentration, a blinding light filled the room, and her body and the plate of bones vanished into thin air.

•••

Aldous's head jerked up. Eddie had *moved* somewhere, and if they were lucky, she was still in the school. Astrid took his hand into hers, and the three of them waited for her to return. The suspense was killing Aldous, and his father's new-found interest in Eddie was unsettling. He let go of his sister's hand.

Eddie was a gifted person, yes, but they didn't know the depths of her capabilities yet, and his father would likely call on her again if he knew that she was capable of *movement* majik. Practicing majik freely was unheard of in the First Kingdom, maybe in some of the lesser villages, but certainly none in the First.

When Eddie returned, hunkered down beside his father's couch, Aldous nearly collapsed onto his sister with relief. Waja Molhata watched Eddie carefully now and asked her questions about *moving*. It *was* an uncanny skill to have, his father explained, and not many were able to move without talismans or agents used for travel. Aldous could tell that his father was envious Eddie's ability to do this, and it made him afraid for his friend.

Even though the interaction only lasted an hour and a half or so, it felt like eons to Aldous. Every meeting with his father was unbearable, and despite his sister offering her assistance and words of encouragement, Molhata barely looked Aldous's way and didn't bother to acknowledge his departure. Aldous couldn't recall a time when his father showed him love or kindness. When his mother was alive, he had feigned an interest in his son at least. His father had yet to attend one of Aldous's track meets, and despite receiving awards for academic achievements in horticulture and chemistry, he never congratulated Aldous or acknowledged those accomplishments, maintaining the stance that horticulture was nothing more than 'glorified gardening.' Of course, it didn't matter that Aldous kept his mother's gardens alive, or that most of the potions they used in the potion arts class were made from herbs and flowers taken from it. No, of course not.

On the walk back to their dorms, Eddie seemed more distant than usual. Aldous wanted to apologize for his father's behavior, but he didn't, because he was too embarrassed to even broach the subject. They reached the halfway point in the school before parting ways.

After Aldous got back to his room, he walked over to his bed and fell face forward onto it, arms outstretched. Mister Fluffy could sense the emotional outburst coming, so he got up from his spot on the bed and went over to Aldous.

Aldous felt horrible.

Why was his father so awful? And why did he have to embarrass him like that in front of Eddie?

"I don't get it, Fluff. Why doesn't he love me?"

Furiously, Aldous slung his glasses across the room and then rolled over onto his back, not able to fight the angry, hot tears spilling from his eyes. He didn't want to be alone, but he didn't want to disturb Eddie, either. The fortress of isolation he had created for himself before her arrival was starting to crumble. He reached into his shirt and pulled out the stone he wore around his neck. Eddie's safety and well-being were the only things that currently mattered to Aldous, and if his father did anything to jeopardize either, Aldous would never forgive him.

Behind him, a speckle of purple light grew and expanded until it engulfed the entire room. Seconds later Eddie stood behind him wearing nothing but a baggy brown shirt and a towel wrapped around her head. She searched the room before setting her eyes on Aldous.

"Good god. What the hell happened? Are you okay?" Eddie asked, looking at his unusually red face. "What's going on with you? Have you been crying?"

At that moment, Aldous wanted nothing more than to pull Eddie into an embrace, something he quickly talked himself out of doing, choosing instead to wipe his nose on his shirt sleeve. "It's nothing. I'm fine," he said. "What are you doing here?"

"Did something else happen?" Eddie asked, removing the towel from her head. "Ya know, I could hear you in the shower."

"What? What do you mean?"

"Yeah, dude," Eddie explained. "It was strange. I turned off the water, and I could hear you. It was like you were standing in the shower with me." Aldous regarded this. "Don't be creepy. That's not what I meant. Your voice was clear. It was you."

"What was I saying?" Aldous asked, now intrigued.

Taking a seat next to Aldous, Eddie replied, "I dunno. Some stuff about your dad."

The things Eddie had heard coming from Aldous's mouth were alarming and made her angry—his father's indifference tonight had been a reflection of the past nineteen years. Other than a handful of people, no one in the school seemed to appreciate Aldous's gifts. The loneliness in his words had sliced through Eddie's heart like an Exacto knife, but she didn't know how to comfort him without being pushy or aggressive.

"Well, if you're alright, I'm going back to my dorm," she said, getting up from the bed. "I guess I have a lot of reading to do."

"Wait," Aldous whispered. "I don't want you to leave. Please don't go."

"Are you sure you don't want to be alone right now?" Eddie asked.

"That is the last thing I want." The pain in Aldous's eyes was as visible as his pupils.

Eddie gently pulled Aldous's head into her stomach and caressed it, running her hand through his hair. It was as soft as she imagined. "OK," she said.

"My da has always hated me. If it weren't for Astrid, I wouldn't have a place to stay. I'm serious. I'm basically worthless here. No one would care if I died."

Eddie didn't agree with Aldous, but said nothing.

"I'm a year behind in my studies because I went completely mad the year my mother passed away. If my da weren't the headmaster, I would not be here. I would be in some asylum. So I get it—I understand why Caoilainn doesn't want to be my waja. I'm a powerless suuga, and a boring person. I can't imagine what life will be like for her when we graduate. I feel sorry for her. I know that she wishes I were Salvator. I just don't know, Edwina."

Eddie couldn't believe what she was hearing. "What?" She took his head in her hands and lifted his chin with her thumbs. "Are you crazy or something? You can talk to plants and they will literally do whatever you want." Eddie had witnessed this at the garden earlier that afternoon, the vines had moved for *him*. "Don't say that about yourself. No one is worthless."

"No one cares if I can talk to plants."

"Ya know," Eddie said, letting go of his face. "When my mom died, I went batshit insane, too."

"It's the worst," Aldous replied, pulling Eddie down onto the bed with him.

"Yes, it was," she said. "I still miss her. And after she died, I lost my dad, too. That asshole started drinking every night. Back then, I still had a babysitter, and she was afraid to leave me alone with him in case he fell asleep and the house caught on fire. I mean, that dumb ass used to like to burn omelets at three AM. He never slept, either. Always up and glued to the TV."

"TV?" Aldous asked.

"Yeah, it's a box with moving pictures that tell a story." Aldous scrunched his nose in contemplation. "Never mind. It doesn't matter. It's not important. Anyway, I think he slowly started going insane, too."

"I'm sorry," Aldous said. "That sounds awful for both of you."

"It was." Eddie turned her face towards his, they were so close that Eddie could feel his breath on her nose. "I fell apart right before I started high school. I'm telling you. It was messed up.."

"Is that when the cutting began?"

"Yes," Eddie said after a moment. "After a break-up."

"Did it help?" Aldous asked.

"I'm not going to lie to you—at the time, yes, it did."

"And now?"

"Let's just say I know better now."

Aldous took her wrists into his hands and gently ran his fingers across the scars. "I'm glad that you know better now. If you had died, I would have never met you."

Their bodies were now inches apart.

Eddie reached out and traced his jawline with her index finger.

He closed his eyes.

Eddie wanted him to kiss her and thought he might when he opened his eyes.

But he didn't.

He just rolled onto his back and exhaled deeply.

CHAPTER 12

The weekend arrived much quicker than Aldous expected. Earlier in the week, he had promised to take Eddie to visit the lyärgo, and all it would take was five miles of walking in the cold (and possibly the rain) to get there. That aspect of the trip wouldn't bother him—he could jog in a blizzard and still find his way back to Ashkak's—but Eddie was different. Despite her bravado and larger-than-life personality, she was smaller and more delicate than him, so he decided to pack a small bag in case they needed to stop or rest.

Before long, a knock sounded at the door, and Aldous stopped what he was doing to answer it. When Vada stood before him, it was obvious from Aldous's expression that she was not the person he expected.

"Vada, hello. Is Edwina ready to go?" Aldous asked.

Vada shook her head and closed the door behind her. "What are you doing? Is that a baalazin?" Vada asked, now pointing to the large piece of fabric sitting on Aldous's desk. "Where did you get one?"

"It is," Aldous replied. "Will you help me tie it around my body?"

"Are you sure you've packed enough food? Really, Aldous, it looks like you're preparing to be gone for a week, not a day. Hold still. I hate tying these darn things."

"It's the back that's the problem," Aldous said. "You can't see what you're doing. Do you need me to turn around? Have you got it?"

"Yes, and if you didn't move so much, it would have been easier," Vada chided. "Aldous, I have a question."

"Hmm?" He asked, now stuffing a pair of gloves into the baalazin. "Can you pull it up a little? I feel like it'll fall if I put more than one thing in there."

"Sure," Vada said, adjusting the back. "So, what if I were to tell you that Eddie had a crush on someone?"

Aldous stopped moving and then turned around. "I guess I would ask who? Why?" He asked.

"Because it just so happens that she does."

"Alright," Aldous said, now eyeing his best friend. "Why are you being so mysterious all of a sudden? What is wrong with you? Is that why you're here? To cause me misery?"

"Aren't you curious as to who it is?" Vada grinned and clapped her hands together. "Even the slightest?" She asked.

"Of course I am," Aldous snapped, annoyed by her coyness. "Why are you even asking me when you already know the answer?" They were best friends, but sometimes Vada could get like this. Aldous was normally sarcastic and blunt with people, but from time to time, Vada liked to see *him* squirming at the end of the line, and Vada found his inexperience with girls endearing and charming. "Well, who is it?" Aldous asked.

"Thing is," Vada said. "I'm not really at liberty to say, but it is a boy, and that boy is not Salvator, in case you were wondering. That's all I know."

Slowly pulling the baalazin around his chest, Aldous stopped in front of Vada. "Just tell me who it is. Stop messing with me."

Vada shook her head and placed a small canteen on his back, then put her hands on his shoulders.

"I am not going to tell you," she said, firmly. "But I will say this: before you ask her anything, I think you should really consider your feelings toward her, and what it will mean for the both of you if her answer is the one you seek," Vada replied, dropping her hands. "She is going to die out there, you know. She's little, and she isn't a great sportsman like yourself. You may want to prepare yourself for several stops."

Walking over to his door, he replied, "It's just a crush, Vada. And why do you think I've packed so many snacks?"

After a hearty breakfast of oats and cream, Mister Fluffy, Eddie, and Aldous set off for the pujari. It was still dark outside when the trio left Ashkak's.

As they walked through the fog and dewy grass, Eddie found herself admiring constellations that were unfamiliar to her. There was a vast universe out there, and Eddie had travelled through it. She had ended up on Aldous's floor by accident. Things could have gone wrong, but for whatever reason, they didn't. Like pearls at the bottom of an ocean, the stars shone brightly in the darkness. Eddie sighed. Somewhere out there, another person was staring at the same sky and marveling in its wonders.

This kind of beauty is universal, she thought to herself, while increasing her pace to match Aldous's.

For the majority of the morning, Eddie kept close to her tall friend and his lyärgo. Leading the way, Aldous had a large staff in one hand and a lantern in the other. Eddie had no idea where they were, or how long it would take to get to the pujari.

"Aldous, how do ya know where we're going? Can you even see anything?"

"I can see well enough in the dark. Call it another one of my freak qualities. Don't you worry. Are you warm enough?"

"Yes, I am," she replied, and she was. Earlier that morning, Vada had given Eddie a pair of fur-lined, leather boots. Normally she would have objected to wearing fur and leather, but allowed herself this onetime exception. You can't help animals if you die from hypothermia, she had told herself.

The three of them walked in silence for the first mile, or at least Eddie did. In the darkness, there was no way of telling if her two companions were communicating with one another. When Aldous finally broke the silence with a story about his grandmother, Eddie was relieved, because other than the sound of twigs snapping beneath their boots and the wind whirling around them, the valley was eerily somber.

"Gran lives by herself," Aldous said. "In a cottage, along the northern edge of the Wyldewood."

"Does she practice majik as well?" Eddie asked.

Aldous nodded. "She did. But then she married my grandfather and was forbidden to practice thereafter."

"Why?"

"Do you remember when I told you that waja are not permitted to get married unless it is to one another?" He asked.

"Yes." Eddie replied. "I do."

"Well, my grandfather was not her waja," Aldous said, matter-of-factly.

"They take it that seriously?" The information was hard to swallow. "Why," Eddie asked. "I don't get it."

"Yes," Aldous said. "I'm afraid so. It was during their first year of marriage that the council stripped her of the sight."

"The sight?" Eddie asked.

"Watch your step. It's really soggy there. Yeah, Gran could see the future, or rather variations of it."

"DAMN." Eddie hopped over a huge mud puddle and said, "That's brutal."

"Gone. Just like that."

"What did she do afterwards?" Eddie asked.

"Do," Aldous said. "Well, I suppose she became an ordinary housewife, much like the villagers she once served."

"Damn," Eddie exclaimed. "That sucks."

"I'm afraid I have to disagree. You have no idea what it's like to be forced into this life, Edwina," Aldous said, slashing at some tall weeds with his staff. "I know that our world is new and different from yours, but Ashkak's is like a prison, and after we graduate, we're forced into a life of servitude. We have no freedom. We have to accept everything the way it is."

Eddie took the lantern from Aldous and then slipped her hand into his. "I'm sorry. I didn't think of it like that. I didn't mean to insult you."

"I'm sure most people are content with the system," Aldous said, squeezing her hand briefly. "But I can't be the only one who thinks it's crummy. Who does it benefit? What is its purpose? To maintain order? To control those of us who have the great misfortune of possessing gifts?"

Until now, Eddie had held the university in high regard. During her short time at the school, she learned that only the best of the best attended Ashkak's—that villagers were eager and even thankful to send their children to a school that would not only teach them how to use majik, but that it was free of charge, in exchange for a lifetime of service. Though, she had not stopped to consider those who did not want to serve—the ones who wanted families of their own—the ones who grew up wanting to be sujii instead of suuga, but were denied permission based on their gender. How many children truly understood what was being asked of them when they agreed to go? She squeezed Aldous's hand in solidarity.

By the time they stopped for brunch, the sun had settled directly above them, and while it offered little warmth, they were grateful for it, nonetheless. The two friends sat down on two large stones alongside the bank of a creek and shared bits of fruit and cheese with one another.

After the small meal, Eddie reached into her pocket and pulled out a cigarette. Upon seeing the small flicker of a flame, Aldous got up and fled in opposition, moving several feet away. Eddie took several drags off the cigarette and regarded the lush green scenery.

Back home, it was spring. Autumn and winter had come and gone, and she had been looking forward to the change of seasons—but here it was cold. For the next few minutes, she sat with her legs crossed and rubbed her hands against her thighs, while Aldous stared at her from the side of the bank.

"What are you lookin' at?" She asked, the cigarette now hanging from the corner of her mouth.

Aldous hesitated before answering her, instead turning his face toward the creek, and said, "I'm sorry for blowing up at you about the forced-waja-prison thing."

"Hey, no way. I'm glad you said something. I'm a visitor here. I don't know anything about this place. I've only been here for a week."

"Right."

After only the butt was left, Eddie smooshed the cigarette on the large stone, then put it back in her pocket and stood up. She took a deep breath. The crisp air burned Eddie's lungs, but also made her feel alive, possessing a renewing quality at times. The air was cold, however, and despite wearing twenty pounds of wool and cotton, she could feel the cold penetrating every limb of her body.

"So, you've been here for a week," Aldous said. "What do you think of it?"

"Mmm. It's different, but I like it. I like the people I've met, anyway."

"Even Salvator?" Aldous asked, with a tone.

"Him I can tolerate, but that doesn't mean I like him," Eddie said, getting pissed off. "How many times do I have to tell you that?"

"I don't think it will ever be enough."

"Do you hate him that much?" Eddie asked, getting up from the rock. "Really?"

"If I asked you to never speak to him again, would you do it?"

"Yes, of course. I already told you that I would. What the hell's gotten into you?"

"Nothing, never mind," Aldous replied. "I meant nothing by it. Just forget I said anything." He was angry, and Eddie didn't know why. Was it her? Was it Salvator? What had flipped his switch?

"Hey, don't do this to me. Not now." Eddie reached for his hand. "Talk to me."

"I have something I need to tell you, but I'm afraid of how you'll take it." Aldous let Eddie take his hand, but kept his eyes on the creek. "Really afraid, actually."

"You can tell me anything," Eddie said, turning his cheek toward her with a finger. "Anything."

"I like you. I really like you," he confessed, his words barely audible. "And I hate Salvator because I don't want him to take you away from me like he did with Caoilainn."

"That is not going to happen."

"How do you know?" Aldous asked. "You're both from the same place. That seems pretty desirable."

"Because that doesn't matter to me." Eddie was the one getting irritated now.

Does he expect a full confession from me? What is he trying to get at?

Eddie took his other hand and forced him to look at her. "Aldous, look at me. You are right about Salvator. We are both from Earth, and I need him. I do," Eddie replied. "I need someone to talk to about this shit. You even said it yourself—I have no idea what things are like here."

"I didn't mean it like that."

"Let me finish," Eddie said. "I need him to help me get back if that's even an option anymore. But that is the only reason I need to talk to him. The only person I care to talk to is standing in front of me currently."

Eddie's lips were on his before she had time to realize it. Once frozen from the wind and cold, her face and hands were now thawing from the heat their bodies generated. Aldous's mouth was clumsy and inexperienced, but that excited Eddie more than it probably should, and she wanted to taste more. When Eddie finally pushed Aldous away, it was because she needed to breathe.

"I'm sorry."

"I'm not," he replied, then leaned in for another kiss.

•••

After hours of walking and stopping (twice), they came upon a clearing in the brush.

The pujari was enormous, unlike anything Eddie had ever seen, with several barn-like structures scattered throughout the hundreds of acres. Workers adorned in gray uniforms, rushed from one building to the next, with woven baskets strapped to their shoulders, and pushing wheelbarrows full of feed. Eddie admired their dedication given the temperature and windchill.

The pujari was off-limits to villagers, Aldous explained, because the lyärgo required special care, and this sanctuary was not a zoo—these animals were trained to assist waja, not entertain or provide comfort. Eddie thought about Aldous and his lyärgo's relationship, and how strained it appeared at times. The lyärgo was not a pet or a companion animal and there seemed to be little reason for him to stay other than some mystical bond.

When Eddie followed Aldous into the third building, a low whirring sound filled her ears immediately, like the sound of a washing machine. Aldous didn't acknowledge or mention the hum, so she didn't either. The first two buildings they entered did not house lyärgo, but were used for storage, hence the difference in smells, Eddie realized. The nets and large cages confused Eddie, as she assumed lyärgo came to waja of their volition. She made a mental note to discuss this later. Eddie and Aldous walked from stall to stall and greeted each animal. Some animals were kept apart, while others shared their dwellings, but unlike animals in a shelter, none of the lyärgo made eye contact with Eddie or acknowledged her existence. Most of the animals in this building were missing feathers, she observed, and had discolored fur and malnourished bodies.

"Most lyärgo are found wounded or injured in some way," Aldous said, upon seeing the concern in Eddie's eyes. "The pujari finds them and nurses them back to health. That is the trade-off."

"Jesus. That one looks really bad. And what do you mean by trade-off?" Eddie asked.

"Yes, these animals are chosen for their resilience and ability to fight. As for the trade-off, well, the pujari rescues them in return for service."

"What happens to the animals who don't agree to servitude?"

"They die," Aldous replied. "I suppose, or whatever else happens to them. I'm not quite sure."

"The pujari doesn't sound like a sanctuary at all, Aldous."

"Yes, you could argue that."

Most of the lyärgo they encountered were dissimilar to Mister Fluffy. Animals that were normally wingless back home had wings, and some animals had beaks and horns when they usually wouldn't. Aldous knew the breeds of each lyärgo and shared information with Eddie about their care.

The last animal they encountered before leaving the building had the body of a wolf and the wings and beak of a bird. A lamassu, Eddie would learn. The lyärgo did not scare or intimidate her, and she had hoped that Aldous would further discuss the bond they were forced to share, but he didn't.

Both waja and lyärgo were forced into serving others for the greater good. Eddie couldn't help but wonder what life might have been like for Aldous and his lyärgo had they been given different opportunities.

After they stepped outside, Eddie shivered and rubbed her hands together. It was cold, and she didn't see how Aldous was just standing there, hands and face exposed to the harsh conditions.

"I gotta say that I'm surprised to see house cats here," Eddie said, dropping one knee to the ground. "I imagined that this place was for wild animals only. Here kitty kitty."

Aldous replied with a chuckle. "Don't let that cat fool you. That is a mountain cat. Smaller than the wild cat but just as fierce, if not more so. He has been watching you this entire time, too."

Eddie responded with a nod, "He has. He hasn't moved from that spot. It's kind of weird."

The cat was beautiful, and Eddie could now see that he was making his way over to them. With a sleek coat, full of black stripes and brown spots, and a reddish-orange nose, the cat possessed whiskers that were as white as snow and as long as his body. On his feet were little white boots of fur and claws that didn't retract, Eddie noticed. They were long and thick, like talons, but not quite as long as a hawk's or an eagle's. When he got closer, Eddie could see that it had thick, gray, scar tissue over where its left eye should be. But despite being haggard, he was still a mighty cute cat.

Eddie had always wanted a cat but figured she would have to wait until she moved out on her own because of Natalie's allergies. The little cat did not look at Eddie until after he had glowered at Aldous for a good long while. Then he walked up to Eddie and rubbed his short body along her boots. Eddie had been told bad things about cats, stuff about being coy and sly and deceptive, but after one look at this cat, all of those assumptions melted away.

The cat and Eddie visited with one another for what seemed like an eternity. Eddie had made another friend today and would be bummed to leave the pujari, to leave this amazing creature behind, not knowing if it were to live or die.

Aldous bent down and scooped the small cat into his arms. At first, it had seemed as if the little cat was irritated, but after a few minutes of being held, the loud sound of his vibrating body signaled otherwise. He was purring. *Really* purring. And Eddie found great delight in it, clapping her mittens together and laughing. Aldous then placed the cat in her arms, and the cat walked onto her shoulder and rested its paws and head on it.

"Are you comfortable? Do you think he looks comfortable?" She asked, wondering if the little cat had chosen her. A lyärgo. This was not just some ordinary house cat after all. He had magical properties beyond her wildest imagination.

"I know what you're thinking, Eddie. He looks plenty cozy, my friend," Aldous said and laughed, while the little cat rubbed his nose against Eddie's skin, its whiskers tickling her rosy freckled cheeks. "Say, are you hungry?"

Throughout the three-hour-trek, they had stopped twice and had eaten both times. Eddie wasn't necessarily hungry, but she wouldn't turn down a snack, so she gave Aldous a shrug and nodded in response. "Sure," she said. He then carefully pulled out two small brown bags from his pack and handed one of the bags to Eddie.

"Aldous, are we really going to eat out here? In the freezing cold?" Eddie asked, her mouth agape. "Are you out of your mind? There has to be a better place to eat lunch."

Then as if dumbfounded by her request, Aldous replied, "Oh yes. We can find a table and chairs. Come on."

The dining room was small and plain.

No chandeliers and no stained glass windows like Ashkak's.

The idea of laughter or children running around the room, playing hide and seek or tag seemed utterly ridiculous to Eddie. This room was meant for one thing, and one thing only: eating.

Strategically lined up in five rows of four, long wooden tables occupied most of the gray concrete floor. At one of the tables, three workers sat in silence, eating bowls of soup. Despite being thankful for all the trouble Aldous had gone to, Eddie looked at the steaming bowls with envy. It was frigid outside & a bowl of soup would surely warm her extremities.

After they found a table on which to set their belongings, Eddie slowly removed the overclothes she wore, all the while carefully avoiding the cat on her shoulder.

During lunch, they sat across from one and another, and Aldous explained the dynamics of the sanctuary more thoroughly to Eddie. All the workers were women—consisted mostly of elderly women and orphaned girls—and everyone seemed content to work alongside one and another. It sounded like a social service to Eddie, something that would interest Natalie.

Natalie?

Women often outlived their partners, and the pujari needed workers to help animals get back on their feet. The pujari existed as a sanctuary, but also as a haven for orphans, widows, and childless women. It was seemingly beneficial for both the animals and its occupants, though Aldous added that he didn't know if anyone could be truly happy in such a dreary place.

"The animals," explained Aldous. "Come from within the Wyldewood. The Wyldewood is a dark and daunting place, unfit for mankind. The trees in the Wyldewood are thought to be alive, *really* alive, and it is rumored that the way to the Fourth Kingdom is through the Wyldewood. Strange creatures dwell there, and it has been said time and time again that some woodland creatures steal infants from villages and replace them with monsters."

"Like the thing from the book," Eddie said, chewing on a piece of dry fruit. "So, these babies, or monster baby things —has anyone ever seen an adult? Sorry, I think I may have already asked you that."

Aldous shook his head and replied, "You're really hung up on this, aren't you? No. Remember? The villagers destroy the monster by drowning it, and then they throw the body onto an open flame and watch it burn."

"What," Eddie exclaimed, a look of horror now settled on her face. "You didn't mention that part." The whole thing sounded so barbaric, so unnecessary. The thought of drowning a baby and setting it on fire stole away the rest of her appetite. "Whoa, dude. That is way cruel," she said, feeding the little cat a piece of cheese. "I can't imagine taking the life of anything, especially an infant. I hate killing spiders and cockroaches, and they're disgusting."

Aldous shrugged and rolled his eyes. "Yes, but spiders kill other insects. They serve a purpose," he said. "Changelings are like parasites. If allowed to live, they will strip you of your majik. They are truly terrible creatures. They are useless beings."

"Yeah," Eddie replied with a grunt and snuggled up against the cat. "I guess I just don't see it that way because I wasn't brought up here, because that still sounds hella wrong to me."

"Look, can we just drop it already?" Aldous bristled. "It's not like it affects you or anything. Soon you'll be back in West Virginia, and you'll never have to worry about changelings or monsters or waja ever again. So let's just stop talking about it."

"Alright," Eddie said, shaken by Aldous's sudden hostility. "I'm sorry I even said anything."

"It's fine. Are you done?" he replied. "Let's get out of here."

CHAPTER 13

When Eddie awoke from her nap later that evening, Vada and Simone were giggling and moving around on the bunk below. Thoroughly irritated that she had not fallen asleep until the next morning, Eddie rolled over and groaned. It had been like this every night for the past week. Then after hearing a soft, muffled moan escape from underneath the covers, Eddie decided that anywhere would be better than here, and grabbed the talisman from her bedpost. Within seconds, a bright light consumed the top bunk, and she suddenly found herself in a crouched position on Aldous's floor.

Welcoming her with a kind smile, Aldous turned around on his stool and said, "Hey there." His mood had lightened since the incident at the pujari.

"Hey," Eddie said. "What's up? Um, Vada and Simone needed some um, alone time, if you get my drift. I hope you don't mind me being here."

With a nod, Aldous turned back to what he was doing, and Eddie took a seat on his floor, and then pulled the large sweater she was wearing over her knees. "Yeah, so sorry to drop in unexpectedly like this. I know I keep doing it and saying I'm sorry, but I don't really know where else to go," she said. "I'm terrible with setting and maintaining boundaries."

As if startled, Aldous turned around, shaking his head vigorously. "No, no," he said. "I told you that you are welcome to come and go as you please. I'm just—I'm working on a project right now. I apologize for being preoccupied. And I'm sorry for what happened at the pujari. I blew up at you, and I'm sorry. It was uncalled for. You didn't deserve that. I really regret it. I'm sorry for being a jerk all the time."

"It's okay," Eddie said. "I'm sorry if something I did upset you. I have a knack for saying the wrong thing."

"No, it's nothing you said. It's just—what if I told you that…?"

"Yeah? Is everything okay?" Eddie asked.

"Nothing," Aldous said, changing his mind. "It's nothing. Never mind. But, don't ever feel like a burden, because you're not. Honestly. I like you being here."

With the elephant no longer in the room, Eddie stood up and then walked over to Aldous. Noting that he had not changed out of his heavy boots or removed his winter coat, she looked around the rest of the room. It was in a state of chaos again. His closet door was open, and his mom's broom now leaned against the wall for all the world to see. It was as if he had given up on hiding who he was.

"Come over here," Aldous said. "I'd like to show you something."

"Wow," Eddie said, as he placed an unusual-looking hat in her hands. "What the hell is this?"

"A hat."

Now slowly shifting the hat in her hands, hundreds of tiny gems sparkled in the dying lantern light, while flecks of light danced on the dark walls, much like a kaleidoscope. Or hundreds of tiny bubbles being popped one by one. It was easily one of the most beautiful things Eddie had ever seen.

"Yes," Eddie said. "I can see that, Sherlock, but what does it do? And don't tell me nothing."

"Ah, yes," Aldous replied. "Well, it's what's referred to as the Helm of Darkness. Don't you find it intriguing?"

Helm of darkness? Like a helmet? Odd. I thought helmets were meant to protect.

Before Edwina could answer, Aldous placed the large hat atop her orange curls, and when she looked down at her body, waves of dizziness and nausea rolled into her, forcing her to stumble backwards and knock over Aldous's chair.

Eddie was invisible again. Her body was gone. She sighed.

Not again. Will I ever get used to majik?

Knowing Aldous, he had this peculiar hat sitting out on purpose, so she carefully removed it from her head and handed it back to him. "Here," Eddie said. "Take it. It makes me feel real strange." She didn't want to imagine why. Was her body truly disappearing underneath? What would that even mean on a molecular level? Eddie shuddered, then said, "Aldous, what are you planning on doing with it?" He dropped his eyes and looked back to his desk. "Is it dangerous?" Eddie asked.

Aldous shrugged his shoulders. "It might be," he said. "Would you be willing to help me?" Aldous placed the hat on his desk, then kicked off his boots, and unbuttoned his coat. "I'll need help getting back here. I think you're the only person who could help me." Underneath his coat, Eddie could see long underwear that clung to his slender body.

Looking away, her mind wandered back into the forest. He hadn't mentioned the discussion since then, and she wondered if he had forgotten everything she said. Their conversation had been a big deal to her, but perhaps it wasn't nearly as important to him. Eddie felt like a pathetic idiot for even thinking about it.

"Well," Eddie replied. "I guess that all depends on what you're planning on doing."

"I am going to break the seal on my father's door," Aldous said, matter-of-factly. "I was wrong. I know that I can do it. He usually leaves his study around midnight. He had a pile of books on his desk that I'd like to check out. If I can manage to slip past folks in the halls and break the seal on his door, it shouldn't take me longer than five minutes to gather everything in my pack. When I'm done, you *move* me back to my bedroom. Then we're finished."

The plan did sound simple enough, and yet Eddie was too smart to believe that everything would just go Aldous's way. But Eddie also knew that regardless of her answer, Aldous was going to attempt this heist anyway, so she agreed to help him under one condition: she go with him.

"No, absolutely not."

"Why?" Eddie asked. "We could just *move* there. We wouldn't even need to use that hat."

"No. Listen to me, it's too risky. I can't ask that of you."

"You didn't ask me." Eddie corrected him. "I'm telling you that I want to go."

For the next several minutes they argued until Aldous finally caved in and agreed to let Eddie go.

It was well after eight o'clock when Eddie looked at her watch. She was sure it had been later than that when she *moved* into his dorm room. Time was wonky here, though, and it certainly felt later.

"Alright, well, I think I'll go back and change out of these clothes."

"Really?" Aldous asked. "I was hoping that you might be interested in hanging out for a little bit, maybe play a few hands of cards with me."

"Cards?" Eddie knew how to play Uno and Old Maid, but that was the extent of her knowledge. She agreed anyway and took off her sweater. "Oh, okay. Sure. If you think we have enough time."

After Aldous made a pot of tea from the dry herbs they had gathered a few days earlier, they both sat on his bed. It was very dim in the room, to the point where Eddie could not see the pictures on the cards, so she waved her hands in a circular motion, and two lanterns sprung to life. Aldous raised an eyebrow at her, and she half-smiled, then shrugged in return. "What? It's just majik, right?"

"Yes," Aldous agreed. "It is just majik, and I am glad that you've finally accepted it. But I have to say, you are more powerful than you think, and I believe the books in my father's study will provide us with more answers, and quite possibly the answer that will return you to your home."

"Home," Eddie repeated the word, and then the two of them stared at one another. Eddie hadn't thought about home in the past couple of days.

Home. They knew what it meant, but neither wished to say it.

They would never see each other again.

"Okay," Eddie said, finally. "Perfect. That sounds great." Did it, though? Neither of them were keen on her leaving, but both kept their opinions to themselves.

While they played cards, the two friends discussed what the 'end of school' meant to them. Eddie would move out of her parents' trailer and into a dorm, preferably in downtown Huntington, while Aldous would soon move out of his dorm and into a little house he would share with Caoilainn.

"Have your parents chosen a bride or groom for you?" Aldous asked.

Eddie choked on her tea. "What?"

"Well," Aldous said, turning over a card. "Hah! I win. You are too loose with your Kings. It gets you every time."

"Wait, what?" Eddie asked, again. "Go back to what you just said."

"About what? You drop your Kings too early. You've done it every hand."

"No." Eddie shook her head. "The bit about a groom. What are the hell are you talking about?"

Aldous picked up the cards and began shuffling them. "Well, I know you said that you're going to finish school and then move out of your parents' home. Aren't you going to get married? Is that something you do back where you're from?"

"Getting married at eighteen is definitely not on my agenda of things to do."

"I don't mean right now," Aldous clarified. "I mean, like in the future, are you going to have children?"

Eddie gulped. Talking about having children and getting married were not things she openly discussed—with anyone, not even her girlfriend.

"I don't think about that kind of stuff. It's not really something I've ever considered doing," she replied.

"No?" Aldous asked, placing ten cards in front of each of them. "It's something I think about all the time."

"Really? Wow. Yeah, it's not something I think about at all."

"I guess it's because I am not allowed to get married. Your turn."

Eddie flipped a card over and placed it on top of Aldous's card.

"See, there you go again." He picked up the card and shook his head. "You're terrible at this."

Eddie laughed and then threw two cards down. "I never said I was good."

"Is it so weird that I want to be a dad?" Aldous asked.

"No, I don't suppose it's weird, just unusual for our age, I guess."

Aldous placed his cards beside the pile of cards Eddie had discarded and then leaned back on his elbows. "In the villages," he explained. "Boys and girls are matched by a maker, then they marry and have children."

"Oh, you mean like an arranged marriage. Isn't that basically what waja are?"

"Yes, and no. We are matched, but there is little assumption (or hope) that we will procreate. I have no idea how my parents got together. Da looks like a troll & my mother looked like a woodland nymph."

"So, she looked like Astrid?"

Laughing, Aldous agreed, then said, "Most villagers are expected to marry after they turn sixteen."

"Whoa," Eddie exclaimed. "That's extreme."

"I agree. Is it my turn? We don't have to play anymore. You're just going to lose again."

"What?" Eddie asked. "Are you saying that I suck at this?"

"You should just come over here and lie beside me instead," Aldous said softly. "I won't bite, I promise."

Eddie looked at the cards in her hand and placed them on the pile beside Aldous, then in one swift move, Aldous shoved the cards off the bed and onto the floor.

"There, that's better. Get over here."

This is dangerous, Eddie thought to herself, cautiously climbing over pillows and a wadded up comforter. *He's never been with anyone, and I'm terrified of screwing things up between us. My body needs to calm the hell down. This is what I want though, isn't it?*

Once beside him, Eddie lay her head next to his and silently wondered if Aldous was as nervous as she was.

Sliding his hand into hers, Aldous whispered, "I can't believe this is happening. You're the most incredible person I've ever met, Eddie."

Eddie squeezed his hand and then turned to face him.

"I mean it. I don't know what I did to deserve this, but being with you is incomparable to anything I've ever experienced."

"You're just saying that," Eddie said. "You're crazy."

"No I'm not, and why would you think that? Do you think me a liar?"

Eddie shook her head and released his hand. The room was hot now, like an inferno.

"I love you."

What? Eddie seized up and looked away, disbelief now consuming her thoughts.

"What I mean to say is that I am in love with you. I know it might seem pointless, given our obligations and the current state of things, but I want to spend as much time with you as possible while you're here. It's selfish of me, I know, but that's what I want."

The confession took Eddie by surprise.

Aldous was so forthcoming with his feelings and thoughts that it didn't seem real. Never before had she met someone so innocent and pure, but how was she supposed to act in this situation?

"Look," Aldous said. "I didn't say that because I expect you to say it back. Please, you don't have to say anything you don't mean. Just accepting it is enough." Aldous turned his face to stare at the wall next to the bed. "Really."

"Alright then, I accept it," Eddie said after a moment, then sat up. "I accept your love. Thank you."

The slow-forming smile that appeared on Aldous's face made Eddie's heart stir. Things were never this awkward with girls. If she liked someone and could tell they liked her, it was usually smooth sailing, but not with Aldous. She knew he liked her—loved her, even—yet being intimate with him was still intimidating.

So when Aldous reached up and pulled her down beside him, Eddie recoiled in fear.

"I'd like very much to kiss you," Aldous whispered. "May I?"

"Yes." Eddie turned her face to meet his.

Even though things were awkward at first, the kiss itself was soft and warm, like a batch of fresh cookies straight from the oven. Aldous's mouth was gentle and sweet, and he didn't know where to put his hands, but Eddie didn't want him to stop. She enjoyed the hint of chocolate on his tongue. They held and kissed each other until they ran out of breath.

For the first time in her life, she was touching a man's body, and enjoying it without inhibition.

"Is this okay," Eddie asked, as she slid her hand up his shirt and ran it across his bare stomach. Aldous nodded in response but said nothing. His body was unfamiliar in more ways than one. Muscle and bones replaced the soft curves and mounds of flesh she had grown accustomed to.

Eddie didn't know what she was doing and felt self-conscious while doing it, but if Aldous felt the same, he was doing a good job of not showing it, even allowing Eddie to remove his shirt. She knew mentally and physically that she wanted to be with him, and made the split-second decision to remove her shirt as well.

Now sitting bare-chested on his bed, they both stared at each other in silence.

Aldous's eyes drifted across Eddie's chest in shock as she reached for a pillow.

Breathing heavily now, Aldous exclaimed, "Stars above! I'm sorry. I can't do this."

Then after grabbing a pillow and shoving it under her armpits, Eddie looked down and replied, "Oh my god, I am so sorry. I don't know what I was thinking. I'm so sorry. I just thought-."

"Oh no," Aldous stammered. "It's not you. The stars know it is not you. That's not what I meant at all. It's me. You're perfect. God, really perfect actually." His eyes returned to the pillow now covering her chest. "I just-I'm just not comfortable with it. Yet."

Eddie blinked back tears of shame. "Okay. I'm so sorry."

Things turned out the way she feared they would. *I do have a knack for mucking things up,* she thought to herself, wrapping her arms tightly around the pillow. *I'm such an idiot.*

"I'm going back to my dorm now," Eddie said. "Things got very weird all of a sudden, and I am mortified beyond words. So just *move* me here when you need me."

Aldous whimpered in response and then shook his head. "No, please don't go. I'm the one who is being weird here," he said. "I must be out of my mind right now, but it isn't you. I really messed things up, didn't I?"

Before Eddie could answer, Aldous threw his arms around her shoulders and leaned his body up against her back. His chest was cool to the touch, but felt really good against her hot skin.

"I guess I've been waiting for this moment for so long," Aldous said. "And I wasn't sure it would ever really happen."

He set his chin on Eddie's unruly curls and squeezed her and the pillow.

"You're crazy. I am sure that in this school someone has thought of being with you like this."

"No," Aldous disagreed. "I doubt it."

"It's just sex, Aldous."

"No." He shook his head. "Maybe with somebody else it would be," he said. "But not with you."

"When you say stuff like that," Eddie replied. "I find it very hard to believe that you're single."

"Well, you've only known me for a week. Just give it time."

Eddie turned her head to look at Aldous. "Yes, it has been only a week. I should get dressed and head back to my room."

But Aldous didn't budge.

"Can we just stay like this a little longer? Or is that total jerk request?"

Eddie laughed. "Well, at least let me put my shirt on." Aldous tightened his arms and pressed his bare chest against her back "Or not. I'll stay if you tell me the real reason for going into your dad's study."

"The real reason?" Aldous sighed, then began. "I guess there's no hiding anything from you, huh?"

Eddie shook her head. "Nope. Spill it."

"I am going there to get those books, but there's also a bag of items on his desk that I want to search. I've been looking for something that he might have in there."

"Like what?" Eddie asked.

"Just some stuff."

Eddie turned her head slightly and eyed him. "What kinda stuff?"

"Okay. So, the story goes that when the kingdoms were all united, it was understood that sujii and suuga didn't need spell books or majikal objects."

"Ooh," Eddie said, leaning into him. "Story-time."

"Yes," Aldous replied, after kissing her bare neck. "Story-time. Anyway, I don't think they used those words, honestly. The majik flowed through them much like their blood did, and their power came from the wind, fire, seas, everything. But then they became too powerful. Horrible beings, really. So horrible that the earth decided it was time to end their reign, and opened itself up, forcing the mountains to cry fiery tears, eventually covering everything in darkness. Of course, back then people were fools and believed that the stars had spared them and left them with this black stone that held majikal properties. The Coterie is what they called themselves. Some people still believe that the ancestors of the Coterie walk among us. It's quite ridiculous." Aldous shook his head. "The stone left behind-."

Eddie interjected with great interest. "What, like obsidian?"

"Yes," Aldous said. "You've heard of it?"

Eddie nodded. "Are you kidding me? Of course. I love all of that stuff—glass, gemstones, you name it. Obsidian is beautiful."

"Right, and unless you're a fool, you know that the mountains didn't really cry. Anyway, you won't find very many objects made from the stone anymore. Long story short, it was banned several centuries ago after the Great Necromancer, Tomas the Seventh, crafted a majikal sword from the stuff, and decimated an entire village. It's a highly unstable substance. I don't believe we should have ever crafted weapons of destruction out of it, honestly. It's far too powerful. And in the wrong hands, it's capable of destroying… everything."

"Jeez," Eddie said, pulling herself away from Aldous and then reaching for her shirt. "Have you ever seen it?"

Aldous smiled, then nodded. "Obsidian?" He asked. "Oh yes. I have. My mother once had jewelry crafted from the stuff. A wedding gift. My grandfather went to great lengths to have it made and sent to her."

"Wow," Eddie said, then looked down at her watch. It was a quarter after ten. "I don't mean to change the subject, but should we discuss the details of this heist?"

"No." Aldous shook his head. "Not really. It's fairly simple. I put the cap on & then we make our way to my da's study. Once there, we grab the stuff, and then head back."

"You are against *moving* there together. Why?" Eddie asked.

"Because we don't know enough about your abilities yet, or the repercussions yet. What if we end up somewhere far more dangerous?"

Eddie pulled her shirt over her head. "That hat is not gonna cut it, man. You're already as tall as the ceiling. How is it going to cover two people?"

"That's why you should stay here," Aldous said, stealing another kiss. "Wait for me. I will be extra careful. I won't put myself in any harm if I can help it."

"What will happen if you're caught?" Eddie asked. "What will happen if your dad finds you sneaking around his room and stealing his crap? What happens then?" Eddie said, reaching for Aldous's shirt before he could get to it.

"Double-standard much, Miss Burke?" Aldous laughed and then pulled Eddie into an embrace. "Don't worry too much," he said. "I've got everything under control. If anything, they'll just expel me, or maybe place me and Caoilainn in the Third Kingdom."

At that, Eddie pulled away and got up from the bed.

Did expulsion also mean that he would have to stop practicing majik like his grandmother? What would he lose? What would it cost him?

"I still don't like it," Eddie replied. Aldous reached for her waist and tried pulling her back into the bed, but she grabbed his hand instead, and kissed the back of it.

"Where are you going?" Aldous asked, his eyes full of desire again.

"Back to my dorm," Eddie replied.

"Why? Why don't you stay with me until it's time?"

"Nuh uh. I don't think so. I need to process some things," Eddie said. "A lot of things just happened, ya know."

"Alright. Are you mad at me?" Aldous asked.

"What? God, no," Eddie said. "Not at all. Why would you even think that? I'll see you in a few, okay?"

Both Vada and Simone were sleeping soundly when Eddie reentered their dorm room. She was nervous, anxious to the point of throwing up. Aldous was prepared to risk life and limb for some stupid books and a bag of junk.

Damned idiot.

Before she could stop herself, Eddie was hugging the wastebasket and throwing up.

Vada, startled by the noise, sat up. "Edwina, is that you? Are you alright?"

Eddie wiped her mouth, then apologized and shook her head. "No, I am not alright. Aldous is about to do something stupid, and he asked me to help him. I tried talking him out of it, but he won't have it."

Vada paused, then asked slowly, "What do you mean? Where is he going? What is he planning on doing?"

"He's going to break into his father's study and steal some stuff. Tonight. Books, or so he says. And a bag of stuff. I don't really know what's going on. He just sprung it on me a couple of hours ago." Eddie groaned. "I'll clean that up when I get back."

"For some stupid books," Vada growled, kicking the covers off of her and Simone. "Hey, get up. That idiot is up to something again. What is he thinking? He's lying. I just know it."

Vada and a startled, but sleepy Simone exchanged looks with one another. *Aldous had been acting strange lately,* Vada thought to herself, *even before Eddie's arrival.* Most of his free time had been spent pouring over books from the school library. He had even ventured off the school grounds a few weeks ago and brought back a few books from town. Of course, he had visibly changed because of Eddie, that was a given—he was absolutely smitten with her—but his behavior had been bizarre for the past couple of months. Running outside in only a pair of shorts was severely out of character for Aldous.

Vada scrunched her nose and folded her arms.

Clearly, he had been going through some changes and did not feel comfortable going to her about them. Vada was his best friend and had been since they met on the day of orientation. So why then did she suddenly feel as though she had failed Aldous? What exactly was the nature of their friendship? What did she mean to him?

Vada wasn't quite sure what to do, but she had to do *something*.

"Alright. Well, we aren't going to be of any use to him sitting here all willy nilly. We need a plan. I won't stop him from getting those books, but I will make sure that he makes it out of that wing safely. Simone, will you help us?"

"Of course I will help you. I love that idiot like a brother. You should know this by now."

Vada turned to Eddie. "Got any ideas?"

Eddie sighed to herself. *Crap*.

Their resolve to help their friend assuaged her fears somewhat. But not much.

Eddie watched the two girls rush around the room, throwing clothes and boots onto the messy bunk, then she thought about earlier, about how she had made an absolute idiot of herself. How quick she had been to jump the gun and embarrass herself. All because Aldous had confessed his love for her—or was that the reason? What did love even mean? Alice loved her, and she loved Alice, but she accepted that their views of love were different, and ultimately the reason the relationship had failed.

Being with Aldous meant fire and ice.

Being with Aldous meant unconditional acceptance.

Being with Aldous meant being with someone she loved.

At first, his words had shocked her, maybe even angered her because they had caught her off-guard, but now she had time to consider them. She was an Earthling, Aldous was not. Maybe. But she had been drawn instantly to him upon arrival, and there was no denying it now: Eddie was in love Aldous, too.

"So, what's the plan?" Simone asked, fastening her cloak.

CHAPTER 14

Aldous glanced at the clock on his wall.

In fifteen minutes he would attempt to break into his father's study, and he was a bundle of nerves. Even with his satchel full of potions and herbs, he was still a poor excuse for a suuga. He knew this.

If he had been born a girl, he might have been an amazing sujii, the best ever if given a chance, but he was a boy and a pathetic excuse for a suuga.

At the moment, the best Aldous could do was manipulate plants into do his bidding—and he didn't like that. Manipulating the plants. Every time felt like a violation. It felt wrong. The other day when he had forced the vines to grow back over the door in front of Eddie, he could feel their reluctance. *Really feel it.* They fought him with every ounce of energy they had, and it wasn't the first time, either. He had been able to communicate with animals and plants since he could form words in his mind.

At first, he thought it had to do with his father forcing him to become a suuga instead of a sujii, but recently he had discovered some things about his birth that seemed dubious. For starters, he had never seen any documentation of his birth. No birth certificate. Nothing. But in the First Kingdom, it was standard practice for the midwife who delivered you to accept the role of your godmother, and Aldous had never met with his midwife (or godmother for that matter), which seemed out of the ordinary because Astrid knew hers and often wrote to her.

And that wasn't the only thing...

Aldous knew every detail about his sister's birth, and not simply because his mother had died giving birth to her, but because it had been recorded in the Book of Life in the town where they had lived before coming to Ashkak's. Aldous would soon turn twenty-years-old, and he hadn't celebrated his birthday since his mother died. His father treated his birth date with great indifference, which had always been alarming to Aldous for a number of reasons. Of course, their striking differences had always bothered Aldous, but recently he seemed to notice things about himself, about his body that didn't seem to make much sense, like sitting outside for hours without being affected by the weather. Why just last month he had waited in the freezing rain for six hours and had been fortunate enough to evade the cough of death the next day. His ability to stay alert for many days without sleep was also a concern. And when Eddie had touched him, his senses went haywire.

Eddie. He put his head in his hands and shook I back and forth. *What am I thinking? What am I doing? What are we doing?*

Things had not gone well. Everything had happened too fast. Until this afternoon, Aldous had thought of Eddie as a friend. Of course, he had wanted more than that, but his usual shyness and awkwardness had prevented him from asking her how she truly felt. Until today. And then she kissed him. He had even seen her without a shirt, which had come as a major surprise to him. He had never seen a girl or woman without clothes, except for his sister and mother, but that didn't count. And stars, was she lovely.

It all happened so fast.

Such a small act seemed like a daunting task within a matter of seconds.

Aldous knew how to please himself.

He had done it plenty of times, but a girl? That was a whole 'nother ballgame.

Aldous shook his head. Just thinking about the scenario made him dizzy. What kind of loser turns down a woman offering herself to him? What kind of man does that? Aldous looked at the clock through his fingers. Eddie would be here any minute. He dropped his hands and sat up straight. He felt like crying or yelling, he wasn't sure. Aldous had a thousand different emotions running through his mind right then, but knew that if he didn't go to his father's study tonight, he might lose his gumption, and something on his father's desk *had* caught his eye: a necklace with a thin silver band and an enormous black jewel. *His mother's necklace.*

After the meeting with his father, Aldous went to his room and opened a keepsake box that had belonged to his mother, a box she had given him right before her passing. Given what Aldous had traded for it, he was certain that the box's enchantment was strong enough to keep out even the most powerful suuga, but when Aldous opened the box, nothing was in it. *Empty.*

His mother's spell book and several pieces of her jewelry were missing. Somehow his father had managed to take the last little bit of his mother away from him. He blinked away tears and balled up his fists. Aldous had never hated his father—but this time, he had gone too far.

When Eddie finally arrived, Aldous noted her change of clothes—black clothes, black boots, and a black knitted hat. She had changed into something darker, something inconspicuous, something that would attract less attention if she were seen, signifying that she still meant to go with him.

"Let me guess," he said, not wanting to pick a fight.

Eddie raised one eyebrow and said, "Well?"

"What do you mean, well? Why are you dressed like that? Aren't you coming with me?" Aldous asked.

Eddie shook her head and folded her arms. "Nope," she replied. "You're on your own. Unless you want company?" Eddie tilted her head and raised both eyebrows, but Aldous only shook his head, then pushed himself up from the stool.

He placed the hat over his head and suddenly disappeared from Eddie's vision. It was creepy, seeing him push the stool back under the desk, and hearing his light footfall across the hardwood floor. Aldous had just reached the door when Eddie said, "Wait." Then she walked over to where he stood and felt for him by the door. When she could feel his shoulder, she pulled the hat off, surprising him with a hard kiss.

"You're absolute an idiot, ya know?" Eddie held his gaze for a moment, then saw a slight smile form right before he placed the hat back on his head.

"I know."

After Aldous closed the door behind him, Eddie looked down at Mister Fluffy and said, "You didn't really think I'd let him go alone, now did you?" Then as if in response, the fox jumped down from the bed and walked over to the door. "Alright," Eddie said. "So with any luck, Simone and Vada should have arrived in the south wing a few minutes ago. Simone said that she knew of a cloaking spell, one that would help Aldous. Now, she said it was a tricky spell and that she had never attempted it, but that's on her. We're just going to have to hope she's right."

Eddie walked over to the door and bent down to console the large, concerned fox.

"The plan is to have Vada and Simone interfere if there's a problem. Create a distraction or step in if he can't break the seal for whatever reason. I'll be the first to admit that it's not the best plan in the world. Hell, it's not even a good plan, but it's the only one we could come up with that didn't involve fireworks or a Trojan Horse." The fox put his paw on the bedroom door and scratched. "Fluffy, I can't go there. What if he needs to be *moved*?"

But the fox didn't expect her to go after him.

"Alright," Eddie said, finally. "But be safe." The fox then fled into the hallway, running so fast that he seemed to disappear right before Eddie's eyes.

Had he disappeared?

She closed the door and walked back over to Aldous's desk. Books were scattered everywhere. Most of them appeared to be reference books from the library, all covering the same topic: Monsters from the Fourth Kingdom. It was an odd topic to be researching given his outburst at the pujari, but Eddie opened the first book and found Aldous's bookmark.

Changelings.

Damn, he must be obsessed. Eddie thought to herself as she looked at the illustrations on the next few pages. *Aldous must really hate these things.* Other tabs included fairies, pixies, and elves. Dark elves. Bewitched swords. You name it, there seemed to be a tab for it. All of these creatures were depicted with fangs and dark, foreboding eyes, which led Eddie to consider the reason for Aldous's budding obsession.

They had yet to discuss the difference between "good" and "bad" majik, which struck Eddie as odd.

Could it be that Aldous was interested in practicing a darker, less safe majik?

Eddie closed the book.

Aldous was such a caring, kind person. She couldn't imagine him using his powers for evil, or in a way that would harm another being. She knew that people always had deep, dark secrets, of course, and that everyone has a few skeletons in their closet, but the thought of Aldous seeking knowledge with the intent of destroying or hurting someone didn't mesh with her view of him. Then again, he was determined to break into his father's study and steal items from him. That had come as a surprise. None of it made any sense, and after speaking with Vada, Eddie rejected his reason for the break-in.

Aldous was lying to her, but why?

Without noticing it, Eddie had nibbled a nail down to its quip. She was nervous now. She looked down at her useless watch. Aldous sure was taking his sweet time. Didn't he say that it would take no more than five minutes? It took every ounce of self-control to not *move* to where he was. With a deep breath, she lessened her grip on the talisman hanging from her neck and dropped her hand. Regardless of his hidden motives, Eddie wouldn't allow herself to think poorly of Aldous. If he needed her help, then she would be there for him because he was certain that he would do the same. For anyone, really. After all, isn't that what it means to love?

•••

It took Aldous a little longer than he had anticipated to reach the south wing. The Helm of Darkness had done its job, but there were several students wandering through the halls, and Aldous had not anticipated seeing (and almost being knocked down) by them. Not to mention, wearing the special garment meant that he had to be extra careful about lighting the lanterns. The halls were dark and drafty, and if he hadn't been so lithe and nimble, he would have surely tripped or rolled over sleepy children walking to the bathroom.

By the time Aldous reached his father's hall, the lanterns' flames had been extinguished. There were only four doors leading up to the end of the hallway. Two on the left and two on the right. His father's door was at the end of the hallway, and seeing that everything was still and tranquil now, Aldous placed his hands on the door, only to be flung back several feet.

After having the wind knocked out of him, he looked down at his hands. They had burst into flames much like Eddie's had done. Now momentarily paralyzed from the sight of blue fire, Aldous's body refused to obey his commands.

Then as if from out of nowhere, an invisible force smothered the fire with an unseen cloth.

"Aldous," the unseen force said, with a familiar voice. "Are you alright?"

Vada. Eddie. He sighed loudly to himself, then whispered, "What are you doing here?"

"I should ask you the same thing. Shh. And be still. Let me help with the swelling." Vada then placed her hands on his palms and softly chanted the phrase "Quil no muria."

To Aldous's immediate relief, the simple healing majik had worked. The loud, scorching heat he could feel thrumming throughout his hands silenced, replacing the once violent drum beat with a dull ache. He rubbed his hands together and shook his head.

Just what had happened? It didn't make any sense. And why was Vada here? Had Eddie spoken to her about his plans?

Aldous brushed himself off and stood up, then walked back over to the door which slowly creaked open before he could attempt another break-in.

On the way into his father's study, Aldous could hear whispering.

Was it Vada and Simone?

"Is there any way you two could show yourselves? Do you have hats or capes as well?" Aldous asked, cautiously approaching his father's large desk. "Be careful. Try to be as quiet as possible."

"No. A cloaking spell, actually," Simone admitted, opening the heavy drapes. "There, that's better. It's like a dungeon in here. Though I must say, Aldous, I'm not entirely sure how to reverse the enchantment now that it's been cast. We came fairly unprepared, you know. You didn't exactly give Eddie ample time to rally the troops."

Despite the moon's insufficient lighting, Aldous could tell that the room was filthy and cluttered—dishes, cobwebs, piles of discarded paper—it was an absolute wreck. While keeping his head glued to the ground during their last meeting, Aldous must have missed it. *Was his father so afraid of others learning his secrets that he kept the servants out as well?*

"What exactly are you searching for, Aldous," whispered a very concerned Vada.

"Some books and a necklace. And we probably shouldn't talk. We don't know what sort of protective spells my father has cast in this room," Aldous answered, spotting the bag and books he had set out to retrieve. The bag was much heavier than he had anticipated, but he slung it over his shoulder, anyway. "Hey Vada, can you lift those books and then place them in my arms?"

"Sure thing."

While Vada collected the books, an enormous black figure darted across the room. Had Simone not bent over to pick up a precarious looking scroll, she might not have spotted it. The figure then rushed at Aldous, knocking him down on the ground. The contents of the bag spilled out onto the floor, and the books went flying into the air. Vada lunged at the dark figure, trying to grab onto their cloak, but they were too swift and slammed her into the wall instead, Vada's head snapping back and forth like a limp doll. After that, Simone growled and dove as hard as she could into the figure. Simone was strong, a lot stronger than she appeared.

Vada groaned and slumped against the wall, momentarily stunned by the shock of impact. Simone threw herself at the cloaked assailant and wrapped one arm around their neck, but before she could gain purchase with her other arm, the assailant slung her body into a wooden table nearby. This did little to deter Simone, however, as protecting Vada was her number one goal.

"A little help here, Aldous!" Simone said, her voice strained.

For the next few minutes, Simone struggled with the dark figure on the floor and cried out in pain, until Aldous finally exclaimed, "Enough! Simone, Vada, come to me." Scrambling to place the books and miscellaneous items back into the bag, Aldous kept his eyes on the black-robed figure, who now pinned his friend to the ground. "Dammit."

Much to Aldous's chagrin, the stack of books was far too bulky for the small canvas bag, so after ditching a few of them, he re-positioned the bag's strap over his shoulder and dashed over to the dark figure.

"Dammit. I can't see you," Aldous exclaimed, trying to figure out who was where and doing what. "Where are you?" From the way the figure writhed and grunted, Aldous assumed that both Simone and Vada were wrestling with the unknown assailant. "Stars, please work. Edwina!" After feeling around for Vada's hair and grabbing at the floor where he assumed Simone was, he called out, "Edwina! Can you hear me? We need your help!"

Within seconds, every inch of the room was filled with a silvery light, and before Aldous could shut his eyes, they were suddenly transported back to his dormitory. Standing there before them Eddie clutched at her talisman, her face bathed in pallor.

After the initial shock wore off, she dashed to Aldous to help him up, but tripped over an unseen force and tumbled onto the floor. Vada grumbled a sorry and then helped Aldous up. Simone lay on the floor next to Aldous and said the words that would hopefully undo the invisibility spell.

Slowly their figures began to reappear, and Eddie looked at them in horror. The palms of Aldous's hands were black, charred even, and Simone was bleeding profusely from her left nostril and the side of her mouth. Vada's dress was missing a sleeve and had been torn at the neck.

Just what the hell had happened in that study?

The three sat in silence for a moment before Eddie blurted out, "What the hell happened in that room?"

After propping himself up on his elbows, Aldous replied matter-of-factly, "We were attacked by something. Or someone. I'm not entirely sure." Astounded by his steady voice and calm demeanor, Eddie crawled over to him and took his charred hands into hers.

"What is this?" Eddie asked.

"Oh," Aldous replied. "We're alright, Edwina. Just a bit shaken up."

"Are you serious? Have you seen your hands? They're freaking black, man. Or haven't you noticed?"

"Ah," Aldous said. "Yes, well, that. Um, I'm not sure what kind of seal my father had on the door, but I wasn't able to

—Simone and Vada had to open the door. I guess I'm still bad at setting and breaking them. But thanks to Vada, they don't hurt nearly as much as they did." Aldous looked over at his friends who were now sitting in a tight embrace. "I'll have to make an herbal salve. Really, it's not that big of a deal. I am certain I can heal my hands. All I need is some redleaf cat's paw. Really. I should be fine."

Eddie, still in shock, snapped at her injured friends. "How can you all just sit there and act like nothing happened in that room? Won't someone tell me what the hell is going on?"

But no one did, instead choosing silence and exchanging worried glances with one another, making Eddie feel more like an outsider—which was fine because that's what she was.

"Y'all have nothing to say? Ya know what? I don't know what's going on. I'm going back to my room now. If you need me, it can wait until the morning."

Eddie opened Aldous's door, then stepped into the hallway.

Life at Ashkak's was becoming too complicated, too frightening.

She would refocus her attention on returning home. How had she become so entangled in these people's lives in such a short period of time?

Things had to change. She had to change. She was always doing this—getting caught up in the moment and thinking only of others, never of herself.

Before Eddie knew it, she was running.

Down the stairwell.

Into the large common room.

Through the dining room.

Into the kitchen.

Down the hallway.

Swiftly waving lanterns and candles to life like a human matchbox.

Eddie didn't know her way around the school yet and was certain that her footsteps weren't nearly as graceful or stealthy as Aldous's, but she didn't care—she needed to get outside.

But every door Eddie encountered was either locked or sealed by an unseen force.

A prison, she thought to herself. *I'm trapped inside of this majikal prison, and I can't get the hell out.* It wasn't until she came upon a heavy, double-sided, steel door that Eddie lost all hope.

"This shit is getting too out of hand for me," she said to no one in particular, sliding down the metal door. "I need to get the hell out of here!"

The next few minutes Eddie spent talking aloud to herself and crying until her eyes were red and puffy. Frankly, she didn't give a damn whether the headmistress discovered her in the kitchen. It wasn't like she could get expelled or suspended from a school she didn't actually attend. After all, she was a guest. Eddie wasn't one of them.

Feeling oddly rejuvenated from weeping, Eddie got up from the floor and looked out the window beside the steel door. Outside the wind howled and angrily thrust itself up against the cold pane of glass.

"Alright," Eddie said to herself, pulling a cigarette out of her hoodie pocket. "I'm going to smoke this damned thing one way or another."

With the cigarette now hanging out of her mouth, she placed both hands squarely on the door and pushed as hard as she could. "Come on, you son of a bitch," she screamed loudly. Seconds later, a bright white light that traveled from her toes to the tips of her curls consumed the entire room, and the door slowly, but surely, creaked open.

"That's more like it." Eddie pulled up her hood and walked into the cold darkness.

After the first exhale of smoke, she slumped her shoulders and walked down the steps. It was cold like the walk-in freezer at the grocery store, so Eddie pulled the strings on her hoodie, tightening the hood around her face and blew smoke out of the tiny opening. Once finished with the cigarette, Eddie put the butt back in her pocket, it hadn't calmed her nerves, but it did provide some warmth.

Now feeling rather emboldened and intrigued, Eddie looked around the darkened facility. Nothing stirred. Blackness enshrouded the school grounds, and it was eerily silent. It wasn't until Eddie had walked several yards away from the school that a glimmer of white light caught her eye, and despite hundreds of hours invested in horror movies in which the victim is almost always an unarmed teenage girl, Eddie blindly walked deeper into the blackness.

She crept upon the white light and discovered the entrance to a densely wooded area. By now it had to be two or three in the morning, but the LED light on her watch had stopped working months ago work so she couldn't be certain. Now squinting, Eddie could see a seemingly endless stream of bright white orbs floating into the dark woods. But before she could take another step forward to investigate, something gently tugged on the back of her hoodie.

"Thank the stars I found you," Aldous whispered, standing behind her with a lantern. "You must be freezing. You're going to get sick if you stay out here any longer. I went to your room, but you weren't there."

Aldous was right. It was dark and cold, and Eddie knew that she had no business being out here so late at night. Still, she turned her back and looked at the forest.

The light had been *calling* to her, and so beguiled was she by the idea of following the light that she hadn't seen or heard Aldous approach. If he hadn't broken the trance, she would have followed the light into the dark woods,.

"I saw a light. Several lights, actually. I was smoking and felt drawn to the forest. So I came down here. It sounds absolutely bonkers, I know, but I felt as if the forest was calling my name. Pretty silly, huh?"

Aldous lowered the lantern, then put his arm around her shoulders and shook his head. "No, not at all. I've heard nothing but bad things about those woods. If there's one thing I'm sure of, it's that evil, disgusting things dwell deep within. It is best if you avoid it. Come on, let's go back in-side," he said. "I'll walk you to your dorm."

Eddie stopped before they got to the steel door. "Are you ever going to tell me why you went to your father's study, and why those books are so important to you?" She asked. "And what happened with Vada and Simone? You owe me an explanation, and no lies, Aldous."

"It's a long story, but I will tell you—tomorrow—I prom-ise. The hour grows late."

Eddie looked up at Aldous. Under the moon his long, white hair shone as bright as starlight and his skin *was* translucent, it didn't just appear that way. If she looked hard enough, she could see through it.

"Aldous," she began. "I—I'm sorry for being such a spazz. Really. I shouldn't have freaked out like that. Everyone is having a rough time. I'm sorry for blowing it out of propor-tion. It's just—you can tell me anything, ya know?"

For the next several seconds, Eddie looked into his green eyes, silently searching for answers. Then taking his now-poorly-bandaged hands into her own, Eddie said, "I mean it —no matter what happens, I hope ya know that you can trust me. We haven't known each other very long, but you can tell me anything. No matter what it is. As long as you're honest with me, I will never judge you."

"Thank you. But please allow me to apologize for earlier as well. I'm not very good with people, and I usually make a fool out of myself. But when I'm with you, I feel like a dif-ferent person altogether, and I'm not sure what I'm doing half the time," Aldous replied, leaning in for a kiss.

Forceful and demanding, the kiss startled Eddie. "Aldous," she breathed, dropping his hands.

Now pressing her body up against his, Eddie could tell their desire was mutual. His lips and fingers were soft, and his white hair shimmered under the moon like a diamond. *Am I dreaming? Is this real? Is he Aldous real?* It took a few minutes for her to regain control of her senses—and while Aldous seemed unaffected by the cold weather, Eddie was afraid her fingers were going to fall off if she stood outside for much longer. Once inside, they slipped their hands into each other's, and Aldous walked Eddie back to her dorm.

CHAPTER 15

When Monday morning came, Eddie was almost glad. Even though she was at Ashkak's, it was still a school which presented itself as a normalcy of some sort, at least. The past few days had been a hodgepodge of emotions and danger for Eddie.

Yesterday Eddie had spent the morning with Aldous going through his bag of goodies as promised. An exceptional historian he gave thorough explanations of the items within. The books were fascinating as well, but she had been surprised to find Aldous's mother's spell book in the mix. There were several pieces of jewelry in the bag, as well as a dagger, five crimson-colored candles, a sachet of dried herbs and flowers, and a scroll. The scroll was written in a language that Eddie couldn't read (surprise), and if Aldous recognized the writing, he kept it to himself.

She and Aldous were getting closer, too.

The development of their friendship seemed sudden, and their relationship even more so. All throughout the day yesterday, Eddie caught Aldous staring at her several times—which usually ended in acute embarrassment, because he hung on her every word, and thoughtfully responded without interrupting. Being with Aldous was unlike being with Alice.

When Eddie rejoined Aldous in the dining hall that morning, he was sitting next to Caoilainn, smiling and engaged in a lively conversation. Her other friends were sharing bowls of fruit and eating bits of ham from a large silver dish. Because of their past interactions, it seemed odd to Eddie that Caoilainn and Aldous would be sitting so close to one another, but she tried to bury the curiosity and unusual feelings she now felt.

When Aldous saw Eddie, he waved her over and moved his satchel onto the floor.

"Good morning. Looking forward to more of Abjou's class?" He asked. "You look tired."

Eddie smiled slightly and poured herself a glass of orange juice. "Not really. That man hates me for some reason. Will you please pass me a plate?"

While getting ready in her room, Eddie had been hungry—hungry enough to eat an entire pan of croissants, now she could barely keep juice down. Aldous handed her a small dish and a bowl of cinnamon rolls, then squeezed her gently on the shoulder. Eddie graciously accepted both and reached for the butter.

Breakfast seemed to fly by—and Eddie was thankful for it.

At lunch, they gathered together once again and spoke about the upcoming exams. During Abjou's class, Caoilainn and Aldous sat close to one another and spoke often. The barrier of awkward silence between the two was slowly dissolving. Knowing that she wouldn't be there for the exams, Eddie sat silently and picked at her pumpkin ravioli. After she finished her lunch, she stood up and made her way to the next class. Halfway to the classroom, Aldous caught up to her in the long corridor. Eddie was in a sour mood and didn't really want to talk, but she turned around and put on a fake smile, anyway.

Aldous had his hair pulled out of his face, and there was a bounce to his walk. He looked happy and cute. The knife twisted further into Eddie's fragile psyche.

"Hey there," he said, greeting her with a smile. "Sorry about all of the dull discussion at the table. We're going to have to study hard for the exams. I'll probably have to spend most of my life in the library until then." Noticing Eddie's silence, Aldous caught her arm. "Hey. Are you alright?" She stopped and nodded at him. The fact that she might not be here for the exams hit her hard. She was just now getting to know Aldous, and she would miss all of her friends.

"Yeah, sure." Eddie didn't know what else to say. If she opened her mouth any more, her voice would crack and betray her feelings, so she just looked up at him in silence. In response, Aldous bent forward and put his arms around her. "You all are planning for the future," she said, finally. "And I'm not going to lie, it's hard as hell listening to you all talk about it because I know that I won't be a part of it."

Aldous hugged her tighter. "No one would object if you chose to stay, Eddie. I know I wouldn't. Why don't you stay? Here, with me?"

Eddie withdrew from his embrace.

Last night was the first night she had thought about staying—about staying with Aldous. But in a few months, he would leave for a village with Caoilainn, and she might never see him again, which would be worse than if she went back because at least then, she would have her baby sister and Natalie.

"I can't, Aldous. Even if I stayed here, you will be leaving soon, and I couldn't stand that. In the end, no one would get what they wanted. I have to go back."

As the two friends made their way to the Za'tari classroom, Aldous suggested that Eddie come with him to meet his grandmother over the upcoming weekend, explaining that he had made plans to visit her months ago, and would feel guilty about canceling those plans. The only thing Eddie cared about at the moment was spending as much time with Aldous as possible, so she agreed to go with him.

While in class, Eddie noticed that Aldous was wearing black fingerless gloves. The salve must not have worked as well as he had hoped. Yesterday, he had been spent looking for spells and potions that would help heal his hands, because the wounds wouldn't stop scabbing over and breaking open, oozing an awful substance from them. The only advice Eddie had for Aldous was to keep them clean and dry and to change the dressing as often as needed, but he proved to be a poor listener.

When Eddie, Vada, and Simone showed up to Aldous's room that afternoon, his door was slightly ajar, and the contents from the other night were scattered all over the bed. Aldous greeted his friends, then hurriedly closed the door behind them. Eddie looked around for Mister Fluffy, who had been missing since the night of the altercation.

"What is all this stuff?" Vada asked, walking over to his bed. "Jewelry and candles? You risked your life for some candles, Aldous?"

Behind Vada, Aldous and Simone spoke softly to one another, out of Eddie's earshot. By the frown on Simone's face, it was obvious they were discussing something important, so Eddie joined Vada on the bed and lifted up a silver necklace.

Astonished, Vada took a step back, then said, "Aldous, is that what I think it is?"

The black jewel hanging from the silver band sparkled brilliantly in the lamplight. It was the most beautiful stone Eddie had ever seen.

"What is that," Eddie asked, eyeing the gemstone. "I know it's not onyx. Black tourmaline?"

"Close. It is obsidian," Aldous replied, walking towards Eddie. "But those were good guesses. And the reason why I called you all here this evening."

Vada and Simone exchanged worried looks. "You stole obsidian from your father?" Simone asked.

Eddie handed Vada a necklace and then picked up a pair of earrings.

"Those were my mother's earrings," Aldous said, dodging Vada's interrogation.

"Oh, they're lovely," Eddie said, as she tried handing the earrings to Aldous, only to have him ball her hand into a fist. "Huh?"

Aldous replied, "Those are yours."

Vada and Simone exchanged raised eyebrows with one another, but kept quiet.

"Thank you, but no. I'm sure your mother gave those to you for a reason, dude. I can't take them. It wouldn't be right."

"Why?" Aldous asked. "You're as good a reason as any. Please, take them. My gift to you. Besides, I won't wear them, and I want you to have them. They've been hidden away for long enough."

Eddie knew from Aldous's tone that there was little point in arguing, so she shoved the tiny handful of silver and black into her pocket, and turned her gaze to the rest of the stuff on his bed.

"So." Vada cleared her throat. "What's the rest of this junk?"

Aldous sat down on the bed, then held up each item, and explained its significance. "This junk is very important," he explained. "This necklace here was made of obsidian as were the earrings in your pocket, crafted by my late grandfather as wedding gifts. And this here," Aldous said, picking up a sheathed knife from the bed. "It is rumored that a blade made from obsidian can penetrate any armor due to its majikal properties. Simone, I'd like you to have this." He handed her the hilt then turned to Vada. "And Vada, I'd like you to have my mother's necklace. You've done so much for me these past few years. I don't know how else to repay you. Besides, you've been eyeing it since you walked through the door."

Speechless, the two girls stared at their gifts in awe and wonder.

"I have not," Vada scoffed, taking the necklace from his hand. "But thank you. I will cherish it."

"You're welcome," Aldous said. "These candles here are made from fat." Eddie reached for the candles, then hesitated. "And colored with blood."

"Whose blood?" Eddie took a step back.

"Well, I mean to find out. And now that you are all here, I have something else I'd like to discuss: forming an order."

"A what?" Eddie was the first to speak.

"An order?" Vada asked, cautiously. "You know we can't do that. It is forbidden. If you think breaking into your father's study was heavy stuff, just wait until they find out you're talking about forming an order."

"Have you lost your damn mind?" Simone was furious. "At what point did you decide that these rules we've followed our entire lives are arbitrary and frivolous? Do you know what they do to people like you, Aldous?"

"Think about the price your Gran paid," Vada pleaded. "You're out of your mind."

Aldous shook his head. "Calm down and just listen to me, OK? I have a theory."

But Vada wouldn't. "I don't know what's gotten into you lately. I thought it was her," she said, pointing to Eddie. "But now I'm not so sure. You've been acting weird for months now. Is this why you're obsessed with all of these books?" Vada asked. "Is that why you snuck off to Chimla a few weeks ago? And I don't give a damn about your theory. You are talking straight heresy."

"You know better than any of us how cruel and vicious your father can be," Simone said. "If anyone practices majik with anyone other than their waja, bad stuff will happen. It is simply the way of things."

"Wait," Eddie interjected, her hands now in the air. "Will everyone just calm down and stop yelling? What the hell is an order?"

The tension in the room made it hard for everyone to breathe.

"Do you want your lives controlled by the Council for all of eternity?" Aldous asked, furious. "Don't you realize what becoming waja means? You'll become a slave to their system. You already are! Wake up!"

"Ya know," Eddie said. "I think it would be best if everyone just left. It's clear y'all need to calm the hell down and clear your minds."

At Eddie's suggestion, Aldous's door suddenly flung open like a sail in a rainstorm.

"Fine," Vada said. "You don't have to tell me twice. Let's go, Simone."

"Wait, please listen to me," Aldous pleaded. "I'm not done. This is important. Don't go yet."

For the next hour, Aldous lay on the bed curled up.

Just what had gone wrong?

Their reactions had caught him off guard. Never before had he seen Simone like that. The vitriol in her words could have curdled milk.

Had he been foolish to think they would accept such a dangerous suggestion? But didn't they see how bad things were at Ashkak's? Aldous had called the school home for as long as he could remember, and every year things just got progressively worse for him. The bullying, the outright hatred his father displayed in front of others, as well as a slew of other horrible things that he had to endure day in and day out.

Besides those items were in his father's study for a reason.

Molhata is planning something, but what?

Aldous sat up. Maybe he could speak to his sister. Surely she would listen to his theories.

"Here you go," Eddie said, handing him a cup of tea.

"Thanks." Asking his friends to accept such a truth was like asking a badger to marry a wolf. "Sorry about earlier," Aldous said.

"It's alright. I have accepted the fact that there are just some things that I won't understand."

"No, that's not it," Aldous replied. "You asked what an order was earlier. Do you still wish to know? Even after all of that?"

"Yes, please tell me."

"So an order is simply a group of sujii and suuga that get together and practice majik."

"OK? I don't get it. What's the big deal?" Eddie asked, confused.

"It's a big deal because the Council forbids it. Being discovered means expulsion, and not just from school, but from society as a whole. Vada and Simone have each other, and they don't want to risk that. So I get it."

"What's the benefit of forming an order? Why do you want to do it?"

"Strength and power."

"But why do you need that?" Eddie asked.

"Because," Aldous said. "I believe my father is up to something, and I'm going to find out what it is. Are you aware that all of this stuff, aside from the candles and two of the books, was in my room before? He came in here while I was gone and took it."

"What? He stole some jewelry and some books from you?"

"Yes," Aldous replied. "None of it makes any sense. Why would he need such useless jewelry?"

"Didn't you say that obsidian was highly unstable, though?"

"Yes, it is, which is the reason behind him stealing from me. Or at least that's what I am assuming."

Now sitting next to her, Aldous looked down at his free hand and groaned. "Oh, crap." His poor bandage job had come undone, and blood was seeping through the dressing. "Not again."

"What the hell, dude?" Eddie said. "Have you been cleaning this like I told you?

Gently unwrapping the bandages from his hands, Eddie shook her head. "What did I tell you? If ya let the wound get dirty, there's a chance that it will become infected. It's dangerous to let them get like that. I doubt you all have antibiotics here."

While Eddie finished cleaning the open blisters with cool water, Aldous found himself tingling all over. If it was the chill from the water touching his tender skin or the comfort of her soft hands against his, he couldn't tell

"Thank you," Aldous said, now inspecting his freshly bandaged hands.

"You're welcome," Eddie replied. "What would you do without me?"

"I have no idea," he responded, placing a kiss on the side of her head. The thought of her leaving him made his insides ache, but he was too much of a coward to say so.

"Thank you again for the earrings. I shouldn't accept them. They belonged to your mother. You should really give them to Astrid."

"No, please. They are yours. As I said before, I will never wear them, and I'll never have a chance to give them to my wife, which is why my mother gave them to me. Er, I mean–"

Eddie froze in his hands, her eyes full of something.

Is it fright?

Have I said the wrong thing again?

But Aldous was just being honest with her. His mother *had* given him the necklace and earrings to give to his Waja, should he be fortunate enough to find love in the relationship. But everyone in the school knew how that turned out. The next best thing Aldous could think of was giving them to his friends whom he loved.

Aldous was exhaustively confused. *Not again.*

He didn't understand the energy now coming from Eddie.

What could I have said that was so terrible?

"Aldous," Eddie started. "I can't do this." She removed the earrings from her pocket and stuck out her hand. "Here, take them."

"I won't force them on you, but are they not to your liking?" He asked, not taking them from her. "I don't understand. What did I do?"

"I can't do this anymore," Eddie whispered. "I can't act like it doesn't bother me that I'll probably never see you guys again once I'm gone." She rubbed her temples. "Aldous, I like you. I like you a lot. And it isn't fair." Eddie dropped her hands and continued. "It isn't fair that we should meet each other, not like this. Living thousands, maybe millions of miles away from one another. I don't know. Long-distance relationships are unmanageable when you don't live in the same state. They are impossible when you don't occupy the same solar system."

Aldous put his arms around Eddie and pulled her near. "I don't know what to say. I don't know how to make things better," he said. "I don't know how to make these things untrue."

These were the facts they both had to face. What Eddie said was true. One day she would leave, and they would likely never see each other again. It was a harsh reality, one that Aldous didn't wish to recognize. So he held her.

Eddie spoke, after taking a few deep breaths. "It's just unfortunate that we can't do anything about it, ya know."

"I know," he replied. "And it doesn't feel good."

"Well, I don't know about you, but I am exhausted. Today has been eventful. So I'm going back to my room." Eddie gathered her belongings, and placed the earrings back in her pocket, next to several cigarette butts. Aldous didn't say much, just sipped on the now-cold tea Eddie had made for him, looking as thoughtful as ever.

"Maybe we should," Eddie said, then paused. "I don't know. Focus our attention on getting me back and not spend as much time together as we have been. We're getting too wrapped up in things. We need to readjust our focus." As each word helplessly spilled onto the floor, Eddie couldn't help but feel like a phony. She knew how generic it sounded, like something from an old black-and-white movie. "We should just, ya know, give each other space. Some room to breathe. You have all of these tests coming up, and I feel like you're spending all of your time with me. And it's not right or fair. I came here at a bad time. I can do research on *moving* alone." Eddie's hope was that their separation might lessen the tension between the two of them, and give Aldous time to refocus on his studies, to spend time on things that actually mattered, like his exit exams.

"What?" Aldous asked. "No, absolutely not. That won't do us any good. I don't really understand the benefit of us spending time alone if you could leave at any moment." At first, Aldous objected indignantly, trying to highlight all of the positives, but Eddie would not budge on the matter, and the hole it left in his heart felt absolutely dreadful. "Why wouldn't we try to spend as much time together as possible? I don't give a fluff about those stupid tests, either. You can't really want this. Is it something I did? Or said? Was it the earrings? You don't have to wear anything you don't want to wear. Certainly not for me. I don't care what you wear. Eddie, please. Think about this. It doesn't make any sense."

"I have thought about this, and it's what I want." Saying the words aloud didn't make them any truer, but Eddie said them anyway. "I'm serious."

"Alright," Aldous said, defeated. "If that is what you truly want, I'll respect your wishes. But it's not what I want. I just need you to know that."

"I'll see you tomorrow."

Later that night, Aldous tossed and turned in his bed. He had spent every day with Eddie since her arrival, and now she wanted space. *Space.* To put an undetermined amount of distance between them. It didn't make sense to him, seeing as how they would eventually be apart forever. Aldous stared at the ceiling. They would both get hurt in the end. He rolled over and picked up the pillow next to him. It smelled like Eddie. Apple cinnamon pie or whatever the hell it was. He squeezed it.

Before Eddie showed up, Aldous felt alone and sad.

What would life be like once she returns? Maybe he should go back with her, to West Virginia, to Milton. Aldous was resourceful. He threw the pillow on the floor. No, that wouldn't work. There was no way around their separation. They would part ways, and things would go back to normal. He dreaded the feeling of isolation, of desperation. He removed the talisman from his neck and tossed it across the room onto his desk. The last time he had unknowingly called out to her and brought her to him.

That's not going to happen again.

Not when she wanted to put distance between them.

Just what did I do that was so wrong? I don't understand. I don't get it.

Deep down Aldous wished Caoilainn would show him the same affection. He knew that it was shallow and heartless to think of her immediately after chucking Eddie's talisman to the side, but he couldn't help it. He loved Eddie, adored her, but she would be gone someday soon, and he would be left with Caoilainn. *His waja.* Conversation hadn't been so awkward lately, and they had even discussed getting together to study for their exit exams. At some point, things had changed between them. Why or when, Aldous couldn't say, but the thought had planted a seed of hope in his shrunken heart.

Aldous knew that Caoilainn wanted to be with Salvator, but she would eventually have to forget him as well. Things were going to be pretty sour fairly soon for both of them. If only there were some way to find out how Caoilainn truly felt about him. To see if it would ever feel right between the two of them. Now that Aldous had emerged from his voluntary solitude, loneliness no longer seemed like an option.

Right before drifting off to sleep, Aldous crafted a plan, one that was sure to settle things once and for all. Or at least some things. It was a truly terrible plan, actually, one that could backfire on him, but if Eddie wanted some space to think, Aldous would give it to her, of course—because he had some things to take care of, too. He would need to run things by Vada first, though; that is—if she wasn't still mad at him when he saw her next.

Chapter 16

The next morning Aldous caught up with Vada in the hall before heading to Waja Abjou's. With an armful of books and her head hanging low, Eddie deliberately hurried past both of them. After last night's conversation about the order, Aldous wasn't sure Vada would speak to him, but he was desperate.

Once the hall cleared, he grabbed Vada's arm and pulled her into an empty classroom. "Well, good morning to you, too. I'm surprised to see you're still interested in coming to class, given your new affinity for breaking all the rules."

"She broke up with me, Vada."

"Who?" Vada asked. "Eddie? Broke up with you? Were you together?"

"Okay, no, not officially, I guess, but we kissed and stuff. I thought, maybe, there might be a chance of something. I told her how I felt. I told her that I loved her."

"You went and told her that you loved her and then you gave her your mum's earrings in front of everyone. I'm no expert here," Vada said. "But methinks you came on a bit too strong. What were you thinking?"

Aldous slammed his satchel down on a desk, then threw his hands into the air. "Dammit. I don't know what I'm doing here. I'd never even kissed a girl, and then things happened in my room a couple of days ago, and here we are. I'm navigating a ship without sails."

"What kind of things?" Vada asked.

"Things. Does it matter? I saw her without a shirt. I thought I was going to pass out. It was not a pleasant experience."

"Not pleasant? Why? You didn't...you know?"

"Stars, no," Aldous exclaimed. "I embarrassed her, and she left. It's not like I didn't want to, you know, but everything happened so fast, and I couldn't breathe. It was bad. Horrible."

"So," Vada replied. "Something happened last night after we left."

"Yes, she said that she needs time. Time? How can she want time? There's no telling when she'll *move* back to West Virginia. Eddie could up and go, and we'd never see each other again. Why doesn't she want to spend time with me anymore?"

"You do love her," Vada said, processing everything Aldous had said.

"You're not helping by pointing out the obvious."

"Why are we standing in this room?" Vada asked, suspiciously. "What are you up to now?"

"Because I made up my mind about something last night. I'm going to ask Caoilainn if she's changed her mind. If she's willing to give it a chance. We're both-"

"Wait, no." Vada raised a hand and shook her head. "You mean to tell me that you love this girl. And that she was willing to be with you in *that* way, but you pushed her away. Then on top of that, you told her you loved her and gave her a pair of earrings that were meant for your future wife. Now, you're not willing to give her the time she needs to think about things and throw her to the side instead? What the hell is wrong with you?"

"No, you are misunderstanding me. It's not like that. That's not what I'm doing."

After placing her hands on his shoulders, Vada looked up into her dear friend's eyes and said, "You are very confused. I get that. And I love you. But if you want things to work out with Edwina, I suggest you talk to her. Tell her about this. This overly stupid plan of yours. If you don't tell her and she finds out on her own, things will go south, very quickly. And nobody wants that to happen. Think about what she means to you. Think about how you would feel if she did this to you."

•••

Even though it took her twenty-some minutes to walk back to her dorm, Eddie cherished the silence and solitude. Everyone was either in their dorms already or still down in the dining hall having dessert. She walked slower than usual because she didn't want to face Vada. Eddie had been avoiding everyone all day, and she wasn't very good at masking her emotions; she needed a considerable amount of time to prepare herself for the inevitable conversation that was to come. Because last night, in front of God and everyone, Aldous had given Eddie his mother's earrings and unloaded an enormous amount of heavy stuff on his friends. She hadn't been very forthcoming about her relationship with Aldous simply because she didn't quite understand it herself. And now everyone knew how Aldous felt about her.

When Eddie got back to the dorm, she was relieved to discover that her roommate had not returned. She threw her stuff on the floor and clambered up the wooden ladder, then withdrew the pair of earrings from her pocket and looked at them. They were the most precious gift anyone had ever given her. No one had given her jewelry, and because of that, she had always turned her nose up at it.

But not these earrings. They are different. Special.

Eddie placed them back in her pocket and looked down at her small hands. Only recently had Eddie begun to believe in the power that rested inside of her. She had never been physically strong, and her mother's death had weakened her emotionally and mentally. But majik made her strong, had awoken a power that she had not known existed.

And if what Aldous said about the order was true—then their powers might increase if they all worked together. Eddie had not been brought up in the First Kingdom, so she did not understand the look of sheer terror in Simone's eyes when Aldous had mentioned the word, and she wouldn't bring it up again, either, but she would secretly work on her craft even if she didn't have a waja waiting for her.

For the next few minutes, Eddie let the majik take hold of her. At first, she imagined the majik flowing into her like waves of water, then she closed her eyes, and let that water consume her. It felt like actually being submerged in water, only she could breathe. When Eddie finally opened her eyes, it felt as though she were opening her eyes for the first time.

Something was happening to her. But what?

When she looked down at the talisman hanging from her neck, Eddie knew with certainty that she could fight the sensation to *move* into Aldous's room—that she was in control. Before it was as if the talisman had all the power, but now Eddie understood.

She was the one who controlled the majik inside of the stone.

The majik inside of her.

Eddie grabbed the talisman with her hand and thought about Aldous. About the kiss he had given her outside. Then suddenly, the talisman shone more brightly than ever, and a shimmering, golden light engulfed the entire room. Eddie could now feel the energy coursing through her veins, through her blood, through every cell in her body. Her legs began to lift off the bed, and before she could *move* into his room, she let go of the thought and the talisman. It was the hardest thing she had to do yet at the school. The force of the talisman slammed her down on the bed and left her panting and aching all over. Somehow she knew that the talisman had gotten angry with her, that she had left it feeling like an unsatisfied lover.

It was a bizarre yet fulfilling sensation, knowing how much power she possessed.

By the time Vada returned from studying with Simone and Caoilainn, Eddie had managed to rearrange the furniture in the room. The bunk bed now sat on the opposite side of the dormitory, the dressers had switched places, and a large wooden trunk was now slowly spinning in the middle of the room. When Eddie first moved into the dorm, the two girls had discussed *movement* majik a few times, but Vada had not seen Eddie in action.

"Aldous," Vada whispered to herself, horrified by what she now saw. "You're just like Aldous. You're just like him."

The next day Eddie tried to avoid Aldous as much as she could, to decrease the frequency of their interactions. It was difficult, especially since she wanted nothing more than to share her epiphany and newfound abilities with him. But it wasn't until the last class of the day that they actually spoke to one another. The exchange was awkward and consisted of four words only. Normally Eddie would sit and listen to Aldous talk about herbs and ask questions afterward. But today he was quiet and kept his nose in a book. A few times she nearly talked herself into striking up a conversation, but self-doubt always won and she would return to taking notes. The lecture must have taken an hour, but Eddie was sure she had been there for much longer. When class was over, she excused herself from the table and hurried out the door. Things were much too tense in that room, and she needed a cigarette.

In the dining hall, things weren't much different, except that Caoilainn was missing, and that Aldous had put together a plate and stole away to his room five minutes into dinner. Vada and Simone sat together laughing and talking about the solstice festival that was next weekend—the ewinoju. The festival sounded wonderful to Eddie, a lot like the fall festivals that were held in Milton—with tents, hayrides, hot cider, homemade candy, and maple-flavored everything. Until that morning, Eddie had assumed she would attend the festival with Aldous, but it appeared as if her plan had backfired, and she would be going stag. If she hadn't found a way home already, that is.

Eddie picked at her food until it was cold, then got up and walked back to her dorm. No one said anything to her at dinner, because Eddie assumed, they were probably still upset about that order nonsense. *Who could blame them?*

While walking through the noisy halls, the thought to *move* into Aldous's room crossed Eddie's mind a couple of times, but with their new arrangement, the thought made her feel uneasy and even guiltier. When she finally got back to her room, she put her things away, and then picked up the earrings on the vanity. Maybe she was wrong. Maybe they were going about things all wrong. Besides, it was too late to turn back, wasn't it? Eddie had already told him how she felt and had even offered to sleep with him, which at the moment had seemed like a good move—a great idea, even —but now the thought provoked an overwhelming sense of shame. Eddie always rushed into those types of situations, and it had embarrassed both of them.

Things were awkward now, but they were unnecessarily so.

"I'm going to make it right," Eddie said to herself, carefully sliding the earring posts through her tiny ear holes.

After running fingers through her orange, curly hair, she looked down at her watch. It was two minutes past six o'clock. If she walked remarkably fast, she could make it to his room in less than fifteen minutes. Together they could spend time out in the garden, or take a walk around the track, and she could smoke. It would be nice to clear the air.

Before leaving the room, Eddie looked in the vanity mirror at her face.

Who is the girl standing before her? Where the hell did she come from?

The curls and freckles were familiar, but the expression she now wore was foreign. Aldous, majik, the talisman, the school, something, or perhaps all of those things, had changed Eddie in such a short period of time. *Who is the girl in the mirror?*

Getting to Aldous's room took longer than Eddie had anticipated. A gaggle of girls in colorful robes blocked most of the hallway, preventing her from walking past. It was irritating, but she also envied them immensely. They would learn and grow together, and Ashkak's was a great place for both learning and friendship. This made her think of Aldous and hastened her pace.

When Eddie finally reached his door, she knocked three times and then walked in when no one answered.

What she saw was unexpected.

Both Caoilainn and Aldous were seated next to one another, leaning in for a kiss. When their lips met, Eddie's jaw dropped, and for a brief moment after the kiss, they exchanged warm smiles with one another and then shook their heads. The familiar feeling of betrayal slammed into Eddie with as much force as a moving school bus.

Baffled by what she saw, Eddie took a step back and stumbled over a pile of clothes. Aldous, wide-eyed and in shock, turned to her.

But "oh no" was all he could manage.

Saying nothing, Eddie turned around and swung open the door as swiftly as she could. Rushing down the hall, she could hear Aldous shouting her name.

I've screwed up everything. Nothing is right. Why was I brought here? I want to go home.

It didn't help that Eddie had no idea where she was going, but she knew that she needed to get out of the school as soon as possible.

Once she made it outside, Eddie felt the anger and rage melt into sadness.

A bitter sadness that she had felt before.

The kind of sadness that steals your breath and replaces it with violent sobs, sobs so jarring it feels like your chest might cave in after each one.

By the time Eddie realized it, a light snow had already fallen from the gray sky and covered most of her body. She was grossly under-dressed for such weather, but she didn't give a damn, because Aldous was a liar, and she had misjudged his integrity. Just like her past girlfriends, he was a jerk, a loser. Eddie fell to her knees, then placed her hands over her eyes and cheeks. What she wouldn't give to have that stupid image of them smiling at one another out of her head! It was awful, horrible, the way they both looked so pleased with each other after the kiss.

Eddie felt so alone.

She just wanted to go home.

There was no telling just how long Eddie sat outside in the cold, but when she looked at her hands, they were as red as rubies. She pulled her hoodie over her head and shoved her hands inside her pockets, then walked around the school grounds, trying to soothe herself.

It didn't matter where she was, people wanted to treat her like crap for no reason.

As she turned a corner, she spotted a figure in the distance.

Aldous.

Hoping he hadn't seen her, Eddie dashed behind a tree.

"Eddie, I know you're hiding back there."

"Damn it," Eddie growled. "Go away."

"Will you please just come out so we can talk?" Aldous asked. "It's not what you think. It's the opposite."

Eddie then cursed herself and stepped out from behind the tree, meeting his gaze a few yards away. Aldous's face was red, and his eyes were just as puffy as hers, but that didn't matter, not right now, not ever.

He lied to her. Had it all been an act? Had Aldous been with Caoilainn the whole time? Is this how they got off on things? None of it makes any sense.

She only asked for space, not a severance of their friendship.

Eddie took a step back, and Aldous took two forward.

"Stop," she warned. "Don't come any closer. I mean it, Aldous. Don't."

Aldous stopped walking toward her but reached out his hands. "I'm sorry. I'm an idiot."

"Please just go."

When Eddie finally met his gaze, tears had formed in the corners of her eyes. Under the bright moonlight, Aldous looked mesmeric, with eyes that shimmered like green gemstones, and his long, white hair that sparkled like starlight. His beauty angered her even more. "You have a severely screwed up the definition of love, ya know. I get that you're weird and royally messed up because your family sucks, I do, I get that, but you lied to me. You literally deceived me. If I could *move* myself back home at this moment, I would," Eddie said, shaking from the cold, from the rage.

With great urgency, Aldous moved toward her. "Ok. Whoa," he said. "Please don't do anything hasty." Eddie ran her finger along the band around her neck. "Eddie," he replied, with a loud sigh. "I didn't do it to hurt you. I meant to tell you, but I couldn't bring myself to do it because I am a huge coward. I'm sorry." Aldous's hands hung helplessly by his side. "All day I wrestled with it, but I couldn't do it. I kissed Caoilainn to make sure that it wasn't a mistake." Aldous paused and looked directly into her eyes. "That we aren't a mistake."

As much as his words stung, Eddie knew they were true.

She knew that by being with her, Aldous was giving up on being with Caoilainn. His waja. His partner for life. Someone he could potentially marry, maybe even start a family with.

But Eddie was too pissed to think logically. She put up her hand to silence him.

"I don't want to hear any more about it," Eddie replied. "Just go back inside."

"Please, it was one kiss. It meant nothing to me, to either of us. Really."

"How can you even say that," Eddie cried. "It meant everything, Aldous."

"That's not what I meant."

"You're not very good at this, ya know. What if you had walked in on Salvator and me?" Eddie asked. "What if you had walked in on us and he was, I don't know, putting his hand up my shirt?"

Aldous clenched his jaw in silent response.

Eddie's words struck a nerve. "What then? What if we were on my bunk? Clothes off, really going at it? Would it mean nothing to you?"

"No," Aldous said. "You know it wouldn't."

"That's what I thought. Some typical double-standard male BS."

Eddie turned around and ran as fast as she could in the opposite direction of Aldous. Then after a couple of minutes, Eddie could hear Aldous running after her. Her lungs burned and her thighs ached. She wasn't used to moving like this and knew that Aldous was a much faster runner than her, so she grabbed onto her talisman tightly and thought about *moving*.

Move me, dammit. Take me home. Take me home now.

Within seconds, a blinding, white light suddenly covered the field, and then Eddie was gone. Aldous stopped running and slung an arm across his eyes and forehead.

He knew that white light. It had been a light Aldous had feared all his life.

Eddie had *moved* into the Wyldewood.

Acknowledgements

I'd like to thank the Creator of this World and Universe for supplying me with endless opportunities to revise the poorly written chapters of my life. Without your guidance and free-range style of parenting, none of this would have been possible—you're to blame for this book! I hope you're happy! Secondly, I'd like to thank my family for putting up with me since I began writing seriously—the messy house, the frozen pizzas, the canceled plans; I don't know how we made it, but here we are. I'd also like to thank my beta readers (in no particular order) for reading the first few drafts, Adicus Garton, Lacy Lawhon, Audrey Linville, and Kelly Mayhugh—your input and often tough criticism made this book better, and I cannot thank you enough for your support. Thirdly, I'd like to thank the Collectibles Etc. Ladies' Night for listening to me go on and on about the stories inside this brain; I would have never started this book without someone suggesting NaNoWriMo to me—*thank you*. Finally, to my eighth-grade language arts teacher who told me I was a bad writer, *this book is for you.*

If you enjoyed this book, please consider leaving an online review. The author would appreciate reading your thoughts, and most sales are prompted by reviews from readers like you.

About the Author

JC Garton is a fantasy writer and LGBTQ activist hailing from the hills of Appalachia. They currently reside in Kentucky with their partner, daughter, and four cats. When JC isn't reading or writing, you can find them in the paranormal section of their local bookstore, or planning their next ghost hunt.

Visit the website at
www.theywritefiction.com

You can also follow the author on social media

Instagram: www.instagram.com/jacksonwritesfiction/
Twitter: https://twitter.com/jcwritesfiction
FaceBook: www.facebook.com/gartonjc/

About the Publisher

Sulis International Press published fine fiction and nonfiction in a variety of genres. For more, visit the website at https://sulisinternational.com

Subscribe to the newsletter at
https://sulisinternational.com/subscribe/

Follow on social media
https://www.facebook.com/SulisInternational
https://twitter.com/Sulis_Intl
https://www.pinterest.com/Sulis_Intl/
https://www.instagram.com/sulis_international/

www.ingramcontent.com/pod-product-compliance
Lightning Source LLC
Chambersburg PA
CBHW050346190726
48284CB00007BB/2171